SCION OF THE SORCERESS

LISA BLACKWOOD

SCION OF THE SORCERESS

GARGOYLE & SORCERESS TALES / BOOK 8

Lisa Blackwood

Scion of the Sorceress

Gargoyle & Sorceress Book 8

COVER DESIGNED BY: Heather Hamilton-Senter

PROOFREAD BY: Tracy Vandervliet

Special Thanks to Stan H for his eagle eyes.

PRINT ISBN: 978-1-990608-54-4

EDITION: 10/27/2021

❀ Created with Vellum

BOOKS BY LISA BLACKWOOD

Gargoyle & Sorceress

Dawn of the Sorceress

Sorceress Awakening

Sorceress Rising

Sorceress Hunting

Sorceress at War

Sorceress Enraged

Legacy of the Sorceress

Sorcery & Firedrakes

Scion of the Sorceress

Sorceress Eternal

In Deception's Shadow Series (Epic Fantasy Romance)

Betrayal's Price

Herd Mistress

Maiden's Wolf

Death's Queen

The Prince's Gryphon (forthcoming)

Ishtar's Legacy Series (Epic Fantasy Romance)

Ishtar's Blade

The Blade's Beginning (short story)

Blade's Honor

Blade's Destiny

The Blade's Shadow

First Queen of the Gryphons

The King of the Anunnaki (forthcoming)

The Anunnaki's Blade (forthcoming)

Huntress vs Huntsman (Epic Fantasy Romance)

Master of the Hunt

Night Huntress

Dragon Archer

Soul Mage (forthcoming)

FREE BOOKS

GET TWO FREE STORIES FROM MY
BESTSELLING SERIES WHEN YOU SIGN UP FOR
MY NEWSLETTER.

I send regular monthly newsletters with details about new
releases,
special offers, freebies, and other bookish news.
If that's something you'd be interested in, just follow the
link below.

http://lisablackwood.com/join-the-newsletter-here/

SCION OF THE SORCERESS

Sometimes the forces of Light just need a little help from a villain to get the job done.

Commander Gryton has always watched his own back. It goes with being at the top of the magical food chain. But for the first time in his existence—thanks to his devious gargoyle father—he's been slapped with a partner.

This infuriating female soldier also has the distinction of being a Null, a mortal sent by the Divine Ones to influence an outcome. A Null's natural immunity to all types of magic allows them to battle even the most powerful of magic wielders, even demigods.

His sire and dam are certain the Divine Ones have sent the Null to aid the Light in defeating the Battle Goddess.

Gryton doubts it's anything so innocent.

And if he's correct, he has just been partnered up with his doom.

But if the Divine Ones think he'll just roll over and allow one of their Nulls the chance to kill him, they'll be disappointed.

Very disappointed.

SCION OF THE SORCERESS

CHAPTER ONE

Gryton

Tapping one talon-tipped finger against his thigh in boredom, Commander Gryton allowed his gaze to slide along the perimeter of his small, clear-sided cell again. Not that there was anything new worth seeing. The spartan area was intentionally devoid of everything that could be turned into a weapon. With a disgruntled sigh, he settled on the narrow pallet that served as a bed.

His captors didn't trust the Avatars' word that he was now an ally. Not yet. Perhaps the humans never would fully trust any of the magic wielders, especially him. He gave a mental nod regarding that bit of wisdom. Trust was something too easily betrayed. He fingered the raised skin around his neck, rubbing at the tattooed collar encircling his throat.

And hadn't he gone to great lengths to gain the Battle Goddess's trust only to betray her within weeks of meeting his birth mother? With a grunt, he adjusted his position and braced his back against the wall.

As it was prone to do, the garment pulled tight around his neck, pressing against the tattooed slave collar and reminding him of its existence for the hundredth time that day. After a few angry jerks to settle the shirt back into place, he crossed his arms over his chest and glanced down, his frown deepening.

The outfit they had forced him to don after his gargoyle sire had stripped him of his natural protective armor left much to be desired. The dull grey fabric of the 't-shirt' was the blandest tone he'd ever laid eyes on.

And the lower half of the garment?

He shuddered.

The muddy mix of greens reminded him of blight crawling up a doomed tree's trunk. The design was to help a warrior hide in a forest's underbrush. And was he in a forest? No.

Though he'd much rather be hiding in the woods, he reflected, than in his present location.

Even mortal servants back in the Battle Goddess's kingdom possessed better attire and lodgings. As for himself, when he wasn't covered in his natural plate armor, he'd worn the finest fabrics. The Lady of Battles had liked to remind her subjects they weren't savages, that living under her rule had many benefits.

He snorted. Not that the benefits outweighed the many life-threatening drawbacks, but if he'd been forced to tell the truth, he'd have to admit that he'd grown to like the luxurious velvets, smooth silks, and the finest of leatherwork.

He'd even admired the expert craftmanship needed to master each bit of gold and silver embroidery and intricate beadwork. His own nature was so chaotic and destructive, the intricate patterns woven into the various fabrics appealed to him on some level he'd never allowed himself to dwell on too long.

Yes, he admitted, *more than a bit vain of me.*

But there was a pleasure in having one's outward appearance match the elegance of a disciplined mind and body. And being able to wear such items had been a personal benchmark that he was in control. Mastery over his elemental fire had been a long and bitter fight. In his youth, it had been a battle just to maintain this body. He couldn't count how many times his power had overwhelmed him, and he'd burned everything around him to ash.

As he glanced down at himself again, his mood darkened further.

He'd betrayed all that discipline. Everything that he'd worked for gone. He'd thrown away the hard-earned respect of the warriors serving under him when he'd agreed to become his mother's apprentice.

And for what?

Grimacing, he admitted he'd envisioned himself working with his sire and dam in a partnership. Instead, he found himself locked in a box two paces in width.

While the last four days hadn't been what he'd intended, that didn't mean he'd always be in this box. He would behave and prove to his parents he was trustworthy.

He'd prove it to the humans if that were the only way to escape this box. After he was free, and they defeated the Battle Goddess, he could strike out on his own. The Magic Realm spanned many worlds. He could find a new lair.

He'd barely finished that thought when the sleeping pallet shifted under him, his braced weight shoving it farther from the wall. The back of his skull smacked against the transparent barrier behind him. Cursing, he braced his hands against the floor to prevent himself from sliding farther.

The last thing his ego needed was for him to end up sprawled in an undignified heap.

Grunting, he admitted even the sleeping pallets of the Mortal Realm conspired against him.

And predictably, his infernal 't-shirt' chose that time to strangle him again.

Cursing, he leaped up from the ground and kicked the pallet back in place while simultaneously tearing the shirt from his body. Slinging it against the wall with every bit of disdain he could summon was mildly satisfying.

"That performance deserves a few bills tucked into the waist of a pair of ass-hugging leather pants," said a female voice possessing a rich, almost husky tone.

The female guard. How had he forgotten about her?

While he didn't have a clue what she was talking about, by her tone, he knew it was derogatory.

"Did your superiors forget to warn you not to talk to me?" he questioned without turning to face her. "I might steal and eat your soul, Mortal."

"It was probably covered in the stack of reports they handed out as they were briefing me, but they rushed me here so fast, no one gave me a chance to finish reading even the first page."

She'd been specially selected to be his guard? His eyes narrowed. Perhaps she wasn't human at all?

No. Impossible. He'd have sensed it if she was a magic wielder. The more he thought about it, the stranger it seemed. From the first day, he'd thought it odd and vaguely insulting that they'd only assigned a single guard to him. When the human was off duty, it was always the leshii Greenborrow who took her place.

"Don't get me wrong," the female began, "They briefed me on some of what has been going on here. Thought it was bullshit. Then ten minutes after I disembarked from the transport, I found myself facing your gargoyle father. Just about jumped out of my skin the first time he materialized out of thin air. Got another swift briefing and was rushed here. But after watching your sullen ass for the last four days, I'm pretty sure you aren't in any position to be eating souls."

His back stiffened as a growl formed in his throat. "I was the Commander of the Battle Goddess's army. Do you know what that—"

"Do I know that you just lost a fight with a t-shirt? Yes. You're scary as hell." Sarcasm dripped off the last words.

He tilted his head in the voice's direction but resisted the urge to look over his shoulder at the speaker. He wouldn't give her that power over him. "You are a mortal, ignorant as all your kind."

"T-shirt one; evil incarnate none."

It shouldn't have been possible, but his mood soured even more. So much so, his expression might almost match what was usually on the female's face. Against his will, and his better judgment, he turned toward her.

A tall, stocky figure with wide shoulders, a broad chest, thick waist, and muscular hips and thighs stood half in shadow outside the ring of light cast by the fixture hanging over Gryton's cell. The first time he'd seen the soldier, he'd mistaken her for a male.

In his defense, without his magic and no breeze to carry her scent to him, he'd only had his eyesight to go by, and at the time she'd been covered head to toe in the strange gear the soldiers of this world wore into battle. The helmet, chin strap, and eye protection had covered much of her face, leaving only broad cheekbones, a prominent nose, and square chin to guess a gender.

It wasn't until the second day when she'd returned without a helmet and wearing somewhat less gear, that he'd realized his mistake. That error bothered him more than a little. He prided himself on always knowing everything about his surroundings, documenting every little detail for future use and to prevent surprises. He hated surprises. Nothing good ever came from them.

Though he soothed himself with the knowledge mistaking her gender had been an honest mistake.

In her bulky uniform, the flat-chested female with short-cropped reddish-brown hair looked manly enough at a glance. Her hawkish nose and prominent brow didn't aid her cause. In truth, she projected an aura of brute strength and assurance. There was very little delicacy or refinement to any part of her body.

In short, while not the ugliest female he'd ever seen, she certainly was no succubus.

He caught her gaze and glowered. She only gave his naked chest a once over and smirked.

"You're a nice looking one. Bet I could bounce a quarter off that ass. And those abs... Shame you're also an evil little prick."

Her words added another layer of insult to his situation. Back in the Battle Goddess's kingdom, no one had dared speak to him in such a way, but this female talked down to him as if he was some lowborn warrior she could summon to her sleeping roll.

"Step inside." Gryton flashed her a smile that displayed his fangs as he gestured toward the locking mechanism on his cage door. "Get a closer look. Perhaps that can help you decide."

"Not born yesterday, Hot Stuff." Her honest laughter possessed a rich, deep tone, and her merriment transformed her features. He realized she had attractive eyes full of mirth and a smile so genuine that it almost called forth an answering one in him. That only infuriated him more.

Scowling at her, he reminded himself that while he may have defected from the Battle Goddess's army because of his mother, that in no way made him an ally to the humans. Certainly not this human. She was nothing to him, unworthy of his notice. Unless she continued to annoy him. In which case, he'd see what he could do to ensure she didn't live long enough to become a thorn in his side.

He dismissed her.

"Aw. Someone is butthurt over—"

Suddenly, the human soldier snapped her mouth closed and came to attention.

He realized he could hear footsteps approaching. He turned his back on the female and crossed his arms over his chest while he waited for the newcomers to arrive. By the sound of the softly clicking talons, he imagined one of them was his father.

Nothing good ever came from facing the male half of the Avatars.

CHAPTER TWO

Gryton

He didn't have long to wait for the Avatars. His sire and dam soon arrived with a unit of soldiers at their heels. Predictably, the male half of the Avatars was in the lead, not trusting Gryton even collared and caged as he was.

He grinned at his father. Gryton wouldn't trust himself either. His father was wise enough to realize that.

"Ah, what a delight. My sire and dam have come for a visit." He cast a glance over his shoulder toward the female soldier, directing his words at her. "Or, in my father's case, to glower while my mother visits me."

The soldier didn't respond. In fact, she stood so still and straight she resembled a statue. Ah, how sad. No distractions from that direction. With a sigh, he turned his full attention back to his parents.

They likely planned to speak of the same things they had for the last four days. Since the first day he'd come to this realm under armed escort, they had visited him once a day to update him on his situation, telling him what they'd been doing to smooth over their alliance with the humans.

And, as much as he hated to admit it, he looked forward to these few short times with his mother even if they merely spoke of unimportant things concerning the humans.

Lillian, when she'd only been a dryad-gargoyle hybrid, hadn't trusted him. But she was now the Sorceress as she was meant to be and could look inside, straight to his soul it seemed, and see all that had happened to him. She knew the reasons he'd become what he was. And, as miraculous as it seemed to him, she still loved him despite his alliance with their greatest enemy.

A year ago, Gryton wouldn't have thought he'd have fallen so far, but now he admitted he basked in the Sorceress's love for him. Yes, he eagerly awaited each visit, weakness though it was.

Then there was his father.

That was another complicated relationship he hadn't yet figured out how to navigate.

Usually, Gregory looked at him like a problem he very much wished didn't exist. Yet on the few occasions when the older male had been examining Gryton's power, the male half of the Avatars had allowed him to peer into that ancient mind.

To Gryton's great surprise, he'd sensed his father's awe.

And if he wasn't mistaken, there was a little pride mixed in with the other less-than-pleasant emotions Gregory experienced when he looked upon his son.

Oh, his sire felt shame, disquiet, and more than a little concern in having betrayed his vows and his honor by producing a son with his Sorceress. Yet there was more than that. Gryton's very survival, his mastery over his chaotic elemental magic, had impressed his father. And that Gryton had flourished in the Battle Goddess's kingdom and exerted control over the rest of the dark army? That had impressed his father more than a little.

Knowing how Gregory viewed him made it harder for Gryton to maintain a proper amount of hatred for his father.

Of course, neither of them would show even a hint of their growing regard for the other. They were still more enemies than allies. It was just how it had to be.

That would only change if they freed him from this cage and allowed him a chance to find a place at their side. If not as an equal, then at least as an honored apprentice.

"We have convinced the human authorities that you will be a far better asset than an enemy." The Sorceress said, studying him in a way that suddenly had him feeling defensive. "We've made it clear to them we won't harm our son or allow harm to come to you. We even laid out the dangers if they tried to kill you. Not that they have the power. But we made it very clear that if you somehow die here on Earth, you'll be reborn as a sun."

"That went over well," Gregory said dryly.

His mother gave her other half a hard stare before she returned her gaze to Gryton. "No one wants to see that happen, and we were able to bargain with the humans. This deal will allow all sides of Light's alliance to work together. Part of the bargain is that after we've won the war with the Lady of Battles, we will take you back to the Magic Realm with us and you will never return to Earth."

Gladly. How soon can we leave? Gryton thought with a touch of rare humor.

"But while we live here, you will cooperate with the humans and allow their scientists to study you."

And just that quickly, his earlier humor was snuffed out. He'd hoped to have minimal dealings with the non-magic wielders of this world. But this wouldn't be the first time things hadn't gone his way. If he had to, he'd learn to ignore the humans and go about his duties as required. Control was something he'd learned at an early age.

"You aren't free to roam." His mother's expression turned guarded.

Gryton stood a little straighter.

When she cleared her throat as a distraction, he knew he wouldn't like the rest. "You won't go anywhere alone. You will obey your keeper's commands without question."

"Keepers?" Gryton questioned with an arched brow. Though, he'd expected as much. He'd killed several humans the first time he'd come to the Mortal Realm. The humans wouldn't have forgiven or forgotten.

As for punishments, there were far worse things than 'keepers' trailing him around.

Perhaps this wouldn't be as bad as he'd expected. He might even earn back his freedom sooner than he'd thought.

"Keeper. Single. There will just be the one," Gregory

clarified and then glanced between Lillian and Gryton, his lips curling back with gargoyle humor. "You tell him the rest. He likes you better."

"Not for long," his mother muttered half under her breath.

Tension grew between Gryton's shoulder blades the longer his mother took to continue.

"The humans demanded a way to control you. We'd expected as much. But there was the problem of finding a human in their military with enough innate magic to allow them to control the command bracelet and then train them on how to use it."

"I wish you well in your search," Gryton said with a hint of a smirk in his tone that he couldn't hide. "Humans are weak-willed creatures. You might as well be handing a djinn over to an ape—the outcome will be just as destructive."

"He is a prejudiced, condescending little narcissist. But he doesn't hide what he thinks, at least," Gregory interjected, humor finding its way into his tone.

Hmmm...

There seemed a touch more humor than the situation warranted. Narrowing his eyes, Gryton studied his sire.

"Something else has presented itself, hasn't it?" he mused aloud, his mind whirling as he tried to leap to a conclusion but came up with nothing.

"Yes." Lillian paused as her eyes slid toward the female soldier still standing like a statue. "The Divine Ones have another plan for you, it seems."

Gregory nodded in agreement and offered a rare bit of free information. "That is why we were late visiting you on that first day. We were called away to investigate why six of our check-point detection spells went dark within the humans' base of operations." Gregory paused and made a face as if speaking the human words left a bad taste in his mouth. "We suspected an attack, but what we discovered was an even greater surprise."

Again, his parents glanced over at the female soldier.

There was something off with the woman. He'd suspected it from the start. She barely looked old enough to be a soldier, even by human standards. His sire's words just confirmed his earlier suspicions.

"If you will leave us for a moment?" Gregory tilted his muzzle toward the female in question.

"Major Resnick said two minutes. That's all the alone time you get." With those biting words, the human left through the room's one door.

Moments later Gregory stepped in closer. Instinctively Gryton tensed.

"Easy. I'm just going to remove your collar and allow you to witness what she truly is."

Gryton was flabbergasted for the first time in his life. They were freeing him with no assurances of his good behavior? That made no sense whatsoever. Had they summoned a djinn from the Spirit Realm and were now turning him over to the creature?

Again, he felt himself tensing, ready for an attack. If it wasn't a djinn, then his father had some other trick planned.

But as Gryton stood there with his hands fisted, his spine straight, and what he hoped was an expression of uncaring on his face, Gregory simply reached out with a small thread of magic and released the spell encircling Gryton's neck.

Freed, his fiery power returned, and he nearly breathed a sigh of relief at having its warmth flooding back through his body. He didn't care if it was chaotic and hard to control. It was a part of him. With its absence, he'd felt fundamentally less.

Lillian turned and whispered to one soldier, and the male marched out of the room. A moment later he returned, the female soldier a step behind. As she came closer, Gryton's power calmed without his will acting upon it.

What was this?

He stepped away from his sire and dam and stared at the soldier. But no matter how hard he tried to read her, there was nothing. She was blank. A void. Air registered upon his senses to a higher degree than she did.

How was such a thing possible?

No spell, no matter how skilled the creator or how intricate the weaving, could hide itself this well, not from him.

Oh, if she'd been skilled in magic and was standing off in another room, he might not have noticed whatever spell she used to hide her true self. But she was standing three paces away, and he felt nothing coming from her. Nothing at all. And yet she was clearly weaving some great spell to trap his power like this.

"Go on," Gregory urged the soldier. "Touch him. Show him what the Divine Ones have sent us."

CHAPTER THREE

Gryton

"I don't know anything about your Divine Ones, but I admit I'm curious what this is." The soldier stepped closer, and then reached out with one hand, pointing to the glyph on his chest. "I thought you were supposed to be unable to call on your magic, but I noticed your glowing tattoo pulsing like it was in standby mode."

Gryton glanced down at the glyph. It normally pulsed with power in time to his breathing, not unlike someone blowing air across the embers of a fire. But now it was dull, only a glimmer of light flared up when he dragged in a surprised breath.

He took a step back, recognizing danger even if he did not understand what it was.

Then suddenly something clicked in his mind. "She feeds on magic."

"No, actually," his gargoyle sire countered. "She gets no tangible benefit from magic, so isn't truly feeding on it. At least not in the way you think."

"Do I look like a vampire to you?" The soldier tilted her head. "Come to think of it, he's the one with the fangs."

Gregory snorted at the female's words and then continued his conversation with Gryton. "She merely absorbs and then releases your magic, but not just yours. She does it with all magic. Even ours."

Suddenly the blank void, the nothingness made sense.

"You're a Null," his voice held a hint of disbelief and maybe a bit of awe.

He'd never met a Null, but he'd heard stories. The Battle Goddess had mentioned having crossed a Null once in her existence. She'd said the Divine Ones created them to rescue djinns summoned from the Spirit Realm against their will, or to kill them if they went insane from their captivity.

Only a Null, an Avatar, or, Gryton supposed, one such as himself could withstand a raging djinn's power long enough to get close and free it from its master. Or, alternatively, kill it and release its soul to return to the Spirit Realm where it would slowly grow in strength over hundreds of thousands of years.

Thankfully, under normal circumstances, a djinn could return to the Spirit Realm on their own given time. But there were a few creatures in the universe capable of corrupting them. Actual pure-blood demons were one. But the Avatars and other djinns were swift to hunt down and eradicate that kind of evil when it tried to escape the void and infiltrate any of the three realms.

But there was a lesser creature that served the beasts of the void. He knew one personally—a blood witch.

He'd not thought Taryin was irrational enough to summon a djinn, or that the Battle Goddess was so far gone that she'd order the witch to do so, but if there was a Null walking this planet, then the Divine Ones had either sent the god-killer for him or a djinn.

"Have the Divine Ones finally caught up with me, then? Is the god-killer here for me?"

"Yes, but not in the way you're thinking," Lillian said, her gaze open and honest. "I'm certain you'd already be dead if that were our creators' plan. While Private Erika Emerson has no memory of her purpose, if she were sent to kill you, her soul would have awakened to carry out her purpose upon first meeting you."

Gryton's brow arched. "So, you just left her here while I was caged and collared to see what would happen? How very reassuring, Mother."

"I thought the plan had merit," Gregory admitted with a chuckle. "However, my Sorceress was greatly displeased by my comment and made me stay and monitor you while she dealt with the human military. Once we were assured the Null wasn't sent to destroy you, it confirmed her real purpose."

Gryton glowered at his parents. "And have you determined what the Null's purpose is?"

"Likely multi-faceted," Lillian said. "But after studying how she interacts with the various magic users, Gregory and me included, I've determined that her ability is most attuned to you. While we all feel the drain of magic when we are near her, it's how she reacts to your power that is the most telling."

"Y'all, for the record, I'm not actively doing shit."

Lillian laughed. "I know. It's as natural to you as breathing. You likely aren't even aware you're doing it. However, I can see what's happening and can say with certainty the Divine Ones sent you to either control Gryton or to aid him in controlling his chaotic magic."

Gryton snorted. "Then she is here to enslave me. I don't need a god-killer's aid in mastering my magic."

Though he knew his words were lies. It had always been a battle to control his power. And dwelling in the Mortal Realm only made it harder. It was possible the Divine Ones knew he'd be forced to spend a great deal of time on this forsaken little world in the Mortal Realm and had sent their pet to ensure he didn't destroy the entire planet in a ball of fire and fury.

The Divine Ones wouldn't have been moved out of concern for him. No, they'd sent their Null to contain him. It was a displeasing notion, but he could still work with this new development.

While magic would be useless against a Null, he had other skills. He glanced at the human, giving her another inspection. With a little effort, he should be able to beguile the human and win her to his side. It would be a nuisance, but to have a pet Null could come in very handy.

"God-killer?" the soldier said with a snort as if she couldn't hold her silence any longer. "Bit melodramatic, isn't it?"

"Perhaps," he agreed, giving her a hint of a smile he hoped showed a touch of friendliness.

She stared at him like he'd sprouted a second head.

Hmmm. Perhaps it was the fangs.

"No one answered my question. What's the mark, and if I do this long enough," she reached out and stabbed a finger against the glyph, making it dim more, "will it kill you?"

The touch chilled him as it sucked away his elemental magic. He held his ground, unwilling to show weakness to the Null, even though he was suddenly feeling as feeble as a newborn foal.

His sorceress mother seemed to have determined the truth. He was more affected by the Null than either of his parents. Though, they were the Avatars and much, much older than him. Perhaps that had something to do with it. In the coming weeks, he'd try to determine what made him more susceptible to the Null's influence or what made the Avatars more immune. If he could crack that mystery, he might combat this Null's power over him.

While he'd been enmeshed with his own thoughts, the Null had stepped back and was now circling him, studying him from different angles.

"You didn't drop dead. Guess that answers that question." She poked him twice more just to see.

A ripple of unease accompanied the weakness. The Null's gaze sharpened suddenly.

No. She couldn't have sensed that momentary weakness. He'd been guarding his thoughts and had a tight rein on his body language.

She smirked and poked him twice more.

Gryton drew himself up and glowered at the Null. "Touch me again and I'll—"

"Do absolutely nothing," Gregory asserted in a deadly calm voice. His expression suggested boredom, but Gryton could see the sharp little bits of shadow magic dancing in the corners of the room. "She was born for a great purpose, sent by the Divine Ones, and you will obey us and do her no harm."

"And her superiors, you won't harm any of them, either," Lillian added and placed a hand on his sire's arm.

The big gargoyle relaxed, his earlier mirth returning. "Not that you'll be able to harm the Null once your mother and I finished soul-binding you to her."

"Soul-binding?" Some of Gryton's shock must have shown on his face because the gargoyle laughed evilly. Instinctively, he took a half step back before he exerted control over himself again. They'd surprised him badly. Servants of the Light didn't do things like soul-binding.

"You can't do that to me. Death would be preferable." If he'd been able to call his power, he would have summoned a defensive wall of fire and attempted escape.

CHAPTER FOUR

Gryton

"Oh, stop whining," the Null said with an accompanying roll of her eyes. "Do you think I'm any happier about this than you? I will have a piece of your evil little soul grafted on to mine. Do you think I'm overjoyed by that? The only reason I'm agreeing is that they say your ass will go supernova and take out the whole damn planet if you lose control. Which, here in this realm, is supposed to be a real possibility."

Gryton snapped his teeth together, allowing the human to speak her mind. Anything that delayed the soul-binding, even if it was only for the time this mortal nattered at him, was a mercy.

"Thought my superiors were playing some kind of joke on us newbies. Nope. I touch down and discover it's all true. Been an all-around surreal week. So, you can just stop whining," she poked him repeatedly in the chest, "and accept that this shit is real. It's happening. I'm getting a slice of your fiery little soul. There's no way I'm letting you destroy my world. If I have to sit on you and suck you dry every day for the next hundred years, I will."

Narrowing his eyes, he glowered at the female but realized her words and reasoning were logical from her standpoint. While she was very young, she possessed a self-assuredness that usually only came with experience, but he sensed he put her off balance and she didn't like that one bit. He resisted the urge to smirk. "Was there anything else you'd like to add?"

"No. I'm good." She straightened her uniform and then stepped back, returning to her earlier position by the wall. Her expression was unreadable once more.

His father's, however, was not. "Something you wanted to add?"

Gregory's grin grew broader. "No. Just wondering when you want to do this?"

How about never? But Gryton didn't utter those thoughts out loud, settling for glowering instead.

"We can begin now if you like since the humans have already agreed to this." Gregory's expression was neutral, but Gryton was sure the gargoyle was still mentally laughing at him.

Grimacing, Gryton reflected that gargoyles were perverse beasts with equally contrary senses of humor.

Lillian watched her mate and her son face off. Then she glanced back at the human soldier for a moment. Not for the first time she dwelled on the fact it was likely no coincidence that the Null was also an old pure-soul and a soldier. A rare combination of characteristics. The Divine Ones were taking no chances that Gryton could corrupt her.

As an old-soul, Erika had lived many thousands of lifetimes—her soul growing stronger each time—and she was now beyond Gryton's ability to corrupt, bribe, or otherwise compromise her morals. She was perfect for this task, and Lillian just grew more certain of the Null's purpose. While she might be useful in hunting down and killing the blood witch and whatever other dark, twisted spells the witch had created, Lillian knew in her gut that Private Emerson had arrived here because the Divine Ones wanted her here to aid Gryton.

The Creators had a way of moving people around like pawns on a chessboard. And while that often annoyed Lillian, in this case, she could only nod at their wisdom.

"If this is truly Divine will, there's no escaping it. Let's get this over with," Gryton said, his voice thunderous.

"Don't know nothing about your Divine Ones, but God put me on this earth, and if my purpose is to make it impossible for you to go supernova, I'm happy to oblige."

Gryton groaned.

Lillian had been fighting back her mirth at her son's grumpiness throughout the conversation and finally lost the battle and started snorting with laughter.

CHAPTER FIVE

Erika

Surveying the scene as the Avatars began fixin' for the magical voodoo surgery, Erika's gaze took everything in and eventually landed on Gryton. After the first day's initial disbelief and doubt, she'd descended into a near emotionally-comatose state where new strangeness just rolled off her like water from a duck's back.

Though she absorbed every new bit of information and reported it to her superiors. Perhaps there was something to this whole Null business that allowed her to adapt to new situations without snapping?

She'd always been resilient.

And she'd already heard rumors of several soldiers scrubbed from the program because they couldn't keep their shit together when faced with magical aliens. Oh, she found it beyond unreal, but the situation was what it was. No amount of denial would make the big gargoyle, his equally strange sorceress mate, or their fire-demon offspring just up and vanish.

After all, life never asked a person what path they wanted to take. It was just shoved in front of them, and a person either stumbled for a couple of steps and then righted themselves, or they tripped and rolled to the bottom of the damned hill.

Erika planned on climbing higher, not rolling down a hill at breakneck speed.

Looking at the creature called Gryton, she knew it wouldn't be easy. She'd need to call on every scrap of patience, perseverance, and fortitude she could summon just to survive dealing with the fiery being. They'd known each other four days and exchanged only a few sentences, but she'd already concluded he was a diva.

If she had her way, she'd start in on his reconditioning as soon as possible. They just needed to get through this soul-binding thing and adjust to their new, and very unwanted, partnership.

It wasn't lost on Gryton as he lay on the cold metal table that he now knew what a sacrificial victim might feel moments before their death. Oh, he wouldn't die from this, but it was most definitely a sacrifice. He was giving up his freedom and his free will.

All because he was so weak as to be swayed by his mother's love.

Bloody blight and plagues! How had he fallen so far?

"Buck up, Hot Stuff. I'm not looking forward to this any more than you."

He turned to glower at the Null where she sat on a second metal table three paces away, grinning at him of all things. His gargoyle father moved to stand between them, but it wasn't enough to block the Null's presence.

His only solace was that this unwanted alliance with a human would be short-lived. Once they won the war, he would return to the Magic Realm, and then there would be no need to ever look upon her again. The Null would remain behind on Earth where she would age and die swiftly like all humans. They'd be free of each other in less than a hundred years.

"We are ready," the Sorceress said as she came to stand beside his sire. "Are you prepared?"

Her tone suggested he should take a few moments to center himself. While he'd never had a piece of his soul sliced off and given to another before, he had enough knowledge that this was darker magic than the Avatars had likely ever used before. He grinned up at them both.

"Do not worry, mother. You'll only be very slightly sullied by this spell work. It is a much smaller infraction than begetting me. You survived that. And this is nothing compared to the dark spells the blood witch was teaching your little brother and his pet human."

She blanched. He instantly felt remorse for reminding her that her younger brother was still missing, his fate unknown.

Gregory grunted, his lips compressing, not finding humor in Gryton's words.

"Keep grinning, Offspring. And know I would have felt much worse for what your mother and I are about to do if you hadn't been guilty of murder several times over."

"The humans?" Gryton shrugged. "It was war. Besides, they were the first to attack intending to kill, if you've forgotten."

Gregory grunted again, and Gryton took it as a sign of a victory against his father.

Just then Lillian called power, drawing their attention to her. A significant current of energy rushed from the Spirit Realm, causing hundreds of small, chilled currents to dance in the surrounding air. A moment later, his sire closed his eyes and bowed his head. Soon his power joined his other half's.

"This will hurt," Gregory warned as the power that had been swirling around the room a moment before formed bands and locked Gryton into place. "The pain will be fleeting at least. Are you ready to give a piece of your soul to the Null?"

Across from him, the soldier had drawn her knees up and now rested her arms against them. The posture wasn't that of boredom. He knew she listened to every word, and her sharp gaze caught every nuance of body language.

Likely other humans were doing the same through their technology even though they'd been forbidden from entering the room. That had caused a few tense moments between his sire and dam and their human allies. Likely his fang-flashing grins did nothing to decrease tensions.

At last, he looked back at his sire. "I am ready. Perhaps you should ask the Null the same question."

"They already did. I'm on board. But can we stop calling me Null? I have a name. Y'all are basically calling me a 'zero' or a nothing. I'll happily respond to Private Emerson, just Emerson, or even Erika."

The Sorceress's eyebrows scrunched together a moment before she apologized. "I'm sorry. I always meant it as a title of respect. It was never derogatory."

"On your part, yes. His?" The Null jerked a thumb in Gryton's direction. "It's always derogatory coming from him."

His mother turned to him with a frown. "Gryton, she has a point. You won't use her title in that way again, will you?"

"If that is your wish, I shall not."

At least not in your hearing.

But that didn't mean the Null had yet earned his respect. She would have to work to prove she had something that resembled honor and nobleness buried somewhere under her unpolished exterior. Only then would he address her with respect. He cast a glower at the Null and decided she might die of old age before he had to honor her in such a way.

In the next moment a gargoyle's tail swatted him across the chest with enough force to make Gryton wheeze.

"What was that for?" He spat out while imagining giving his sire some lasting scars. Though he settled for glowering at his father for now.

"That was for lying to your mother."

Gryton smirked. "I'm still learning the art of truth-telling. It might take a little time."

"And what else might you be learning or planning, I wonder?" Lillian gestured at his naked chest. "I thought the military was supplying you with basic needs."

"We did," the human piped up. "He tore his shirt off. He either has super sensitive skin, or he thought he'd attempt a little seduction to see if I'd let him out of his cage. He was so bad at it, I'm not sure which motive it was."

Gryton dropped his head back against the table. "I hate humans. This is the Divine One's true punishment for my service to the Battle Goddess all these years."

"That is entirely possible," Gregory agreed and then gave him a most ghastly smile. "Shall we continue?"

"Just get it over with. The sooner I'm 'leashed' and no longer a threat, the sooner we can then strike a blow to the Battle Goddess and her monstrous pet blood witch."

"Very well." Gregory flicked his wrist, and a sharp little shard of shadow and spirit magic appeared between his fingers. Then in a motion too fast to follow, the two magics blurred and his sire struck.

It wasn't a killing blow. Nothing that tiny could kill Gryton, but that didn't mean it didn't hurt. He clenched his teeth. The power cut through his weakened defenses like they were water. Then his mother's power joined his father's, and they were digging deeper into his spirit.

Goddess! The two powers were so cold his fire magic hissed and recoiled. Usually, this was when his magic would have returned tenfold, a raging inferno to destroy whatever threatened him.

But this wasn't an attack, and with the Null only a few paces away, his power didn't respond as it normally would. Instead, it coiled tightly, like a banked ember that slept while his sire and dam cut deeper into his spirit.

He lifted his head enough to look down and didn't see blood or fire even though the shadow and spirit magic blade had cut into his chest. Usually, when he was wounded while in a flesh and blood form, he bled like any other creature, but that blood would then ignite, setting fire to anything not immune.

"I'm so sorry," his mother said, horror clear in her tone, "but there was no way we could render you unconscious without causing even greater trauma. We will be swift."

"This tiny scratch? It's nothing." He scoffed at her concern. While it hurt and likely would have rendered most mortals dead and many immortals unconscious, he was a fire elemental and had experienced his flesh burning away far more times than he could count. This was just a dull, barely felt pain in comparison.

As promised, they swiftly separated a tiny sliver of his soul from the rest. Soon their powers were withdrawing from him, leaving him cold and shaking but remarkably whole. There wasn't even a fading scar upon his chest. Though the glyph pulsed surprisingly bright considering the Null's proximity.

He calmed his breathing and that, too, dimmed. Once he'd mastered himself, he turned to watch the Null. She stared wide-eyed back at him but seemed otherwise determined.

The Divine Ones had given her a remarkably calm nature.

It wasn't until the Sorceress approached with the fiery bit of his soul that the human looked about ready to bolt.

"Is it too late to change my mind?" the Null asked, a bit of forced humor in her tone.

"No one will force you to accept this fate," Gregory said in his serious tones. "Not even the Divine Ones. They don't keep slaves, only willing servants to the Light."

The Null grimaced. Gryton could see her practically scouring her mind for ways to back out and still keep her dignity intact. At last, she stared at Gryton. Then her gaze hardening, she turned back to the Avatars. "If everything you told me about what I am is correct, then I suppose I must have already agreed to all this back in the Spirit Realm. Let's just get on with this."

There was still uncertainty in her eyes, but Gryton's sire and dam glanced at each other for long moments and communicated mind to mind. He couldn't hear their words, but he could imagine them well enough. They were trying to determine if the human was up to this task.

Gryton could have answered that question for them.

No, she wasn't ready. No human was a match for him, not even a Null as powerful as this female.

And he planned to use that against her.

If he were to be a slave, he'd make sure she was equally enslaved to him.

CHAPTER SIX

Erika

Erika stared between the two Avatars, willing them to believe her, even if she didn't really believe herself. Who the hell could be prepared for this kind of shit? But it didn't matter if she was ready for this or not. She needed to do this.

While she hadn't been ordered, she knew everyone was counting on her to put a leash on the monster on the other table. But if she couldn't convince herself, there was no way she could fool the two Avatars. Had she already failed in her mission before it had even started?

She held her breath and waited.

And waited some more.

At last, the two Avatars nodded their heads in silent agreement.

"We believe you are worthy of taming our son of his least savory tendencies," Gregory said.

Lillian nodded serenely and then began calling on power again. The second spell was much subtler than the one that had dug in and carved out a bit of Gryton's soul. The sorceress painted a glowing symbol in the air above Erika's exposed midriff.

Gregory came forward then, the fiery slice of Gryton's soul suspended between his talons. With great care, he placed it on the spell the sorceress had woven. A bright flash momentarily blinded Erika.

When she could see again, the shimmering spell and molten soul fragment had merged.

"Excellent," Lillian murmured to herself and then met Erika's gaze. "Are you ready?"

"Yes, ma'am."

The sorceress looked doubtful but merely nodded. "Very well."

Slowly the spell lowered until its chill touched her skin. She shivered involuntarily at the contact.

"Once you absorb this spell, it will draw the sliver of my son's soul along with it. Then the bit of Gryton's soul will seek yours out and merge. It is smart enough to know it is too small to survive on its own, but it will wish to live."

Sounds like a parasite, Erika muttered in her own mind.

"Shall I continue?" Lillian asked.

Erika just waved a hand to indicate the spell and the fiery bit of soul. "Carry on as you were."

"You are brave," the big gargoyle said.

"Or foolish. My family never agrees on anything, but they all thought I was a damned fool for joining up.

Though that might have been because I told them after it was already done. If I'd given them a little more warning, they probably would have warmed to the idea."

Erika eyed the soul fragment and wondered if she hadn't just jumped without looking again. Oh well. Too late to back out now. She motioned for the Avatars to continue.

They did, the gargoyle stepping forward to lock her in place with bands of power like he had with Gryton. "To keep you from moving if you panic."

"I never panic." Her jaw clenched as she willed that to be true this time.

Surprisingly, there was little to cause panic. A faint tickle. A chilled tingle. A slight heaviness in her chest. Then it was over.

"That's it?"

"You were expecting more?"

"Err. Yes. But I will not complain."

The big gargoyle chuckled. "That's good because Gryton is likely to complain enough for you both once he recovers. If he gets too annoying, just let me know. I'll happily aid you with his reconditioning."

Loathsome gargoyles and their twisted sense of humor. Gryton had been about to spit something equally sharp-edged at his sire, but his mother leaned over him. "Ignore him. He loves the challenge of seeing if he can get a rise out of you."

Gryton snorted. The only rising he wanted to do was to

get off this table and limp back to his cage and huddle there until he'd recovered. The pain he could deal with.

This...

This was a violation.

"Did you need help getting up?" His mother asked.

"No." He sat up and swung his legs over the table. Unfortunately, that put the Null directly in his line of sight.

They'd both been moving slowly and cautiously to make sure that everything worked until the moment their eyes locked on the other. A silent challenge resonated between them. They both hopped down. Gryton strode back to his cage; the Null marched to her earlier position by the wall where the light and shadows met.

Behind him, he sensed his mother following.

"You both may want to sit and rest—"

"I'm fine," two voices snapped in near synchronicity.

"You think you are now," Gregory added ominously.

Lillian continued to trail Gryton, and out of the corner of his eye, he noticed his sire had moved to the Null's side. The gargoyle just stood there staring until the Null grew tired of it.

"What? Did I grow horns or something?" Her words came out somewhat slurred. She reached up with a clumsy hand, feeling to be sure she hadn't suddenly grown a set. Gryton almost laughed at her drunken behavior until he understood.

"No horns," the gargoyle replied. "I'm just waiting for you to lose consciousness."

She scoffed at the big male. "I don't faint. Never fainted in my life. You will have a long..." She paused, her eyes suddenly going unfocused. "Oh..."

She slumped forward a moment later.

A bark of laughter escaped Gryton as she dropped where she stood. Only his gargoyle sire's swift reflexes prevented the human from cracking her head.

"Hold your laughter for later," Lillian said in a tone that wasn't a suggestion. "She's just overcome with the sudden stress on her body from absorbing so much magic. Living on Earth as she has, she hasn't had to deal with the magic the three of us naturally give off. Plus, giving her a piece of your soul is another added stress. She now has a direct line to feed on you. You're the straw that broke the camel's back."

"A camel?" He was unfamiliar with the word.

His mother nodded and then touched his mind. Her power carried with it an image of the beast. A large and lumpy and ungainly creature. Ugly beyond measure. And if he wasn't misunderstanding, the beast's disposition was as unpleasant as its appearance.

Gryton gave his mother a beautiful smile.

"What did I say?" Her brows scrunched unhappily.

"A camel. You describe the human accurately. I shall be certain to put that to good use."

"Don't you dare. That's not what I meant at all. It's just a saying." She went into a detailed explanation that he ignored, distracted by a new sensation. Well, not new. He'd felt it the first time the Null had approached him and poked him in the chest.

A chill shivered its way down his spine. Another followed fast on its heels. Shortly, his strength steadily drained away, and his knees grew weak. Bloody blight! She was feeding off him without even being conscious.

Cursing the Null to the Void, he took a wobbling step inside his cage and locked his knees. When he wasn't sure that would keep him upright, he leaned against the nearest wall as if he was equal parts bored and confident. Though he was feeling anything but.

Worry gnawed at him. How much power did the Null need to devour before he lost consciousness? He despised being helpless. If he were going to collapse into a boneless heap, he'd prefer to do it when his mother wasn't there to see it.

"Ah. You're starting to feel it." His mother reached out and placed a hand over part of the glyph marking his chest. "Better lie down before you fall down."

Gryton just flashed his teeth at her. "I'm fine. A little weakness will not knock me flat."

A frown marred her features, and then she planted her fists on her hips. "Fine. Be stubborn. You get that from your father."

She glanced over her shoulder. "Gregory, my love, bring the human here. Gryton will need her once she drains him dry."

As Gryton watched his sire obey the Sorceress, he finally unbent enough to ask, "What are you talking about?"

"Young Nulls, new to their gift, will continue to feed until they glut themselves on power, only then will their bodies release it back into the surrounding environment. Normally, we would just separate you, but now that she has a piece of your soul, she'll feed upon you, regardless. Or at least until she learns to master her new abilities."

Gryton made a hissing sound of denial, but his mother just ignored him.

"To restore your strength, you'll need her close so you can begin feeding off the energy she'll release once she's maxed out her gift's ability to absorb."

Narrowing his eyes, he glanced over her shoulder to watch his sire carrying the unconscious human toward his cell.

"No!" Gryton stumbled forward and then slammed his cage door shut. "You can keep the camel. I'd rather starve."

The gargoyle merely stood outside the cage and gave him a toothy grin. "I can wait."

Gryton returned his sire's look with a glower, but the longer he stood there defiantly, the weaker he grew. Soon he was shaking with cold, and he had to grit his teeth to stop them from chattering.

With a muttered curse about the loathsomeness of gargoyles, he collapsed to his knees and bowed his head in a useless attempt to keep his vision from greying out.

One of the last things he heard was the cage door opening. Shortly he was dragged over to his sleeping pallet. A moment later, a warm body was being placed next to him. He managed to roll over and spear his father with one last hate-filled look.

The big idiot merely laughed. "I'll be back to check on you later."

Don't be in any hurry on my account, Gryton thought as he glowered at the male.

He wasn't sure how long he lay there, barely aware of his surroundings, but slowly the seemingly endless sensation of having his magic sucked away eased and then stopped altogether.

After a brief pause where nothing sinister happened, a warm and mellow power began flowing across his body and soul. It was the purest, most divinely pleasant substance he'd ever tasted. He instinctively wanted to curl around the source, but his body was still unresponsive to his commands.

Slowly it dawned upon him that his mother had been correct. The Null was already releasing some energy. When he blinked open his eyes, he could see ethereal tendrils of magic rising from her body like heat from the sands of a desert.

In time his strength returned enough to move a little. He reached out to grab some part of her so he could absorb the magic faster. His arm was still numb, his control minimal, but he flopped his hand around her neck.

After a time, warmth returned to his hand, and he curled his fingers around her throat. Briefly, the idea of strangling her flitted through his head. That would certainly ruin his sire and dam's plans.

But if he killed the Null now, the delightful power would stop flowing into his body.

He couldn't bring himself to do it.

With a sigh of defeat, he allowed himself just to rest and drink the power she cast off. It was peaceful.

Or at least until his senses expanded enough to realize his sire was still in the room.

"You're still here?" The surly tone he'd been hoping for fell flat and the words came out in a broken and slurred tone.

"You thought I'd leave while the Null was vulnerable?" The gargoyle snorted with disdain.

"Vulnerable? The Null?" Gryton grimaced. "You're demented."

Gregory chuckled. "Apparently. Otherwise, you wouldn't exist."

Beside him, the Null moaned and jerked, coming to wakefulness.

"Since I know you won't actually harm the Null, I'll leave you both to finish recovering," Gregory said with an accompanying little huff. "Your mother is likely growing weary of holding off the team of scientists wanting to run tests on you and your Null."

"She's not my Null," Gryton hissed as he removed his hand from around her throat, but the outer door clicked softly, his father already gone.

Beside him, a second groan issued from the Null.

"What damn fool ran me down with a tank?"

There was more grunting and groaning. A moment later he received a sharp elbow in his side, then the Null was propping herself up. She looked around the cage, saw him sprawled out next to her, and then looked heavenward. "God, help me. How did I end up here?"

"I assure you this wasn't the work of the Divine Father."

She glowered at him and tried to sit up, only to collapse back down next to him a moment later.

"Never mind. Floor's good."

He almost laughed at her tone but held it back.

She turned her head toward him and then blinked

several times as if having trouble focusing her vision. He could understand the feeling.

Presently his eyes were trying to convince him there were two Nulls in the cage.

She was blessedly silent for a time after that.

It didn't last, and she turned to face him again. Her eyes lowered to gaze at his chest. He saw the question before she'd even put it into words. She was that easy to read. He stared up at the cage's ceiling hoping she'd forget her question and just fall asleep.

"You never told me what the mark on your chest means."

So much for that wish.

With a sigh, he turned from staring at the ceiling to spear her with a scornful look. "It's a visual representation of my true name."

"Gryton isn't your real name?"

"No. But you've already gotten all you will ever get from me. You don't get my true name."

She arched an eyebrow at him. "I'll let that one slide. No one's at their best after surgery. I think we got off on the wrong foot. Maybe we should start over?"

After spearing her with a second glower, Gryton turned on his side, facing the wall of his cage. While he might be unable to escape her, that didn't mean he had to acknowledge she existed.

Strangely it helped to ignore her. He didn't feel as vulnerable when he wasn't looking at her, his rage and hatred cocooning him in a protective shell.

"Fine. Carry on being a jackass."

"I shall."

"Great. We'll get along wonderfully. Mutually assured misery." She muttered a few other things under her breath before she fell silent again. After a length of time, he sensed she'd lost the battle against sleep.

He rolled back over and glowered at her a moment before he wrapped one arm around her. At least now he could feed in peace.

CHAPTER SEVEN

Gregory

"Are you sure he's mine?" Gregory waited in the hall, peering through the partially open door into the chamber where Gryton was imprisoned. After Lillian had finished with Major Resnick and his superiors, she'd wanted to see for herself what he'd relayed to her about their son.

Lillian smacked his arm. "Of course Gryton is ours! All he needs is a little..." She stumbled to a halt before trying again. "Hmmm, that is... I am confident that he will learn to adjust. He's just—"

"A prick?"

Lillian kept her face straight for ten seconds, and then she doubled over with laughter. "Goddess, he's such a little diva. I never would have guessed it of the Battle Goddess's most feared warrior."

"Don't call him that in the Null's hearing. There will be no hope of peace between them."

She wiped at the tears rolling down her face. "Goddess. Never tell him I said that. Gaining his trust has been so hard. And I do care for him. He is ours. Our son isn't evil, not truly. He'll come around in time."

Gregory cocked an ear. "If he and the Null don't kill each other first."

"They won't." Lillian said the two words with a confidence Gregory didn't feel.

"Still. It might be wise to station more guards."

Lillian looked down the hall, her gaze lingering upon each soldier briefly. "There are already plenty of guards. Besides, I know he won't hurt her."

"How can you be so certain of that?"

"Because the Divine Ones placed her in his path."

A skeptical snort escape Gregory.

Lillian shrugged. "We took away all his weapons."

"He still has his fangs."

His Sorceress's mouth formed an 'O' of surprise.

"I'm joking. Gryton won't rip the Null's throat out. He likes his own hide too well and is wise enough to know if he hurts her or any of our allies, I will punish him unlike anything he's experienced in his life." Gregory paused when his mate arched a brow at him. "I'd think up a creative but non-lethal punishment, one where he'd be wishing for death."

Lillian snorted and rolled her eyes. "We'll check on him and his Null again soon. However, I have other plans this morning, since Resnick said we'd have the next three hours to ourselves."

Free time? Gregory's wings twitched at the news. Great Father! It had been more days than he could recall since the last time he'd taken flight.

"How have you managed such a miracle? Surely that is something even beyond the Divine Ones' control."

His Sorceress gave him a mischievous smile. "I may have alluded the spell binding Gryton to the Null would weaken us much more than it really would. I pleaded exhaustion."

"My brilliant Sorceress, always planning for all scenarios."

She gave him another mischievous grin. This one lit her eyes with mirth. "Actually. What I want to do next does have something to do with planning for the future. I want to visit my hamadryad."

His heart did that happy little lurch it did every time he was reminded of the miracle that grew within the heart of her tree. Duty had them running in so many directions at once, they hadn't been given the time he'd have liked to spend with his unborn daughter.

At the thought of his daughter, he glanced down at his left hand, gazing upon the simple gold band that encircled one of his fingers. He used his thumb to spin Lillian's gift in a slow circle as he smiled. Marriage was never something he would have thought to propose to his other half, since they were already bound far more tightly than any ceremony could achieve. And, yet, he grinned, pleased by his Lady's gesture. Soon he would set aside time alone to make her his own gift to pledge his troth.

Once they were outside, he called upon his shadow magic to hide their presence and then dropped to all fours. Lillian approached and gave his shoulder an affectionate thump before mounting. Then he was running toward the glade, his Sorceress on his back. All was right in his world.

CHAPTER EIGHT

Lillian

Chuckling at her mate's baffled look, Lillian merely cut into a large bale of potting mix. Earlier she'd arranged fifteen pots on a bench near her hamadryad tree. As she worked, she was very much aware of Gregory's confusion. She had the distinct impression he thought they would be doing something more physical than gardening.

When they'd first arrived in the glade, they took turns linking with the hamadryad and the child within, allowing their daughter to grow accustomed to their minds and the essence of their magic. Then after they'd spent time with their daughter, they'd lazed under the shade cast by the tree for a short time. But Lillian had other plans, much to Gregory's confusion and disappointment.

When he'd paced over and gotten in the way, she'd shooed him off. With a huff, he'd stomped away and thrown himself back down in the shade beneath her hamadryad.

That's where he still sat an hour later. Every so often he'd grumble softly in ancient languages.

"Oh, stop pouting. We can go hunting once I'm finished here." She gestured at the potting mix and the pots.

"What are you doing?" He finally asked.

"I'm going to take cuttings from my hamadryad. I want a big family." She pulled a set of pruning shears from her basket and walked toward her tree.

Gregory bolted upright.

"Got your attention, didn't I?" She grinned and then sidestepped around him when he wouldn't move.

"Lillian, you're the Sorceress once more. We can't beget another child." His words were slow and gentle as if he feared her reaction.

She just shook her head at him. "I haven't taken leave of my senses. I know we can't have another Gryton. The Divine Ones might not forgive their Avatars a second time. But once we defeat the Battle Goddess and restore peace, my hamadryad can become the Sorceress once more. And I can simply be your mate—your wife. At last, we can have a family like we've always wanted."

Gregory had gone still, but she could feel his thoughts, his joy. "I was uncertain if you would wish to return to how you were before. The sacrifice of putting your soul and magic into your hamadryad—"

"Is a sacrifice I am willing to make to finally have a

family." She gestured at the fifteen pots. "I'm planning to have an enormous family to make up for lost time."

Gregory glanced at the pots, his ears flicking gently, revealing his emotions as clearly as any facial features. "You know I've wanted the same thing, but I would never expect you to sacrifice your powers as the Sorceress. I love you as you are. I am content."

She felt what he hadn't said. "I love you too. And I'll admit, while children are a big part of my decision, I miss my mate. I look forward to the day we can join again like that without risking all creation."

Gregory leaned forward and purred softly.

Hmmm. She wasn't the only one remembering the times they'd come together as lovers while she'd been a mere dryad and it had been safe to love each other like they'd always craved.

Something else occurred to her, and she tapped him firmly on the chest. "Don't you dare go getting yourself killed in the final battle. If you do, I'll follow you into the Spirit Realm and bitch you out for half an eternity."

"I'll try to remember that." He shifted closer, his hands settling on her hips.

"Hmmm, hold that thought and let me finish up here and I'll reward you later tonight."

Gregory huffed and stepped back, giving himself a little shake. "You are wise as always. Now isn't the time for play." He looked troubled for a moment. "Perhaps it would be safer if we don't tempt fate again while you are the Sorceress."

Now it was her turn to scoff. "Oh, you can just stop

that train of thought. I just spent a small fortune on toys for us."

"Toys? I don't understand."

She grinned. "Toys for adults, my innocent immortal. Since we can't share intercourse, I ordered a few things to make up for the lack."

Gregory's tail froze, and she grinned at the telltale sign he was processing her words. Then a hint of mischief gleamed deep in his eyes. "I think I understand. Greenborrow showed me many things on this vast, mystical thing called the internet."

He said the terms like they were foreign to him, but his body language was still happy and eager. "I will do anything you want, my Sorceress. Even play with these 'toys' you speak of."

Lillian laughed. "We will figure them out together."

"As we've experienced all things."

Nodding, she reached for him with one hand while the other snatched up the clippers. With a gentle tug, she led him toward her hamadryad and began selecting the tips of branches that would make the best cuttings.

It only took her a half hour to select and cut each one and deposit them into a pail of water that Gregory had blessed with gargoyle blood and spelled to increase strength. Calling upon her dryad magic, she soon encouraged each one to root.

Then, within a matter of minutes, they each had a vigorous enough root system to plant them up into pots. After watering each one, she turned to glance at her other half.

"There. What do you think of the beginnings of our new family?"

"I think I've never seen such a beautiful thing in my life."

"Sweet talker. You just want to go play with the new toys."

Gregory looked momentarily embarrassed. "What can I say? You have triggered my curiosity."

While she was happy with this symbol she'd created for a bright future with her beloved gargoyle, there was one thing sullying her enjoyment.

Gregory must have sensed it for he dipped his muzzle to brush her shoulder. "What darkens your happiness so suddenly, my Sorceress?"

"Shadowlight, Anna, and the Lord of the Underworld."

He stilled, and she watched as his earlier humor fell away. "As soon as we know the Null has Gryton safely contained, we will inform the fae council and our human allies that we must return to the Magic Realm and face Lord Draydrak and learn what has become of Anna and the cub."

"They're alive. They have to be." Lillian glanced down at her loam covered fingers and rubbed at them absently. "I'd know if my little brother was dead."

Though, if Lord Death was no longer an ally, then he could easily hide Shadowlight from her. But one thing *was* certain. She would learn what happened to Shadowlight even if she had to challenge the demigod for the truth.

"Shadowlight lives. I'm certain of it. And I pray Anna has survived." Gregory glanced away from her to look upon her hamadryad. Then he continued in a quieter voice. "But there is no certainty that the Lord of the Underworld is still an ally. By the time we find them, Anna and Shadowlight may no longer be allies either."

His words weren't truly a surprise. She'd thought the same thing more than once. Lord Draydrak couldn't be counted on to think like she or her other half, but he could be very persuasive. He was one of the few beings that could wield truth like a weapon.

It was part of his power that went along with purifying souls before they made their journey to the Spirit Realm. Lillian also knew that mighty being may no longer view them as fitting leaders for his gargoyle legion.

But one problem at a time. Once the Null had mastered her powers and Gryton was safe to leave behind with the humans, then she and Gregory would see what had become of her little brother and discover if Draydrak was still an ally.

CHAPTER NINE

Gryton

"**H**ey! Someone get in here and let me out!" Rhythmic banging on the transparent walls of their prison accompanied the Null's shouts. "I didn't sign up for this shit!"

Gryton glowered at the human. "You might as well stop screaming now. It's the leshii outside. He hates me, which is likely why he erected a shield spell around the outside of the room. The guards in the hall can't hear you, and he also did something to those strange devices on the wall the humans use to look into a room without being present."

She stopped and turned to him. "The cameras?"

"I'm unfamiliar with that word."

She pointed out the devices in the corners of the room. "Those are cameras."

"Yes. The leshii did something to them. I imagine whatever the humans see is exactly what the leshii wants them to see."

"What the hell? Isn't he supposed to be an ally?"

Gryton shrugged. "He's an ally when it suits him. And in this case, his hatred of me likely goes deeper than his common sense."

"What did you do to him?"

"Why do you think I did something to him? Perhaps he just hates me for serving the Battle Goddess."

"Bull. Shit." She turned to face him fully, her arms crossing her chest as she glowered at him.

Gryton felt himself fighting back a grin at her tone.

"While I might only know a fraction of what's going on inside your head, I absolutely know you're lying about the reason the leshii hates you."

He shrugged. "There was an incident between us the last time I was in this realm."

"Why the hell is he punishing me for something you did?"

"I think he's hoping you'll feed on me until you extinguish my life-force enough that he can come in here and kill me without destroying this world."

"You've got to be fucking with me. How did this happen? They put so many safeguards in place, this shouldn't be possible."

"I would prefer not."

"Prefer to not what?"

"Fuck you."

She did a double-take. "What are you talking about?"

"My speech is perfectly logical and clear. It's you that spouts rubbish every other sentence."

"You know what? Never mind the leshii. I will drain you dry and then worry about getting out of this cage later."

"If you wish. At least between you and the leshii, you might put me out of my misery."

"Oh, stop whining. Your fate could be much worse." The Null rolled her eyes. "I don't know everything that's going on here yet, but I know your parents moved mountains to keep you near them instead of handing you over to be dissected by scientists or having you shipped back to the Magic Realm where I hear two demigods would like to sink their talons into you. The leshii is probably the least of your worries."

He grunted. "Did I say I was worried?"

She scrunched up her brows and then gave him the finger.

"Back at you."

Her eyes widened slightly. "Hah. You know what that means but don't know what a freaking camera is?"

He shrugged. "A human soldier followed her young gargoyle friend into the Battle Goddess's kingdom. I learned a few things from Anna and the cub while I was mentoring them."

"Hold up!" She held one hand out in front of her and then nodded and looked at him again. "You know a human and actually speak respectfully of her? Yet you can't even address me by my name. How does that work?"

He'd been about to say Anna had earned his respect but

sealed his lips instead. He'd already revealed more to the Null than she deserved at this point.

"Fine. I can always go back to shouting at the top of my lungs. You've heard nothing yet."

Bleeding Gods! Was she serious?

Of course she was serious.

"I didn't like her in the beginning either, but over time she proved herself capable of mastery over her mental and physical being." He arched an eyebrow at the Null. "You aren't anywhere near that level of mastery yet."

She snorted. "You going to teach me?"

"Not unless I'm forced to."

"Good. The feeling goes both ways." She turned and began pounding on the clear wall.

"The leshii's hatred is warranted."

The Null turned back to him. "Now we're getting somewhere."

Folding his arms and leaning against the wall, he studied her.

"Speak," the Null barked. "Your acolyte thirsts to hear your great words of wisdom."

He merely arched a brow at her words.

When it became apparent he didn't plan to say more, she scowled. "I wasn't joking."

She pounded her fist on the transparent wall hard enough to make it quiver, but it only made a dull, hollow sound. After a moment she looked over her shoulder and began hollering again, never taking her eyes off him.

While she'd intentionally set out to annoy him, she wasn't foolish enough to turn her back to him. He met her gaze and continued to glare without blinking. She met his challenge, never faltering in her pounding.

He had the distinct impression she wished it was him and not the wall her fist hit. But she held herself in check.

She was testing him.

Was this all some part of his parents' plan? An attempt to stress him enough to trigger some response in him?

They would be disappointed.

He hadn't survived this long by being rash.

But after a few minutes, he concluded he'd have to tell her the truth if he wanted any peace. But that didn't mean he'd have to do it on her terms.

Pushing off from the opposite wall, he darted forward and slammed his own hand over her fist, trapping it against the clear barrier. "The leshii has reason to hate me."

Interestingly, the Null didn't so much as blink at him. Her breathing remained even, and she smiled.

"See? That wasn't so hard, now was it?"

He tilted his head slightly, puzzled by her behavior and demeanor.

"So, Hot Stuff, how did you end up in a fight with the leshii?"

"My name is Gryton." He kept his expression neutral.

"And my name isn't Null." She twisted suddenly, showing surprising strength.

While she freed her one hand, the other was darting up to clip him in the jaw. His training saved him, and he jerked back enough her knuckles only brushed along his skin. But then her other hand closed around his wrist, and suddenly his knees were buckling.

He cursed and gasped at her feet. One of her boot toes

caught him in the shoulder and flipped him onto his back. "See what happens when you don't play nice?"

"I will kill you."

"You'll try." To his surprise, she reached down and hauled him back to his feet. A moment later his magic returned in a rush that left him gasping again. "Think I'm getting the hang of this Null thing."

She patted his shoulders and then pushed him against the wall so he could use that as for support until he found his legs again. Of all the embarrassing situations he'd endured throughout his life...

"Oh, stop whining."

"I said nothing."

"Your face sure as heck did."

He glared but admitted the fault was his own.

He'd lost mastery over himself. Again. It kept happening with this Null. No one, immortal or mortal, should have that power over him. But the only way back to mastery was to take that power away from her. He didn't have to rise to her baiting. He would be in control, of himself and the conversation.

"When I became trapped in this world the last time, I attempted to fight my way free. Many of the fae and human soldiers were injured or killed. My fire magic took the leshii's arm."

"That'd do it." Her words were flippant, but the way she studied him was at odds with her tone. She watched him a moment more and then sighed, sounding tired. It reminded him she'd been through a trial as well.

"We good?" she asked with a skeptical look.

He acknowledged her words with a regal nod.

"Good. Because I'm tired." She settled to sit cross-legged on his sleeping pallet. "My name is Private Emerson. Please refer to me as that instead of calling me Null. Or even just Erika. And I'll refer to you as Commander Gryton or whatever other names you prefer."

He came and settled on the pallet beside her because the cage was too narrow for anything else.

"Truce?" She held her hand out to him in the way he'd seen humans do before.

After eyeing it for a reasonable length of time, he slowly reached out and clasped her hand. His talons flexing and digging into her skin as he uttered 'truce' back at her.

She merely barked out a sharp laugh. "I can see life will not grow any less interesting anytime soon."

No, he agreed silently, it probably wouldn't.

CHAPTER TEN

Erika

She'd been drowsing until she heard pounding on the door leading to the hall. Erika jerked upright from her slouch. A glance at her watch confirmed it was noon. Someone had just brought the prisoner his meal and realized something was amiss when they couldn't get the door open. She glanced sidelong at him.

Gryton's lips twitched in what might have been an aborted smile. "I think we've just been rescued from each other's company."

"Sweet baby Jesus! I think you're right." She clapped her hands and stood. No point looking too chummy with the prisoner. Not that they were chums. But appearances.

There was more pounding and then some shouting

from outside. "Hey, I thought you said the spell the leshii wove sound-proofed the room? Why can we hear them?"

Gryton unfolded himself and glanced around. A couple seconds later, the earlier aborted smile returned, forming fully this time. "You've been feeding on the spell."

She didn't miss his change in expression.

"You're happy. Now I'm suspicious."

"It's because you're gaining some control over your natural abilities. From what I've read, most Nulls never learn to control their natural inclination to feed upon all sources of magic."

"Not picky eaters, then?"

"No. Most Nulls absorb the nearest source of magic and then work their way out from there."

"Ah. I see. Since you were the nearest snack in range, I should have feasted on you instead of the shield thing." Her brows drew together over her nose. "But I wasn't even trying to feed on the leshii's spell. Mostly because I didn't think about it."

"It frustrated you to be locked in this cage. The spell stops others from hearing you and coming to your rescue." Gryton waved his hand, gesturing vaguely toward the door. "On a subconscious level, you knew that was the only way out, and you made your ability search further afield for its next meal."

"You make it sound predatory."

"Isn't it? Or maybe Nulls are more like scavengers? I never really thought about it before."

Her glower returned. "You want me to come all the way over there and punch you?"

"You mean take two whole steps just so you can throw

your punch, miss, and then hit the wall behind me? Because you'll never hit me."

"Almost worked last time." She huffed and glanced back toward the noise outside. "How long do you think it will take them to get through the shield?"

"However long it takes my sire and dam to arrive and realize what's going on. Your fellow soldiers likely think the spell is my doing, that I've already killed you and am attempting escape."

"Well. That'll light a fire under their butts."

Gryton's eyes crinkled a moment before he burst out laughing.

He was still laughing by the time a unit of soldiers led by the big gargoyle busted down the door and filed into the room, every gun trained on the still laughing fire elemental. Erika instinctively stepped in front of him and held her arms out wide.

"Wasn't him. It was the leshii." She was pleased to see the big gargoyle believed her. He turned from the cage and glanced behind him at Major Resnick. After a quiet word, the major nodded and ordered his men back out into the hall to go search for the leshii.

Erika hoped he would surrender without a fight. From the reports, she knew the leshii was one of the more powerful fae, which made him dangerous, but she didn't think he planned to do more than annoy Gryton. The leshii didn't deserve to die for that. She'd only known the fire elemental a short time, and already she could relate with the leshii in wanting to wipe that smirk from Gryton's face.

"My sire has already summoned the one called Gran to aid in the hunt for the leshii."

"Did you just read my mind?"

"No. Your body language is just exceedingly easy to read, even for a mortal." Gryton didn't even look apologetic. "Our soul-binding hasn't advanced far enough to allow me into your head yet."

"You're still an ass."

Major Resnick had ordered Erika to stay with Gryton while they hunted for the leshii. Sighing, she'd returned to her usual position by the wall to wait. The entire time Gryton pointedly ignored her. Or at least as much as he was able with the soul-binding linking them together now.

It was the damnedest sensation. One moment she'd be thinking about something mundane, and then the next their link would spark, and she was reliving fragments of his memories. While she couldn't control when it happened, she could free herself by concentrating on something else in the real world.

Luckily it hadn't taken the patrol units long to find the leshii, since he hadn't bothered to hide. And as far as Erika could tell, the leshii had gotten off with little in the way of punishment. But that might have been because he'd claimed to know that she wouldn't feed on Gryton enough to kill him.

Greenborrow had only sought to make Gryton 'a little less of a surly bastard' which made Erika even like the leshii a little.

"We have something for you," Gregory said to Gryton as he approached the cage. After waving his hand at the cage in an almost dismissive manner, the lock disengaged, and the door swung open as if an electronic lock had been triggered.

Erika narrowed her eyes and admitted a touch of jealousy.

Why couldn't her superpower be something cool like telekinesis or the ability to call upon the shadows to hide or a hundred other things she'd seen in Gryton's memories? But no. Her superpower was magical gluttony.

The big gargoyle continued to the cage and held out the armful of clothes. "I asked the sidhe to provide something that would fit you."

Gryton glowered at the one he called sire but snatched the clothing from his father's hands with near eagerness.

"Once you are dressed, there is something your mother and I wish to show you. We've secured permission from the humans." Gregory paused for a moment, glancing thoughtfully at his son. "While the leshii's trick was an attempt to punish you, it actually benefited you. As far as the humans are concerned, you had an opportunity to harm the Null, but did not, proving that you are willing to embrace this new alliance."

Gryton's snort of disdain swiftly turned into a huff of surprise when the gargoyle's tail thumped him across the back.

"If you act out at all, even so much as to glance at me in a way I don't like," Gregory threatened, "you'll find yourself back in that cage. Do I make myself clear?"

Gryton continued to glower, but he nodded before

retreating two steps to lay his newly acquired clothing on his cot. After returning his son's glower, the gargoyle stepped from the cage. He didn't close the door, though.

The woman known as the Sorceress came up beside Erika. "You can wait out in the hall if you wish. Gryton won't try to escape. You've drained him of too much power to even make an attempt."

"I need confirmation from Major Resnick, ma'am." Erika hoped her tone came across as polite as possible. Because, really, one didn't want to go around insulting demigods more than necessary.

"Of course." Lillian glanced back at Gryton and then toward the hall. "I'll go find Major Resnick."

"It's not required. One of the other soldiers will find him if something happens before he comes with new orders. I'll stay here for now. I'm fine."

The other woman laughed. "No doubt you are. However, I plan to spoil whatever my offspring has planned to intimidate you."

"I wouldn't be where I am if I was easy to intimidate, ma'am."

"Yes, I suppose that's true. However, my son has already had too much fun baiting you."

"Think it's the other way around, ma'am."

Lillian just laughed. "Perhaps you are correct."

She would have said more, but the big gargoyle came and whispered something in his partner's ear. Lillian grinned and then nodded once to Erika. "We'll be back shortly to collect Gryton after we've spoken to Major Resnick."

With that, the two Avatars disappeared out into the hall.

Erika was just returning to her earlier spot when Gryton's laughter rang out.

"I'm aware some humans are lusty creatures, but I admit I thought you might have more discipline over your baser instincts, but I see you lack mastery there as well. Look your fill, inferior one."

"Well, I was going to look in the other direction to give you privacy, but since you so kindly reminded me I have uncontrolled animal instincts that must be sated, I'll just have to admit defeat and watch helplessly as you reveal your god-like body to me. I'll try to hold myself back from ravishing you."

A glance in Gryton's direction showed him scowling at her.

She grinned. "Called your bluff, didn't I?"

He merely glowered a moment more before he presented his back to her and reached down to examine the first garment. She had zero interest in seeing his naked ass, but she'd die before letting him call her bluff now that she'd issued a challenge.

He glanced over his shoulder and speared her with a look. A moment later, he slowly turned to face her.

Ah. Shit. She'd forgotten how good he was at reading people.

His grin was huge, positively deviant.

"You're really going to make an ass of yourself, aren't you?" She aimed her best scowl at him.

"Indeed. And you could leave if you wish. I'm not forcing you to stay."

There was no way she was giving ground now. Locking eyes with him, she answered his challenge. His smirk grew even bigger—the asshole.

She returned his smirk. "Guess we're both going to have to just stand here until one of us dies of old age because Hell will freeze over before I march out that door against orders."

"Suit yourself." He slid his thumbs into the waistband of his pants.

Damn. Come on, you can freeze over anytime now Hell.

But just then, God smiled on her, or maybe that was Major Resnick, because two other soldiers marched in. She didn't know either of them, but that wasn't a surprise. She didn't know most of the soldiers assigned to Gryton. They were Special Forces, and she was a raw Private.

The shorter of the men spoke for them both. "Colonel Turner ordered us to take over. He's out in the hall with Major Resnick. They want to talk to you."

Colonel Turner was a full bird colonel overseeing the brigade she'd shipped in with. She'd never met him in person, only having seen him at a distance, but had heard he was a hard-ass and not to be crossed.

By some fluke that likely had something to do with how the Avatars only interacted with a select few humans, Erika had had more interactions with Major Resnick and a few other foreign officers these last few days than with her commanding officer or fellow infantrymen.

But right this moment, she didn't care and would have taken orders from a penguin if it got her out of this room before the fire elemental flaunted his stuff.

"Ah. I see I finally found a way to make my keeper flee my side," Gryton called after her with a laugh.

As she marched from the room, the mocking sound chased her.

"Fate may have forced me to concede this battle," she called over her shoulder as she paused at the door, "Doesn't mean I've lost the war. There's always the next round."

"I look forward to it."

CHAPTER ELEVEN

Erika

When she walked into the hall, more chuckles greeted her. This time from the devil's parents. It seemed everyone had overheard her verbal exchange with the prick. With a scowl, she just took up her place with the rest of the guard unit out in the hall, her face neutral like she hadn't just been yelling at the prisoner over her shoulder. It wasn't the first time her mouth had gotten her in trouble.

Continuing to keep her expression neutral, she waited for Colonel Turner and Major Resnick to finish up their conversation with another officer. She wasn't left to her own devices for long. The big gargoyle halted in front of her.

"Gryton will be a trying one, won't he?" There was still

humor in his tone, but his expression was serious. "If he ever oversteps, notify me. I shall make him regret it."

"Thank you," she hesitated, still not knowing how to address a demigod, "sir. I'll keep that in mind, but I don't think I'll have a problem handling him."

"You're probably correct. The Divine Ones tend to partner up well-matched pairs before they set them on a quest."

Erika was sure the gargoyle was trying to reassure her, but he really sucked at it. Not that she would mention that to the eight-and-a-half-foot-tall wall of winged muscle and sharp talons.

Luckily, Colonel Turner finished up his conversation with Resnick but didn't seem interested in singling her out. And after a moment of studying the two Avatars, he turned and marched away, a few other support staff following. Major Resnick stayed behind, likely to directly oversee Gryton's excursion.

They didn't have long to wait for Gryton. A few minutes later, he joined them.

Erika eyed the fire elemental's new clothing. With his long black tabard, leather bracers, a form-fitting pair of black breeches, and knee-high boots, he would look right at home in either a medieval renaissance fair or a fantasy movie set.

On Gryton the outfit looked natural. Which likely had something to do with how he walked with the natural grace of a warrior or martial artist.

Major Resnick ordered everyone to move out. The unit of soldiers formed up around the prisoner and his parents, then they headed off as a group. Before they left the community center that had become their base, the gargoyle called on his shadow magic. A moment later, he, Lillian, and Gryton all faded. They didn't disappear, though.

The gargoyle glanced behind him and narrowed his eyes before huffing with humor.

"If you wouldn't mind falling back a little, I won't have to waste a greater amount of magic that would be better used elsewhere."

Glancing toward Major Resnick, she waited for his nod before dropping back.

Lillian turned toward the gargoyle and said in a voice designed to carry, "And if you would take on human form once in a while, you wouldn't have to use shadow magic to hide your big gargoyle ass all the time. Then I could just put a glamour on Gryton."

The gargoyle rumbled something back in a language Erika didn't know, but she'd bet it wasn't pleasant.

Their destination turned out to be a maze. A real maze complete with forking corridors, dead-ends, and green twelve-foot-high walls. While it wasn't the strangest thing she'd been exposed to since her arrival, it was so magically whimsical, she half expected to see honest-to-god fairies flying around corners or flitting over the top to vanish into the surrounding garden.

There were no fairies, though. At least none that she'd seen. The day was still young, though.

She continued to maintain her spot near the rear of the

unit as they moved deeper into the maze. Lillian marched forward boldly, familiar with the twists, turns, and dead ends.

Erika memorized their path in case they needed to retreat in a hurry for any reason.

After another ten minutes of fast walking, they reached a clearing in the center of the maze. Smack in the middle was one of the biggest damn trees she'd ever seen. She'd been told it was a hamadryad and was presently gestating the Avatar's daughter.

Really, some things were just too weird, and all you could do was shut your mouth and bob your head.

Scanning the area, she soon spotted something else odd. In the tree's shadow, a stone statue lurked. By its silhouette, it was another gargoyle. If she'd had time, she would have asked about the stone gargoyle.

Major Resnick and Gregory spoke for a few minutes before Resnick ordered his men to stand at the perimeter of the maze. It gave everyone a good line of sight upon Gryton, but also gave him and his family a modicum of privacy.

After waving her over, Resnick leaned close to whisper in her ear. "I don't trust Gryton. Stay near and drain him if he does so much as glances toward the exits."

"Yes, sir!" She nodded sharply and hustled to follow the strangest family on the planet.

Lillian and Gregory led Gryton close to the tree until they were in its shadow.

"We'd like you to meet your little sister," Lillian said.

"I..." Words seemed to fail Gryton.

Erika could see he was speechless by the fact his

parents trusted him enough to visit with his unborn sister. Slowly Gryton reached out and tentatively touched the tree with a kind of reverence.

She arched one eyebrow but held her silence. To the best of her knowledge, he wasn't doing any harm. Besides, she was just supposed to observe and stop Gryton from escaping.

Whatever else he did wasn't her concern. She waited patiently for them to have what was probably their first family time together.

Eventually, Gryton finished greeting his younger sister, and he came to stand next to Erika, surprising her.

"I'm giving you a source of magic to feed on that isn't my mother's hamadryad or my little sister."

Eyes widening, Erika took several steps farther back. "Why didn't someone say something before now?"

"You weren't close enough for long enough to be a threat. My sire and dam wouldn't have allowed you near my unborn sister if they thought you were truly a threat to her. But you are so new to your abilities, I don't wish to risk my sister's life on their possible false belief that you aren't a threat."

Well. Here's to insults all around. But he was in a talkative mood, so maybe she could learn a little more of what was going on in this new, strange world she'd walked into only days ago.

After all, this was a far cry from helping at the new provisional base north of town where she'd initially been assigned to one of the building details. But within an hour of touching down, her destiny had changed and here she was, four days later, surrounded by demigods.

Her eyes tracked back to Lillian and Gregory. The gargoyle was slashing a wrist with one talon. If she hadn't seen weirder shit, she'd have been more concerned. For once, the link was being quiet, so she didn't have the benefit of one of Gryton's memories to aid her.

But after a few minutes of the gargoyle circling the tree's base, dripping blood the entire time, she concluded he was feeding the tree in some fashion. There was likely magic seeping into the ground along with the blood.

Briefly, she wondered if the child would be a demigod like Gryton and the parents. Probably.

She side-eyed Gryton. "Am I supposed to babysit that one once she's born? Kids and I don't get along. More accurately, they hate me and start crying at first sight."

Beside her, Gryton coughed. She was sure the bastard was covering a laugh. "The hamadryad was the Sorceress at the time Lillian got pregnant. Later she gave the child to the tree to gestate and took back her Avatar soul. So, while my younger sister will be powerful, she won't possess the great and destructive powers I and my sire and dam command."

"Interesting."

Gryton rocked back on his heels and gazed down at her. "And what about you?"

"About me?" The question took her off guard. As far as she could tell, Gryton couldn't care less about her, or any human for that matter. Maybe he was bored?

"Yes. Surely you didn't just spring forth from the ground at the Divine Ones' command."

"You already know my name, not that you ever use it."

What else was there to tell? She'd led a relatively uneventful life.

"I was born in Texas. Granddad owns a ranch outside of Austin. Mom died of cancer when I was four. Dad was never in the picture much after that." She shrugged. "Guess we have not knowing our parents in common."

Gryton snorted disdainfully at the idea they would have anything in common. But he surprised her by gesturing for her to go on.

"Yeah, so my grandparents raised me. I'm the youngest of four. My two oldest siblings did the equivalent of running off to join the circus as far as my granddad is concerned. My oldest brother forges swords and other weapons for renaissance fairs and movies. My sister works in Hollywood as a stuntwoman. She's in a lot of fantasy and historical pieces. She also loves cosplay and does the convention circuit when she can. As far as granddad is concerned, my other brother is the normal one—a cattle rancher like him."

Glancing up at Gryton, she could see he didn't understand half of what she was talking about but was pretending he did.

He tilted his head. "And you are the warrior."

"A soldier, yes. At least, that was the plan before all this happened. I enlisted out of high school. This is my first assignment after completing basic training. Or at least, building the new base was supposed to be my assignment. Then everything went to heck."

"Why did you wish to be a soldier?" He sounded curious.

She'd been asked that a lot by her family, but never

really had a good answer. She shrugged. "Guess I wanted to see something of the world more than just cattle and horses and dust."

His typical hostility seemed to have simmered down a touch, and he was actually looking at her thoughtfully. "How old are you?"

"I just turned nineteen last month."

"Nineteen years?"

"Yes."

His expression gave nothing away as he turned from her. After a moment, his shoulders started to shake, and rich, deep laughter burst forth from his chest. "A child! The Divine Ones sent a child to watch over me. Ridiculous!"

He continued to laugh until Gregory looked in his direction. Under the glaring eye of the gargoyle, Gryton eventually got himself back under control.

"Funny, I don't remember you laughing your ass off while I was draining you dry."

His features were a calm mask once more, but she was pretty sure that was a gleam of humor still in his gaze.

"Oh, look. Guess it's back to the cage for you," Erika said as she jerked her chin toward where he watched as his parents approached, finished with whatever they were doing to the tree.

"I've had worse lodgings than that cage."

She almost felt bad for him.

Almost. Not quite.

CHAPTER TWELVE

Obsidian

Stepping through the great portal spell, Obsidian left the Magic Realm for the Mortal. Almost as soon as his talons touched the ground, this realm began plucking at his shadow magic like a starved creature trying to devour a meal too large for it. He gave himself a little shake and took a second step farther into the Mortal Realm.

Behind him, Anna followed him through the portal.

"Well, fuck. That's quite the greeting." She shifted from foot to foot, her talons digging into the loam of the forest.

"It is unpleasant," he agreed.

"Why don't I remember this from last time?"

"I am not sure. Perhaps Thayn will have some insight."

"Of course I do." Thayn quipped as he joined them, but

he took a moment and commanded the portal spell to close before continuing, "You're finding it worse this time because you had only begun your transformation when you'd left. And even if you weren't awake for it, you have spent the last thirteen years in the Magic Realm. You have no more immunity to this place than any other gargoyle. Well, other than being as powerful as you are."

"Still sucks," Anna muttered.

Obsidian had to agree. He remembered the dislocation of crossing the Veil between the Realms when he'd been a cub. But that time he'd been newly born and weak. Now he realized it was more a condition of the Mortal Realm than the fact that he'd been a child.

"I should report to Major Resnick," Anna said as she dropped to all fours and scouted a half-circle around Obsidian, her nose in the air. From her thoughts, he knew she was trying to determine her location by any familiar scents. But they were likely too far from civilization to quickly pinpoint their location.

At least that was the hope. By using a portal spell with a destination anchor this deep into the forest north of town, he'd hoped it would go unnoticed by any humans or fae. Thayn had cautioned them they should scout the area and find out what had happened while they'd been gone before revealing themselves.

From what Truth, the current gargoyle spying on the humans, could determine, a great many changes had occurred in a relatively short time. Truth had confirmed that Gryton was here and a prisoner.

"It still boggles the mind," Anna said along a private link, *"that almost no time has elapsed here, but so much has changed.*

Meanwhile, it has been thirteen years in Haven. This must all be strange for you.”

“It *will be,”* he agreed, not hiding the disquiet that crawled through his soul at the thought of meeting his sister again when the Avatars might now be their enemies or rivals. But he could share anything with his Kyrsu, and she would never judge.

“Oh, I’ll totally judge if the situation warrants it, but I’ll always have your back, my Rasoren.” She slid up next to him and gave him a little nuzzle before returning to her circling.

“I think I know where we are,” she said. “Or at least which direction leads to civilization. I smell a patrol. We can follow the unit back to base.”

“Good,” Thayn agreed. “You both scout the Avatars’ lair to see what you can learn. When you have news, bring it to me. In the meantime, I will do some scouting on my own. I’m sure Truth could use the help.”

Obsidian and Anna nodded at the ancient gargoyle’s words before heading in the direction of the gun-metal and sweat scent.

As Anna had suggested, the human patrol led them back toward town. Once Anna knew where they were, they left the patrol behind and continued swiftly on toward the spa grounds with its maze and glade. The Avatars often spent time there. It was an excellent place to start the hunt.

They entered the maze first, making their way to the center.

"By the scent, they were here recently," Obsidian said as he cast a glance around the glade.

The hamadryad stood tall and proud like he remembered. It wasn't until his gaze tracked to the stone statue resting in its shade that he jerked like someone had punched him in the stomach.

"Obsidian, I'm so sorry." Anna came to stand next to him where he'd frozen in place. She curled one wing around his shoulders and then leaned into him, her compassion flowing along their mental link and into his mind, brushing away the sharpest pains the old memories unleashed.

He hadn't thought they would still hold such power over him after all this time, but they did.

After a few moments of Anna's compassion, he could force his legs to move and carry him closer to Darkness.

Reaching out, he caressed one stone cheek.

"Hello, Father." His throat tightened, and his eyes blurred with tears. He continued in mind speech. *Even after thirteen years, I'm not ready to be without you."*

"He loved you, still loves you. He'll return just as soon as he's able. I know he will." As usual, Anna's words were plain but grounded, and he took comfort in them.

After another whispered prayer to the Divine Ones to speed his father's healing, he reluctantly stepped out from Anna's warmth and sheltering wing. Later, after they'd had their reunion with his sister and her mate, and he'd had a chance to check on his mother's healing, he would allow himself to bask in Anna's compassion and love.

"Do you think my mother still lives? She was in a coma when I was abducted."

"Your mother was one tough lady. She survived a battle with Gryton, I doubt a simple coma would keep her down." Anna nuzzled him again. "But we'll find out as soon as we can."

He nodded and then followed her as they started out of the maze.

"Should we see if we can locate Gryton first or seek my sister and her mate?" he mused.

Anna shrugged. "Gryton first. I know what Truth said, but I'll believe Tin Man's a prisoner when I see it with my own eyes. He's entirely too manipulative. I don't trust him to remain in a cage for long."

CHAPTER THIRTEEN

Gryton

For the first time in days, the restlessness Gryton had been suffering was finally sated. It was also the first time he'd ever crossed swords with his father in a practice ring. The last time they'd met in battle hadn't been particularly enjoyable since they'd been trying to kill each other.

This time had been different. They'd been able to study each other's sword forms. As expected, his ancient father had had plenty of time to master many styles, but Gryton had held his own. Though there'd been a few times where he'd had to sacrifice beauty for efficiency.

He'd even been able to ignore the glowering human guards. Perhaps that was because a particular talkative female soldier was absent, the need for sleep finally catching up with her.

It had been a peaceful afternoon without his new 'partner' trailing after him.

"Session over," Gregory barked, a toothy grin on his face. "Your nursemaid is headed this way."

Gryton's shoulders hunched, but he schooled his expression as he turned. Sure enough, his father hadn't been lying.

"What did I miss?" The Null came to a halt in front of him, the toes of her boots almost touching his.

Instinctively he stepped back as soon as her ability reached out and began dragging at his magic. He realized his mistake as a full-fledged grin spread across her face.

"Made you move."

He sneered, flashing her a bit of fang. "Must everything be a challenge or a joke with you?"

"Nope. You can make it all stop just by saying one thing."

He frowned, not understanding, but not willing to ask her for clarity. To show ignorance in front of her would be like alcohol poured over a wound. Scoffing instead, he turned and headed back toward his prison. When she didn't immediately follow with the rest of the guards, he called back over his shoulder.

"I believe you are supposed to escort me back to my cage and then report to Major Resnick."

She caught up with him swiftly. "You really going to prolong your misery when you could just eat humble pie and enjoy a bit of peace?"

"As usual, I do not understand what you're talking about."

"Yes, you do. It has been three days since I told you my name and you still haven't used it."

He halted and received a prod and a growled order to keep moving from one of the other guards. Gryton ignored him. Instead, he eyed the insufferable female. "I will never dignify your existence by calling you by your name, Null."

He started forward again, his spine straight.

"Well, bless your heart." She started to laugh. "You must enjoy being miserable."

"I am accustomed to pain."

She came up beside him again. "You one of those guys who gets off on insults and pain? I can keep dishing out the insults, but I'm not into the other thing."

"Your words make no sense, and the images I see in your mind are... disturbing. Whips and cages and such are for torture, not pleasure."

"Not my cup of tea either. But that doesn't give you the right to just pass judgment on other peoples' lifestyles—"

He halted, and the human almost ran into his back, but he paid her no more mind, his attention on another female he'd never thought to see again.

"River, I see you survived our last meeting." Last time he'd seen her, she'd been on fire courtesy of his magic.

"You," the dryad hissed, calling bits of shadow magic, which surprised Gryton since he'd cut down her gargoyle mate and she shouldn't be able to call upon that magic. Perhaps her gargoyle mate was closer to waking than he thought.

"River. We're on the same side now. Don't make me kill

you. That might cause an unfortunate rift between myself and my new allies."

"We'll never be on the same side. You stole my son! You killed my mate!"

A swarm of tiny bits of shadow magic raced toward him.

Summoning his own power, he called a shield of fire to vaporize the glass-like shards. He was about to call a secondary wall of magic when a pale, long-fingered hand reached through his fire and wrapped around his bicep. A moment later the Null stepped in front of him, and the dryad's shards buried themselves in her back.

Her eyes widened for a moment in surprise, and he made to push her aside before the next wave struck, but to his surprise, he couldn't move her.

Her eyes glittered dangerously. "Bitch just tried to stab me in the back, didn't she?"

The Null turned to face the equally startled dryad. "I'm going to toss your ass into a cage. You can have the one right next to his." She jerked a thumb back in Gryton's direction. "Give me a reason I shouldn't?"

While the human was threatening River, he studied her back. There was no sign of the shards, no damage to her clothing, no scent of blood. She had sustained no harm that he could see. She'd managed to absorb the magic, unmaking the shards before they could pierce her skin.

Impressive. He'd known she was powerful by how easily she could drain him, but considering how young she was, he hadn't expected her body's ability to react swiftly enough to stop such a rapid magical attack.

Turning his attention back to River, he found the dryad

on her knees, gasping for breath. He might have felt a twinge of sympathy had she not just attacked him.

Gryton had once respected the dryad, and they'd gotten on well enough. And there was a good chance they'd need to work with each other in the future. Though he doubted they'd ever get past the whole 'I abducted your son and killed your mate' event. But with proper incentive, he and River might be able to work together.

If the Null didn't kill the dryad first.

He cleared his throat. "She is Lillian's mother. And she wasn't lying about her son or mate. My actions led to their fates."

"Shit. You really are a Grade 'A' prick. I can't believe I stepped in." The Null glowered over her shoulder at him. "I should have just let you two battle it out. Might have saved me some trouble later."

CHAPTER FOURTEEN

Lillian

After Major Resnick left, having told her about the newest incident involving Gryton, Lillian dropped her head into her hands and cursed softly. Who needed enemies when they had a family like hers? But at least the Null had been there to prevent anyone getting killed.

"Goddess, our son has me calling that poor woman 'The Null' in my head."

Gregory snorted. "Gryton is very stubborn and persuasive. That's a dangerous combination. He'll have everyone calling her 'the Null' before long."

"I wonder where he gets the stubbornness?" Lillian mused with a glance at Gregory.

Predictably he didn't rise to her baiting. "Me. We both

know that. But enough talk of our troublesome son. It has been days since we've been alone."

Lillian grinned at his less than subtle hint. She sauntered over to him where he was reclining on their oversized bed. He gave her a toothy gargoyle grin and then a moment later light and shadow magic surrounded him, blurring his form. When she blinked the spots from her vision, her other half had taken on human form.

"Didn't even have to ask. Wonder why that is?" She grinned at him. "Might it have something to do with the new toys?"

He huffed. "If you'd prefer me as a gargoyle..."

"No. You're too well endowed as a gargoyle for what I have planned tonight."

"I love it when you have plans, my Sorceress." His relaxed posture didn't hide the eagerness she felt in his mind.

She was just leaning down for a kiss when a heavy pounding sounded at the door.

"Fuck. Really?" Lillian turned to glower at the door. Still scowling, she marched to the door, flicked the lock, and then jerked it open wide. And it still didn't convey a fifth of the annoyance she felt.

"If an invading army isn't even now crossing the Veil between the Realms—"

"You might have just gotten your wish," Gran said as she stood looking severe and more than a touch concerned. "A military patrol found a gargoyle. Or maybe I should say he let the patrol find him. We think he might be a spy."

Lillian's breath hissed from her lungs like someone had punched her in the gut.

A gargoyle? Here?

By the Divine Ones. Could it be Shadowlight or Anna? Had they returned home at last?

"It's not Shadowlight or Anna," Gran said, reading Lillian's expression. "Though the newcomer was surprisingly forthcoming with his name."

"What is it?" Gregory asked suddenly.

Gran flicked her gaze in his direction. "He says his name is Truth in Shadows. But we are welcome to just call him Truth. He wants a word with the Avatars."

"I don't know a gargoyle by the name of Truth in Shadows." Gregory's words echoed Lillian's thoughts.

"He must have been born after we left the Spirit Realm." Though Lillian wasn't sure of that at all. Something didn't feel right with her theory. It had only been twenty years since they'd been reborn into flesh and blood bodies. Lord Draydrak wouldn't usually send a child as his spokesperson.

"I don't like this," Lillian whispered along their link.

"Nor do I."

"We'll come at once," Gregory said aloud, then asked, "Where is he being held?"

"Major Resnick has him back at base."

Gregory surveyed the new gargoyle. It was as they'd both expected. He was a young one. Less than a hundred years. Despite his youth, the gargoyle had an excellent command of his magic, and Gregory couldn't push past his mental shields without hurting him. He wasn't willing to force his way into his mind and harm a young gargoyle just because the youth had excelled at his training enough to keep an Avatar out of his head.

Lillian sat at the metal table across from the youth, trying to persuade him into talking. She'd had mildly better success than him, but even his Sorceress was finding the newcomer a tough nut to crack.

"If you won't tell us why you're here, will you tell us what you can?"

"Yes," he said in a friendly tone.

But then he said nothing else, and Gregory noted his Sorceress's eyes narrowing.

"All gargoyles are stubborn."

"I'm aware." She rolled her eyes. *"Perhaps a new tactic is in order. We might be asking the wrong questions."*

"True. While he might not be willing to speak about his mission, he seems willing enough to be here. He allowed himself to be captured, so he must want to tell us something."

Lillian nodded and then turned her attention to their young guest.

"Do you know Corporal Anna Mackenzie or a young gargoyle by the name of Shadowlight?"

The gargoyle's ears twitched. "I know them both."

Ah! They were getting somewhere.

"Are they both still alive?" Lillian asked, leaning forward over the table.

"Yes."

Gregory cleared his throat and asked what his Sorceress hadn't. "Are they the Lord of the Underworld's prisoners?"

"No."

Lillian stood and walked around the table as if her nearness could force the truth out of the youth. "Are they returning to the Mortal Realm?"

"They are already here."

Lillian and Gregory glanced at each other.

If Anna and Shadowlight were already here, why hadn't they made themselves known?

Anna would have reported to her superiors as soon as she stepped back into the Mortal Realm.

Something was very wrong.

Truth in Shadows stood, the chains on his wrists falling away as another spell wrapped around his form.

"Stop!" Gregory barked the order even as Lillian summoned her magic.

But the foreign power built faster than Lillian could weave a counter spell.

"You should prepare yourselves," Truth in Shadows warned. "Anna and Obsidian will seek you out shortly to carry out Lord Draydrak's command."

Then in a blink of an eye, the spell wrapped around the gargoyle flashed bright just as Gregory was leaping over the metal table. He landed on the other side, nothing but empty air between his talons.

"What the hell was that all about?" Major Resnick snapped as he marched into the room.

"I don't know, but it isn't good. Anna and another gargoyle called Obsidian will be arriving shortly to carry out Lord Death's orders. I can only assume they mean to take us back to the Magic Realm to face the demigod."

Gregory snorted. "They are welcome to try."

CHAPTER FIFTEEN

Obsidian

Anna wouldn't admit it to anyone, not even him, but he knew she was nervous about the inevitable meeting with her superiors and ultimately her father. Obsidian wanted to tell her everything would be fine. But that might very well be a lie. He knew very little about the human military or how it worked or what form her punishment would come in for following him into the Magic Realm against orders.

Yet whatever she faced, she wouldn't be facing it alone. He would share in her punishment. And if the humans were foolish enough to separate them, the Legion would have something to say about it.

That, at least, was a surety. It was one of the few

certainties. If he was honest, he was more than a little uncertain as well. Only a few months had passed in this world while they had been away. Yet so much had changed. He had changed.

He no longer knew his place here in this world. And what about his mother?

They hadn't yet been able to discover what had happened to her. And his magic could not track her whereabouts because of all the concrete, metal, and magical shields surrounding the human military camp and the spa grounds. He could only track other gargoyles.

Obsidian had adjusted to this realm well enough that he knew where Gregory was at all times, which was good. The last thing they needed was to stumble upon the Avatars by accident.

Anna had been skeptical, thinking Lillian and Gregory would somehow sense them, but Thayn had only smiled, saying he and the Divine Ones had a few tricks in their arsenal.

That had given Obsidian pause.

The Divine Ones must think their Avatars' allegiance was in question. That did not bode well for a peaceful future.

"What's eating your ass?"

He glanced over at his Kyrsu where she was standing watch. He was supposed to be helping prepare for Truth's sudden return. There was no guarantee that the Avatars wouldn't be following close on the gargoyle's tail.

His Kyrsu's comment reminded him he should stay sharp and stop his woolgathering.

"Well, out with it," she prompted, then added with a saucy little flick of her tail, "Not that I don't already have a good idea what's going on inside that head of yours."

He huffed. "I don't want to fight my sister."

Her expression turned gentle, and she came over to him and gave him a friendly little lick.

Giving her a toothy gargoyle grin, he returned her affection.

He would miss this when they inevitably returned to human forms. He was certain Anna would want to resume that form once she had to deal with her people.

She gave him another nuzzle. "You won't have to fight your sister. If it comes down to that, she's my responsibility. You'll have your hands full with Gregory."

"There is that," he agreed with a laugh.

He leaned in and wrapped his tail around her hips and rubbed his muzzle along hers. It wasn't exactly the most innocent of touches, but he enjoyed her scent and desired her too much to resist.

Plus, he wanted to see how far they could venture before they triggered any unpleasant memories.

So far, they both seemed fine with these little not-so-innocent embraces. Not wanting to press too far, he relaxed his tail and allowed it to slide down her legs.

Once free, she stepped back. "For what it's worth, I'm doing more than a little praying that we don't have to fight the Avatars. I'd hate to see what that would do to this planet."

"Or this entire realm," he offered helpfully.

With that dark thought, he again looked out over the

small ridge that overlooked one side of the town. The trees gave enough shadows even with the sun high in the sky that they could have hidden without the aid of their shadow magic.

But he wasn't so foolish as to risk discovery until after Truth's return.

Obsidian's friend had volunteered to go, saying he was eager to meet his best friend's older sister who just also happened to be the Mother's Sorceress.

After Thayn had finished weaving spells around the young gargoyle, Obsidian and Anna had opened their mental link to track his progress and be ready to trigger the spell that would return him to their side when he gave the signal.

Since Obsidian and Anna had completed the magical bond between Rasoren and Kyrsu, they could now pinpoint and track the location of every gargoyle.

Truth was presently in no danger, though he'd been inquisitive of the human's machines. Obsidian's mind was just beginning to wander again when he detected a change in Truth.

The other male began to broadcast his surroundings in more detail. He hadn't even bothered to do that when he'd been captured by a unit of human soldiers.

"The Avatars come," Truth whispered along the link.

"We'll be ready to pull you out if we sense danger," he reassured his friend.

Anna snorted. "Gregory is a protector and loyal to all gargoyles. He won't hurt Truth."

That was true.

Obsidian turned his attention to the one-sided conversation between Truth and the Avatars. Then, at last, Truth shared his message with Lillian and Gregory.

It was time. Summoning his own magic, Obsidian reached out and triggered the spells Thayn had woven upon Truth.

Immediately the spell responded. Then with a bright flash of light and the scent of the Avatars' startlement on Obsidian's tongue, Truth emerged from a swirling cloud of shadow magic.

"I'd say we just surprised a pair of billion-year-old Avatars," Anna said. "Not sure if that's a good thing, but mission accomplished."

Truth gave himself a little shake and made an exaggerated show of checking all his extremities. "Good. Everything is still where it's supposed to be. Felt like I'd left a few pieces of me back there."

Obsidian reached for his friend to drag him into a hug. "You did well. You kept an Avatar out of your head."

Truth snorted. "Only because he allowed me to keep my secrets. I've never felt such ancient and vast power before."

"You'll get used to the Avatars," Anna offered. "They are down to earth and mellow once you get to know them."

Truth silently mouthed Anna's words back at her. Obsidian chuckled harder and began to explain the phrase to his friend.

When he was finished explaining, Anna tapped Obsidian on his arm. "We need to be ready for when everything goes sideways. And everything in my life always goes sideways."

Obsidian very much hoped his Kyrsu was wrong this

time. If the negotiations with the Avatars went 'sideways' then that would be devastating for all the realms.

But before they could convince the Avatars to return to Draydrak's island, they first had to meet them face to face and discuss giving up their son to Lord Death.

Obsidian's wings flicked nervously a second time.

CHAPTER SIXTEEN

Gryton

The restlessness was rising again. Though Gryton ignored it. Not that there was anything he could do while trapped in his cage. He sat with his legs crossed, eyes closed, and his upturned hands resting on his knees as he projected the appearance of calm indifference toward the leshii.

Greenborrow was watching him again while the Null slept.

While he didn't acknowledge the leshii's presence and the fae endeavored to do the same, Gryton was certain this round of guard duty was a subtle punishment for the ancient leshii's last defiance. Gryton kept his expression neutral, but inwardly he was smiling at the leshii's periodic disgruntled huffs.

It wasn't until another prickle of warning crawled up Gryton spine that he snapped his eyes open and studied the leshii. The alarm intensified, but there was no sense of threat emanating from the fae.

This was something else.

If he hadn't been soul-bound to the Null, her natural ability draining him even as she slept in another building, he would have recognized what he sensed immediately.

After all, the two he suddenly sensed had once been slaves to his collars.

Grinning at the realization they'd both survived what the blood witch had attempted, he allowed the leshii to witness some of his pleasure. Things were about to get interesting.

Perhaps Gryton would even escape his cage for a short while.

"What are you grinning about?" the leshii growled.

"There are two newcomers to this realm."

The leshii arched a brow. "You can sense more gargoyles? It doesn't surprise me that he didn't come alone."

Gryton's merriment vanished.

The leshii already knew of the visitors? Yet Greenborrow hadn't called Shadowlight by name. Perhaps he was unaware of the gargoyle's identity?

But that made no sense either. From what he'd gathered, Greenborrow and the cub had been friends. The leshii would have recognized Shadowlight even if he'd only seen him briefly as the soldiers escorted him elsewhere.

If Shadowlight wasn't the gargoyle the soldiers found, then the other arrivals could only be legion gargoyles loyal to Lord Death. Damnation! Why couldn't it just have been Anna and the cub returning alone? But they weren't alone if there was already another gargoyle spy here.

"You must warn the Avatars of Anna and Shadowlight's return. If they have come with other gargoyles, it is likely on Lord Death's orders. Surely I need not tell you how bad that could be?"

The leshii snorted. "The human hybrid and the cub are no threat to the Avatars or anyone else."

"Underestimating them is a mistake, leshii. Those two youngsters excelled far. They nearly killed a blood witch. There's no telling what new tricks they've learned under Lord Death's tutorage."

Greenborrow narrowed his eyes, and by the set of his jaw, Gryton could tell the leshii would not carry his warning to the Avatars.

"If what you say is true, which I highly doubt, Anna and the cub are likely still scouting for your location so they can kill you as Lord Death wants. I, for one, will not get in that demigod's way if he's commanded his servants to snuff you out of existence." The leshii cackled. "I'll even unlock the cage door for them if they get here before your parents do, misbegotten one."

Gryton flashed his fangs at the leshii but didn't continue the conversation.

There was one thing the leshii had overlooked. While Anna and Shadowlight had advanced quickly, they were both years away from being a real threat to Gryton. Even soul-bound and caged, there was little they could do that would cause him irrevocable harm. They didn't have the strength to kill him unless the Null was working with Lord Death.

But from what he could tell through his regrettable soul link with the insufferable human, she was still deeply asleep.

If she were working with Anna, Shadowlight, and the other legion gargoyles, then she wouldn't be sleeping during an attack.

Gryton frowned.

Lord Death would know Anna and Shadowlight weren't yet a match for him. Why then would he send them? They wouldn't be able to win a fight against the Avatars either.

The human military? But what could Lord Death want with a war with the humans?

No. None of those possibilities made sense. He was missing something.

What did the demigod want if not him?

Gryton's mind stilled, calming even as his elemental magic lashed out in response to what he'd just realized.

There was another being, still helpless and innocent, that might be seen as a violation of Divine will. Could that be Death's plan? To seek out and end Gryton's unborn sister before she matured into something much more powerful?

No! You will not have her. You will not have that beautiful bright new soul.

His sister—the one creature in the universe that might be like him in some small way.

Gryton bolted upright and leaped toward the cage door, bellowing at the leshii. "Let me out now!"

"Ha! You've already caused me enough trouble. I'll not

be stepping out of line again. Gregory threatened to turn me over to the scientists. You're likely just looking for a way to escape and get back at me. I wasn't born yesterday."

Gryton bellowed the order a second time.

"No."

"Have it your way, fae," Gryton hissed as he called on his magic. The spells worked into the walls of his cage and surrounding room flashed a warning a moment before tendrils of power lashed out and wrapped his body in bands of raw energy. One encircled his throat as if it could choke him into submission.

Everywhere they touched, the cold power dug below his skin and stimulated his nerves, blasting him with a wave of agony.

But pain had been his companion from the moment of his birth. Pain was familiar and could be withstood. That was one thing no one understood about him—not the Battle Goddess, not the Lord of the Underworld, not his sire and dam, perhaps not even the Divine Ones understood. No amount of pain could ever stop him. His own magic inflicted more pain upon him than any other being could ever hope to match.

His fiery magic came to his call. It danced along his skin and burned away his clothing. The tendril around his neck continued to grow colder and imposed more agony. But it and the others wrapping his body couldn't contain his power. The spells woven into the clear-walled cage disintegrated, burned away by his fierce, unrelenting power. The bands covering his body fell apart. With a grunt of disdain, he flung away the remnants of the tendril around his neck.

Moments after the cage's ineffective defenses failed, his fire magic expanded outward. Soon holes opened as the material melted, dripping to the ground, where it hissed as it began to eat into the floor below the cage.

As more of his power answered his summons, scales grew from his skin, shaping themselves into armor.

Between curses, the leshii was shouting warnings to the soldiers outside in the hall, but they ignored the fae and came rushing inside instead of fleeing. Greenborrow's curses grew louder and more creative.

The humans continued to ignore the fae and advanced on Gryton's cage. They did not issue a warning—which he would have ignored. Instead, their weapons all pointed at him and began to spit their tiny, painful little projectiles.

As his scales finished growing into impenetrable armor, he exerted control over his magic. When it bucked and fought, he closed a mental fist around the flows of power until only a little fire glowed between the plates of his new armor.

Looking up at the guards, Gryton grinned and released a wave of magic. This flashy show of destruction was for the guards, to inspire terror in the hope they'd be reluctant to engage. On an emotional level, he didn't care what happened to the leshii or the human soldiers. Yet he retained enough sense to know killing them wouldn't benefit his own future.

But if the thought he'd reduce them to ash kept them off his trail for a short time? All to the better.

Turning his hands palm up, he slowly raised his arms, fire magic swirling and dancing around them.

The leshii's eyes widened. "Out now!"

Gryton directed the next wave of destruction toward the soldier farthest to the left of the group.

Greenborrow swore again, pivoted, and then jerked the guard out of the path of the fire and then with an impressive heave, physically tossed him toward the safety of the hall. The soldier cleared the door without issue but hit the opposite wall with enough force Gryton wouldn't be surprised if the male suffered a broken bone or two. The guard collapsed into an unmoving heap.

"Unless you want to die, out now," the leshii roared to the others even as he was grabbing two more soldiers and shoving them toward the door.

To help them decide, Gryton sent another wave of magic racing toward them. The leshii and the four remaining soldiers dived through the door. Smiling, Gryton darted out of the cage and made for the back wall of the room. The entire chamber was ward-spelled, but his destructive magic was swift to burn away that protection, and then it was eating into the unknown substance of the wall itself.

The composition was some strange mix of pulverized native stone, minerals, and sand. It didn't matter what it was. Even if it had been made from the death metal of this world, his power still would have worked upon it.

Under his hands, the material turned molten and oozed like lava bubbling down from a vent of an active volcano. When the hole was large enough, he stepped through and sprinted across the floor of the new room to the next wall.

Soon he was through the second wall and emerged into a dimly lit stairway.

As he raced up them, heading toward the surface, he

called on another of his formidable powers. This one allowed him to touch the minds of mortals and direct their attention elsewhere.

It wasn't foolproof. Some humans had a higher natural resistance to his power than others. And now that the alarm had already been raised, it made his task harder since they were actively searching for him, but he still managed to redirect any eyes that would have landed upon him.

It wasn't as good as a gargoyle's shadow magic, but it was still enough for him to make it out of the military camp.

While he had a head start, it wouldn't last long. Already he could sense the humans mobilizing to give chase. Other fae would soon be on his trail, and his mind control magic didn't work on them nearly as well.

Worse, he could feel the Null. She was awake now and already tracking him. For the moment, she was on foot, but she'd soon find another mode of travel. If she overtook him before he made it to his destination...

That couldn't happen.

He briefly debated weaving a portal spell to get him to the glade faster, but that would alert Anna and Shadow-light and whatever other Legion gargoyles might be there. And then there was the Null.

Even now, over the distance between them, he could feel the slight tug on his power as she fed. But for now, it wasn't enough to incapacitate him. That might change if he created a portal spell and she mistook it as an attempt to escape back to the Magic Realm. She was exhibiting some control over her ability. Now wasn't the time to test how great it was.

He trusted that once he got to the maze and engaged the Legion gargoyles, she would divert her attention to the newcomers if she was even remotely intelligent.

And while the Null might be brash and uncultured, she wasn't a fool. There was intelligence in her eyes that made her tongue even sharper. That same astuteness would allow her to guess his true purpose.

Gryton ran full out, cutting through a forested area that opened onto a street with manicured lawns. Small dwellings lined both sides of the road. It was early yet, the sun just clearing the horizon in the east. He only encountered a few humans. They weren't soldiers and were more easily deceived.

He continued to run, his long strides covering the ground quickly. Soon he left the outskirts of the town behind. The surrounding land opened into fields with crops or grazing livestock. He cut through a field as he had the forest before, making a straight line toward his destination.

Not far behind, he could hear the roar of machines. But once he left the fields for forest once more, they wouldn't be able to follow so easily over the uneven terrain.

While he'd been sure to keep his presence hidden from the gargoyles, they could sense the humans' approach. If the humans tipped off the legion gargoyles, the intruders might hurry to complete their mission before Gryton could stop them. His power rose, testing his control at the thought.

He clamped down on his power.

Later, he promised it. *You can destroy our enemies later.*

And while he didn't think Anna and Shadowlight would

have changed so much that they would kill an unborn child, he couldn't risk the chance Lord Death's other legion servants might act.

He put on another burst of speed, inadvertently surprising a small herd of deer. The startled beasts didn't distract him. Soon he reached the small laneway that led to the stone cottage and the other buildings belonging to his mother's mortal family.

CHAPTER SEVENTEEN

Anna

Walking up to the hamadryad's last line of defenses, Anna placed her hand on the top edge of one of the standing stones ringing the tree. With a small tendril of magic, she pushed her intent at the ward spell.

I am no threat. I mean no harm.

Which was true. After confirming that Gryton was indeed a prisoner, they had then sought out and studied all the other fae who had once been allies. After observing each person with subtle magic, she and Obsidian had sensed nothing new. Everything seemed much as they remembered. If Gryton had influenced the others, it wasn't obvious.

But he had visited the hamadryad more than once in

the time they'd been here, the Avatars allowing him that much freedom. Which is why Thayn had sent them back here today. While Gryton may not have been able to influence any of the other fae or human soldiers, the eldest gargoyle had pointed out the fire elemental might be secretly influencing his unborn sister.

"I can't believe we've been able to slink around with no one the wiser," Anna admitted. *"No one sensed us. Not even the Avatars."*

"They are less than they were," Obsidian said in response to her thoughts. *"Thayn was correct about that."*

"Still, I can't believe they haven't hunted us down yet. They know we're here."

Obsidian shrugged. *"We don't mean them harm. Perhaps they sense that."*

"Perhaps." Anna shrugged. *"Everything seems much as it was when we left."*

"True," Obsidian agreed after a long pause. *"And yet I see things I didn't see as a child. The Mother's Sorceress and the Gargoyle Protector now compromise in a way Thayn says they never did until this life."*

Predictably, her Rasoren sighed when she flicked an ear to convey her doubt.

While Obsidian and Thayn might think the worst of them, if it hadn't been for the Sorceress, Anna never would have reunited with Shadowlight.

"Still, they are less than they were," Obsidian continued. *"It is possible that extends to more than just their power."*

Anna read his next thought before it was fully formed.

"You think Gryton's birth also changed them, changed their personalities?"

"It is possible. To be certain of their motives, we will need to

study them more. But we have another task to complete first." Obsidian glanced up at the hamadryad.

Anna followed the direction of his gaze until she was tilting her head back to stare up at the tall tree.

Approaching the hamadryad, Anna discovered three more very nasty defensive spells.

She chuckled. *"I'd say the only thing the Avatars are guilty of is wisely protecting their daughter from the likes of the Battle Goddess's minions."*

Huffing his disagreement, Obsidian still joined her by the hamadryad's wide trunk.

Closing her eyes, Anna placed her hands upon the tree, careful not to think even a slightly aggressive thought. After a moment, Obsidian mirrored her, and together they examined the developing fetus within.

"Her soul is beautiful. And she's already so strong," Obsidian said with a hint of pride in his tone.

Anna nodded. *"I sense nothing of darkness within her."*

"Nor I."

"She's pure. I don't think Gryton was trying to influence her during his visits. Not that Lillian and Gregory would allow him to, anyway. I'm sure they still don't trust Gryton."

"She feels the same as I remember as a child." Obsidian grinned suddenly. *"I was strong enough even back then to sense it."*

"Did you want some alone time to stroke your ego in private?"

"Would that not defeat the purpose?" He bumped his muzzle against hers before sighing. *"We should be going."*

Anna agreed, and together they moved out away from the trunk, Obsidian a step ahead of her. She was just stepping clear of the boughs when she was suddenly shoved back into the tree branches by a blow from Obsidian's powerful tail.

While she was still momentarily stunned, the wind knocked out of her by the mighty blow, a ball of fire magic screamed through the air where she'd stood only a moment ago.

After scrambling to her feet, she darted around the tree trunk to get a bead on their attackers and to locate Obsidian. Using their link to guide her, she swiftly spotted her Rasoren sheltering behind one of the standing stones ringing the tree. Seeing that Obsidian was out of the line of fire, she began scanning for the threat.

From her vantage point, she could just make out a tall, familiar form in full armor standing in the maze's shadowy south exit

"*It's Gryton,*" she sent along their link.

"*Can you create a distraction? I'm pinned down here. If I call battle magic, he'll sense it even through my shield and know where I am. But, interestingly, he isn't attacking you even though the branches' movement gave away your location.*"

"*On it.*"

Reaching out with her mind, she weaponized the shadows nearest to the commander's position and sent them flying toward him. The little bits of shadow magic weren't a real threat to the armor-clad opponent, but it gave Obsidian the time he needed to leap across the expanse of open ground and reach the hamadryad's shadows. He crouched next to her.

Still uncertain of Gryton's motives, Anna swiftly erected a shield in front of the hamadryad to protect it and the child the tree carried.

"We need to take the fight out of the glade. This is too great a risk to the unborn child." Obsidian's worry for his future niece flowed along their mental link.

Gryton stalked forward, his long strides eating up the distance. It also made him a damn tempting target.

"He wants to draw us out," Obsidian said, his surprise cascading down the link. *"I think he's concerned for the tree and the child. That's why he didn't attack again once we were within the tree's canopy."*

Anna narrowed her eyes as she peered around the tree's trunk again. With his elemental magic snapping around his armor and his molten gaze glowing through the slit in his visor, he looked mightily pissed off, but Obsidian was correct. Gryton wasn't attacking.

"Get away from my sister, gargoyle! Your shadow magic will not save you."

Anna ducked under a large branch, moving with Obsidian as they kept the trunk between them and Gryton. *"Guess that confirms that theory. He's holding off his attack until he's flushed us out."*

"We need to go before the Avatars arrive," Obsidian said, reluctance at fleeing a fight echoing in his thoughts.

"Good point. Time to retreat." As much as she'd like to pin Tin Man to the ground and punch him for a day or two, they needed to move.

"Get ready to run. You go first. I'll cover your retreat."

If Anna hadn't been in Obsidian's head, she wouldn't have agreed. But her Rasoren was correct. Gryton knew they were gargoyles, but he couldn't know it was them. But that would change if he saw a female gargoyle scampering away.

"We'll need another distraction first," Obsidian said, even as he called on his shadow magic.

The shadows under the hamadryad shivered, rising from the ground like a mist. Anna was just adding her own power when another familiar figure arrived at the maze's west entrance.

Obsidian huffed out a surprised grunt and stilled, frozen in shock at seeing his mother for the first time in over thirteen years.

A swirling mix of dryad and shadow magic surrounded River. "Get away from my daughter's child, monster!"

"Shit!" Anna hissed, realizing Obsidian wasn't ready to fight his own mother. She called more power, preparing to send a lance of energy at the ground a few feet in front of the dryad to unbalance River. A moment before she launched her attack, Anna realized she and Obsidian weren't the targets.

Gryton was.

What the hell was going on? But then she knew. *"Obsidian, she thinks Gryton is attacking the hamadryad. River doesn't know we're here. This is our chance to escape without being discovered. We need to move."*

"But..." His words were whispered barely above the rustle of the grass.

"I know," Anna soothed. *"But now isn't the time to face her."*

Nodding jerkily, Obsidian moved at last. Though he paused and glanced over his shoulder at his mother longingly.

"They are allies even if they don't want to be. They won't kill each other. Your mother is a smart lady. Once she realizes there were gargoyles here, she'll switch to hunting us instead of Gryton."

Obsidian still hesitated.

"I'm sorry. But move your big ass."

Obsidian grunted but redirected his shadow magic to cover their retreat. Anna did the same, and then she was running toward the maze's north entrance. Obsidian raced just feet behind. Then they were once again safely within the labyrinth.

Obsidian nipped her in the flank, his teeth leaving a mark.

"What the hell was that for?" she barked at him.

"For saying I have a big ass." His mirth flowed down their link.

She smacked him with the tip of her tail. He was still laughing when they reached the first branch of the maze. She continued to run, and Obsidian kept pace. Neither of them ran at top speed. The twisting corridors didn't allow that.

She was just coming around another corner when she nearly collided with a human soldier she hadn't sensed in their path.

Two things became immediately apparent.

The human could see them.

And the human soldier wasn't human at all.

As Anna stood there, staring mutely, the soldier continued feeding on her magic.

"Avatars, what's happening? Gryton sensed intruders with possible hostile intent. I was tracking him. Then got turned around in this maze. Not sure what's going on now."

"You're draining our magic." Obsidian's tone was ominous enough to send a skittering down Anna's spine in reaction.

The human snapped to attention.

"Shit. You're not Gregory." She sized up Obsidian and then pointed her gun at him. "On the ground!"

Anna leaped to the attack, her need to protect her Rasoren momentarily overpowering common sense. Lashing out, she knocked the gun away in a lightning-fast move. While the other woman was still surprised, Anna hit the soldier in the jaw with a powerful punch. The soldier stumbled back a few steps but didn't go down.

More surprising, Anna's fist had turned numb. The chill in her hand swiftly climbed her arm.

Eyes widening, she stared at the other woman.

That blow should have knocked the human soldier on her ass. Probably unconscious. But she just stood there looking as surprised as Anna felt.

"She feeds on all types of energy," Obsidian said in sudden understanding. "She absorbed the force of your strike."

While the soldier was still surprised, Obsidian jerked the gun from her grasp and then lashed out with his talons. The human blocked the strike with her arm. It was as if Obsidian had hit an invisible barrier instead of flesh.

"Good God. How do we fight something that can swallow magical and kinetic energy? My damned fist is still numb." Then something occurred to Anna, and she darted farther away from the abomination. Obsidian followed; the gun still held in his hand.

They both glanced at the gun and then the stranger.

A look of understanding flashed across the soldier's face. "Fuck it. I'm not staying to find out if I'm bulletproof."

The soldier turned and dashed down a side corridor.

"Time to go." Anna dropped to all fours. As she darted past Obsidian, she smacked him in the flank to get him moving. "I know you want to go after her and find out what she is, but as far as we know, she could be something created by Blood Witch Taryin and the Battle Goddess. If that's the case, then we're deep in enemy territory."

While Anna had felt nothing overtly evil about the soldier, she couldn't be confident whatever power allowed her to drain magic wouldn't also dull their other senses.

"You're right." Unhappiness tinted his thoughts, but he followed close on Anna's tail as they made their way out of the maze. Getting out proved much harder than sneaking in. Dozens of soldiers were now making their way through the maze. Anna and Obsidian had to swiftly backtrack down several side corridors and dead ends to keep out of the soldiers' way. Neither of them trusted their shadow magic to hide them since they couldn't be sure how greatly the female soldier's strange power had weakened them.

They eventually made it out of the maze, but it wasn't until they reached the shadows of the forest that Anna marginally relaxed. But the strange numbness in her one hand prevented her from relaxing completely.

"We need to get looked at by healers to discover what that woman did to us. And then we need to see Thayn and hope to hell he has some idea what she is and how to fight her."

Obsidian nodded, his thoughts in complete agreement with hers.

CHAPTER EIGHTEEN

Erika

*I*f Gryton hadn't broken out of his cage and wasn't presently raging, Erika might have stayed to find out if she was bulletproof. But as far as her strange ability was concerned, Gryton was the greater danger at the moment. His power levels were rapidly reaching dangerous levels.

She needed to secure him and drain enough power that he wasn't a threat to himself or anyone else. Once that was done, she and the others could go find the two new gargoyles. While it was embarrassing that she hadn't immediately realized the male and female weren't the Avatars, and they'd then got her gun, she'd also learned she might be immune to physical assault.

She'd dwell on that later. For now, she needed to reach

Gryton. Thanks to the soul binding, she knew exactly where he was and what he was doing. He was battling more than one magic-user and enraged by that forced distraction. He'd much rather be chasing the two intruders she'd just encountered.

Erika couldn't even blame Gryton. He'd detected the intruders before anyone else. Regrettably, everyone else thought he'd broken out of his cage in a bid to escape. When really all he'd been trying to do was protect the tree fetus.

Her soul-link to the fire elemental opened wide, and she was suddenly in his head.

"Stand down," she shouted into his mind, hoping he would somehow hear her. *"Stand down now!"*

"I can't."

Shit, it worked.

"Why can't you stand down?"

"The simple fact that everyone is trying to kill me." Magic pulsed between them stronger than before, and suddenly she was both running through the maze's confusing corridors and standing shoulder to shoulder with him.

What the hell?

Gryton stood inside the ring of stones encircling the tree, his back to the hamadryad as he fed power into the protective dome of magic surrounding the immediate area. On the other side of the circle, at least four dozen soldiers were firing at the dome, trying to breach it. They weren't alone. At least seven of the fae were also targeting the dome with magical attacks.

"You're fucking kidding me?"

*"I don't know what fornication with baby goats has to do with

anything, but as you can see, I'm unable to stand down without the hamadryad and my unborn sister coming to harm."

She rolled her eyes. *"All you have to do is say two simple words."*

"And what would those two words be?"

"I surrender."

When he snorted with humor, she knew he'd have been enjoying all this if not for the two gargoyles getting farther away by the minute.

"You still don't know me. I never surrender."

Actually, she knew that about him.

The connection between them snapped, or Gryton closed it off. But suddenly she was entirely in her own head again and couldn't see what was happening in the center of the glade.

"Shit," she cursed at the green walls of the maze. "I really hate labyrinths!"

After longer than she wanted to admit, she stumbled across one of the maze's exits. She just burst out into the glade when Gregory and Lillian arrived, galloping through some kind of a magic portal that shimmered in the air on the opposite side of the clearing from Erika's position.

Lillian was yelling for everyone to stop. At least that's what Erika thought she was shouting. Too bad no one could hear the Sorceress over the noise of gunfire and the explosive hiss of magic strikes.

The other woman must have realized the same thing

for she raised her arms wide and power began rising up out of the ground.

Erika was damn sure the Sorceress was about to attack the soldiers and fae targeting Gryton and her tree.

"How do I get myself into such shitty situations?" Erika asked herself and then squared her shoulders.

With a savage grin, she started to run again, envisioning sucking up all the magic in the glade.

To her surprise, it wasn't just spells that fell apart and dissolved, bullets fell out of the air. Even the dome protecting the tree collapsed, revealing Gryton, his magic still rising into the air, snapping and flickering like a bonfire in a stiff breeze.

As Erika sprinted past the two startled Avatars, she shouted over her shoulder, "He wasn't trying to escape."

Gryton's magic dwindled at her approach. When she was ten strides away, he hissed out something unintelligible and slowly collapsed to his knees. A well-placed shove sent him face-first into the dirt. Then with her knee pressed into his lower back, she held him down and reached in her pocket for a zip tie.

"What are you doing?" The grass muffled his question.

"Securing the prisoner."

"You know I wasn't trying to escape!"

"Yep. That's why I just risked my ass to get to you before you got steamrolled by your gargoyle father. Pretty sure he had something nasty planned." She shoved his face into the ground again as she pushed herself up. "You're welcome."

Another muffled curse reached her but whatever else

he might have said was drowned out by the roar of approaching helicopters.

"My sister is still in danger," Gryton managed to say after turning on his side. "Your ability has gone into battle mode. You're draining every speck of power in your immediate vicinity."

She glanced around and noticed the nearest fae looked like they were on day three of a bender. Even the Avatars looked under the weather, their great wellspring of power dwindling. Then she remembered the reason Gryton was protecting the hamadryad tree.

"Crap." She didn't want to be responsible for the death of the tree fetus.

Grabbing Gryton under the arms, she started dragging him away from the tree. He was almost too hot to the touch but swiftly cooled under her hands.

"I'm still feeding off you, aren't I?"

"Yes." His answer was more of a grunt than a word.

"Good. Better you than little sis. You deserve it for this stunt."

His growl became more pronounced. "You most illogical and dimwitted of creatures! On the way here, you admitted you knew why I broke free. You didn't even blame me."

"Yeah." She nodded, not that he could see it. "But that was before I realized all this could have been avoided if you'd just told someone your concerns instead of acting like a firebrand."

"Firebrand?" He swore in another foreign language. "I told the leshii. He didn't listen."

"Fine." While she continued to drag him farther from

the tree, Gregory raced up to them and grabbed Gryton's other arm, and together they quickly dragged the armor-clad prisoner to the edge of the maze.

She glanced up at the big gargoyle. "Am I far enough away from the tree?"

Gregory gazed across the three-hundred-foot expanse of ground. "For the moment you're feeding on Gryton. It is safe."

"Good. I meant no harm. I just needed to stop everyone from trying to kill Gryton."

Erika glanced toward the tree again. The female Avatar was already there, sharing magic with the hamadryad.

"You said he wasn't trying to escape?" the gargoyle said, drawing her attention back to him.

"He was protecting his unborn sister from the two intruders."

"Intruders?" The gargoyle tensed, his body alert, ears and tail not moving so much as the smallest twitch. His eyes took on a distant, unfocused look for a few seconds before they sharpened once more upon her.

"I sense no intruders near, and none of the defenses were tampered with or triggered."

"No idea about any of that, but Gryton wasn't lying. I ran into two gargoyles on my way here. A big male and a slightly smaller female. Thought they were you and Lillian at first."

Major Resnick marched up to them. "Did I hear you say intruders? Another female gargoyle? Full-blooded?"

"Looked that way to me."

He turned his next question to Gregory. "Anna? But you

said she's months or years away from becoming a full-blooded gargoyle."

"From what I could tell from studying her. However, there is no telling what the Battle Goddess or Lord Death may have done to her. More worrying is the fact I didn't detect them."

Erika glanced between Major Resnick and the gargoyle. She thought she knew what the major was thinking. Her suspicions were confirmed a moment later when he tossed an accusation at Gregory.

"If you had allowed us to interrogate him as we wished, we would know Anna could shapeshift."

"Gryton is too dangerous and cunning to be a candidate for your interrogations. He would have used the contact to influence you or your men with his gift."

"So far, I don't see you faring much better. He escaped his cage and made it all the way to the hamadryad."

Resnick prodded Gryton with the toe of his boot. "Tell us what you know."

Erika eased her foot off Gryton's back and then rolled him over. He only glowered at them.

"I've answered all your questions truthfully. How is it my fault you don't know what questions to ask?"

Gregory growled and showed his teeth. "Watch it, pup."

Gryton only laughed. "I don't fear you, father. The Sorceress won't allow you to harm me as long as I don't act out against the humans. If you noticed, I didn't harm so much as one human in my escape. My only concern was for my unborn sister. I feared Anna and Shadowlight had been sent to scout for weaknesses and to terminate her. And if

Lord Death wished to strike out against you, she's your most vulnerable spot."

Interestingly, the big gargoyle didn't deny his words, though he looked like he was about to stare a hole in Gryton's armor-clad chest.

Erika studied the fire elemental and noticed his scale armor was missing in a few places, patches of his pale skin showing. Frowning, she realized it was all the locations where she'd manhandled him while she'd been securing and dragging him over to the maze wall.

"Anna and Shadowlight wouldn't attack in such a cowardly way," Gregory said at last. "You have some other scheme. Tell me what it is."

"They are greatly changed from the human and cub you knew. I should know. I helped with their training. They endured tutelage under the blood witch. Taryin could never break them. But Death? It's said he can whisper the most seductive promises. No one can long resist his influence. And are gargoyles not compelled to serve him?" Gryton smiled, fangs flashing.

His grin faltered as his mother approached. Erika could sense him wanting to know about his sister's condition.

"He wants to know how his sister is," she offered helpfully, "but he's too proud to ask."

"She is fine." The Sorceress's expression had softened at Erika's comment, but now it hardened again. "But what in the ever-loving fuck is going on?"

As father and son explained what they knew, Erika looked toward Major Resnick. "Orders, sir?"

"We need to get Gryton hidden. There are too many reporters. Plus, the locals are getting bolder in their expressions of doubt for our reason for still being here. We've already shot down three toy drones in the last week." Resnick looked up at the sky, and his frown lines deepened. "The last thing we need seen on the six o'clock news is a man in medieval armor being chased by military personnel. As soon as Lillian and Gregory finish with Gryton, I want you and the rest of the teams on location to take him to Gran's cottage. She has a secure ward-spelled room in the basement for just such an emergency. We'll hold Gryton there until nightfall and then move him after the town folk are asleep."

"Yes, sir."

"And, Private."

"Yes, sir?"

"I don't care if you have to sit on him until the transfer, don't allow him to escape. If the new base at Alpha Site were closer to completion, we'd move him there now, but not all the needed security measures are in place there yet. But for now, we'll take him to Gran's dungeon."

'Dungeon?' Her new assignment was never dull, at least.

Gryton laughed, more bitter sarcasm than humor. "You haven't seen anything yet, Mortal."

After that ominous declaration, Major Resnick ignored Gryton and turned his attention to the Avatars, where they were still having a conversation about the intruders. Erika stood at attention a few feet away and waited for them to finish.

Eventually, Lillian broke away from Gregory and Resnick and approached Gryton. "Thank you for your concern for your sister. Even though your decision to act alone was in error, it was still done with good intentions."

The Sorceress patted Gryton affectionately on the shoulder.

"I would never harm you or my sister willingly, Mother."

A few feet away, Gryton's gargoyle father huffed softly as he pinned his ears. And while Erika wasn't able to read the nuances of gargoyle expression, she was damn sure that was an expression of extreme skepticism.

Smart fellow.

Erika didn't trust Gryton any further than she could toss his heavy, armor-covered ass.

Gregory wandered over and studied his son in silence for several minutes. At last, the gargoyle said what was on his mind. "I'm surprised you care for your sister as much as you do. Until recently, you didn't care for anyone or anything besides yourself."

Blunt but honest. Erika tipped her head to the gargoyle in admiration. Here was one unlikely to fall prey to Gryton's manipulations. Erika turned her attention back to the fire elemental. As usual, he was too busy being stubbornly silent to speak the truth she'd glimpsed in his mind. A truth which might have cut him some slack.

"He's honestly not working an angle. For once. He sees the unborn fetus as the only thing in the universe like him if even only a little. He feels a sense of kinship toward her."

And he'll likely make one badass big brother, she added silently.

Erika couldn't place what had moved her to speak. Whatever it was, it would likely come back to bite her in the ass later. As things do.

"Insufferable Mortal! Stay out of my head!" Gryton snapped.

Suddenly the sorceress giggled with humor, surprising everyone. It made her seem much younger.

When she had herself under control, she looked Erika in the eye. "I think my mate is correct. You were put on this earth to force my son to learn to be humble. An emotion that is completely foreign to him."

Erika shrugged.

Soon the big gargoyle cleared his throat. "I will leave my son in your capable hands, Major Resnick. If you'll excuse us, we have two gargoyles to track down if they haven't already used a portal spell to escape."

One thing no one mentioned was that if the two intruders could make it past all the new defenses set in place, then there was nothing to suggest there were only two gargoyles.

They might be looking at an invasion.

CHAPTER NINETEEN

Obsidian

He and his Kyrsu had holed up in a den they'd dug earlier. It was well away from any human patrols or the game trails the fae used for traveling through the forest. And while they'd waited for Thayn's arrival, Obsidian's magic had returned with no side effects that he could detect.

But even with time to think, he hadn't been able to figure out what power the human had possessed that allowed her to drain others of magic.

"You?" he asked Anna, knowing she was touching his thoughts.

"Not a clue. But I don't think she did any lasting harm." Anna dropped to all fours and stalked over to bump shoulders with him before leaning in and giving the curve of one wing a reassuring little lick. As her tongue stroked along the sensitive skin, he purred his happiness.

Huffing softly, he nosed aside Anna's thick mane so he could nuzzle the skin of her shoulder in return. It was during these moments that their link naturally opened wider, and they became as one mind. This time was no different.

Ah. Her grooming had a purpose. She was checking again for any residual foreign magic from a spell that might still be on his skin.

"I detect nothing, but a healer might. Must we really wait for Thayn?" She sounded unhappy. "We could return to the Magic Realm and be back here within a couple of hours."

Obsidian snorted. "You'd leave him here alone?"

"Thayn can look after himself. Besides, Truth is with him."

"It's not Thayn I'm worried about. It's this world," he added with a little chuckle.

Beside him, Anna started to laugh, her entire body shaking with her mirth. "Good point. There's no way Truth has enough hutzpah to keep Thayn in check."

"Truth doesn't have enough 'what' to keep me in check?" Thayn's voice came from somewhere just outside their den entrance.

Obsidian emerged from the den, but he didn't immediately spot the elder.

"*Shit!*" Anna hissed along their link. "*Did you feel him approaching? How the hell can he hide from us? We're the Rasoren and Kyrsu. Thought we were supposed to be able to track all gargoyles' locations? Eh?*"

"With age comes great wisdom?" Obsidian hedged. Belatedly he felt shadow magic tingle along his senses as Thayn appeared before them.

His Kyrsu rolled her eyes. *"We were distracted. That old rascal can smell distraction ten clicks away. Time to be proactive."*

Obsidian agreed. "Thayn, don't bother with your pranks. We don't have time. There is a more pressing matter to discuss."

Thayn snorted and released his hold on his shadow magic, appearing at Obsidian's shoulder.

"You're no fun." The eldest of the gargoyles continued to laugh at his disgruntled look.

"We just had our asses handed to us by a human soldier," Anna piped up as she settled on a fallen tree trunk that doubled as a bench.

Thayn's ears perked forward inquiringly, and Obsidian continued where Anna had left off. "We encountered a new threat. A human female. She fed on magic and was easily able to drain us. I couldn't detect any of the spells she used to attack us."

"She was also near impervious to physical attack," Anna added. "It was like she just absorbed most of the blow without damage."

Thayn looked thoughtful. He dropped to sit on the tree trunk bench beside Anna. Tail flicking slowly, ears twitching every few heartbeats, he muttered things to himself.

At last he looked up. "Interesting. Fed upon your power but you weren't able to detect what spell she used?"

"Correct." Anna's statement had a little questioning lilt at the end.

"Hmmm. Very interesting."

"Out with it, Old Man," Anna barked.

Thayn's grin stretched his lips wide, showing rows of gleaming teeth. "I might be old, Young One, but that means I've learned patience. Something you're clearly still struggling with."

"Can't deny that," Anna muttered.

"I need to meet this extraordinary mortal to confirm my suspicions," Thayn said and then dropped to all fours and sprinted away.

"Damn it," Anna shouted. "Wait for us!"

After a swift run, Obsidian was once again in the extensive gardens and pathways that surrounded the spa complex. He followed as Thayn continued unerringly to the large stone cottage where Gran and her family lived.

"Is it just me," Anna asked, *"or does he seem rather too familiar with this area? Do you think the old fart has been spying on the Avatars on his own even though he said he wouldn't?"*

"I think that is a very accurate guess," Obsidian agreed. *"I wonder what all he's learned and kept from us?"*

"Probably all the good stuff."

"If you two are finished talking about me," Thayn whispered into their minds as he halted in the path ahead, *"we're here."*

They came around a gentle curve in the pathway to see the back wall of the stone cottage come into view. At the moment, no one was in this section of the garden or sitting on the porch, but they could hear voices from within.

Thayn strutted boldly up the stairs and onto the veranda where he peered into the back windows.

A familiar smell drifted to Obsidian and old memories surfaced. Gran's cookies. Chocolate chips and peanut butter and something that smelled like tri-berry pie.

Thayn drew in a deep breath and made a purring sound of appreciation. Obsidian shouldered the elder aside and gazed into the window. Gran was within, using a spatula to remove freshly baked cookies from a pan. His stomach rumbled, reminding him he hadn't eaten in hours.

"Watch your step. Or you'll slip in a puddle of your own drool," Anna whispered into his mind as she moved past them and made straight for the door.

Disgruntled that his Kyrsu had entered what might now be unfriendly territory before he had, he hurried into the house.

Thayn followed them in.

On the lookout for squeaky floorboards, he followed Anna deeper into the kitchen. His Kyrsu was stealthy, making no sound that would betray their arrival.

Thayn came last but cut out around Obsidian and boldly approached Gran.

Obsidian's adopted mortal grandmother stood with her back to them, unaware of the gargoyles invading the kitchen.

He was about to suggest Anna take human form and alert Gran of their arrival—a familiar face would be a lot less intimidating than the sudden appearance of three gargoyles—but Thayn acted faster.

Obsidian froze as the eldest of the gargoyles leaned

around Gran and stole a cookie off the cooling rack. He popped it into his mouth whole and his tail stilled.

It took to the count of thirty for his tail to swing back into motion. But it was the slow flick of contentment, rather than curiosity or mischievousness.

After a brief hesitation, the elder leaned forward and stole another cookie. He was reaching for a third when Gran smacked his hand with the spatula.

"An exchange of names would be nice before you steal any more of my cookies." Gran's stern voice rang out across the kitchen.

The gargoyle elder laughed and released his hold on his shadow magic shield. Gran turned and looked him up and down, not rattled by the gargoyle leaning over her with the cookie still clasped in his hand.

"And you are?" She asked, the spatula smacking rhythmically against the palm of her other hand.

Thayn stepped back and gave her a bow. "I am called Adept Thayn and have the dubious distinction of being the most ancient of the gargoyles. And by what name may I call you, most delightful of cooks?"

She arched an eyebrow, taking in Thayn's form. "You don't look very ancient."

"Gargoyles do not age physically, but I assure you, I am very old. And your name again?" He bowed a second time, then caught her hand and brushed a kiss across her knuckles before he straightened.

Gran laughed at his deep bow. "Vivian. But most around here just call me 'Gran' for grandmother."

Thayn tilted his head, his lips stretching with humor. "You are far too young to be called Gran. Vivian is a beautiful name. I shall use that if you are not averse to its use."

"I'm not." Then Gran grumbled in an attempt to hide her blush. "Wouldn't have told you my name if I didn't want you to use it."

Anna bumped Obsidian's shoulder. *"Is it just me, or is Thayn flirting with Gran?"*

"I," Obsidian paused and tilted his head as he studied the elder's body language. *"I think you're correct. Though I'm not sure what game he's playing. They only just met."*

Anna broke out in sudden laughter. *"I think I can guess. Dryads have a phrase that is very similar to one we have on earth. It means the way to a man's heart is through his stomach. Truer words I've never heard when it comes to gargoyles. You all love food."*

"That goes for you too," Obsidian remarked.

Anna's eyes narrowed.

Obsidian was still holding back chuckles when Gran held out the plate of cookies in his direction, though her words were for Thayn.

"Why don't you tell the other two gargoyles to drop their invisibility acts and come over here and have some cookies and make introductions?"

Anna glanced at Obsidian. *"How the hell did she know we were here?"*

Thayn just looked in their direction. "You've been found out. Might as well show yourselves. I imagine Vivian will be happy to see you both."

With a shrug, Obsidian released his magic. Anna followed a moment later.

Gran eyed his appearance. "Well, aren't you a big one!"

Then her eyes shifted to Anna and froze. Whatever she'd been about to say forgotten on her tongue.

After a count of ten, Gran closed her mouth and nodded to his Kyrsu. "You're female. Which can only mean you're Anna. Welcome back, my dear! Gryton told us what the blood witch did to you and that Shadowlight took you to the Lord of the Underworld to save your soul. But even Gryton wasn't sure if Lord Death could save your life."

"It was close," Anna agreed.

Obsidian felt when Anna's mind turned back to that time. Instinctively, he reached out and gave her a comforting lick.

Gran didn't miss the little intimacy. She focused on him with greater scrutiny. He could see her battling with her disbelief and doubt until she gave herself a little shake as if it was that easy for her to cast aside her doubts.

"Shadowlight!" She opened her arms wide. "Come, give your Gran a hug."

Obsidian stalked across the space and scooped her up in his arms. Chuckling, she returned his hug as hard as she could. When he allowed her feet to touch the ground, she reached behind her and grabbed the plate of cookies and held them out to him.

"Go on, I know you want them. You cannot have changed that much." Then she gave his height and broad shoulders another look and shook her head again. "Or maybe you have. Still, I can't see you not liking my baking."

"I've missed it and you a great deal," he admitted as he scooped up a cookie from the plate. She offered them to Anna next. His Kyrsu just shrugged and then grabbed two of the still-warm cookies.

"How did this," Gran paused and gestured at his height, "happen in so short a time?"

"It has been close to fourteen years for me," he admitted, seeing no point in lying to Gran.

"Fourteen years?" Shock registered on her face before she schooled her expression.

"It has only seemed like a few months for me," Anna interjected, "since I took a stone nap for the rest of it. I can relate to the shock of seeing the new Shadowlight for the first time."

"Goddess of the Moon," Gran breathed, "this will be a long tale, won't it?"

"Indeed," Thayn agreed. "Best we bring all this lovely food with us. If my memory isn't failing me, the male half of the Avatars always has a healthy appetite."

"He still does," Gran said as she turned back. "I was just getting this ready to take to them and the others, anyway. Let me just get the tea ready, and we'll be all set to have a long chat."

The kettle was just starting to boil when the door between the kitchen and living room swung open. "I came to help carry the goods down to the—"

Jason stopped short at the sight of three gargoyles occupying the kitchen. Obsidian would have called greetings in the human tongue, but presently, his mouth was full of cookies. Not that Jason gave anyone a chance to respond. With a shout, he darted back through the kitchen door faster than Obsidian thought humans could move. Jason's footsteps swiftly receded deeper into the house.

Gran sidestepped Thayn to glance around his wings. "Was that my grandson?"

"Yep," Anna said, pushing the door open to glance into the empty living room. "That was Jason, and I'm pretty sure he's gone for reinforcements."

"Hmmm. It will save us all having to carry this down to the dungeon, I suppose."

"A dungeon?" Thayn asked, sounding delighted by the news.

Gran faced him. "You never know when you will need a nice cage with stout bars and powerful warding."

"True."

Anna's thoughts brushed Obsidian's a moment before her voice was in his head. *"Gran and Thayn. I'm not sure if any of the realms are ready for their meeting."*

Obsidian laughed, drawing the gazes of the two in question. *"I think Gran and Thayn will hit it off to the detriment of everyone else."*

"Goddess, imagine the pranks the two of them will get up to!"

"It will be interesting."

Gran cleared her throat to get their attention. "It's not nice to talk about us behind our backs."

"It is not," Thayn agreed, a note of mock threat in his tone.

"Ah, fuck," Anna hissed mentally. *"We're in deep shit now."*

CHAPTER TWENTY

Lillian

After an unsuccessful hunt to find the two trespassers, Lillian and Gregory had returned to the cottage. Now she stood in the secret chamber one level below the basement. Off in one side of the room, three cages sat looking ominous. Only one of them was occupied.

A part of her hated to see Gryton locked in a cage, but she also knew it was the safest place for him and everyone else. Thankfully, Private Emerson had a strong moral compass, and she'd been quick to come to Gryton's defense since he'd been acting to protect the hamadryad from gargoyles with unknown intentions.

The alliance didn't need a greater wedge between the

different factions than already existed by the revelation that Commander Gryton was their son.

But at the moment, Lillian had a more significant concern—a mother's worry. "I don't like that two Legion gargoyles were examining our daughter."

"They did not harm her. And I can't believe that any gargoyle would harm an innocent child. Perhaps they were only reassuring themselves that she will not grow up to be another demigod like Gryton."

His words were full of confidence, but she knew her protector well. He, too, feared another attempt at her hamadryad which was why he'd taken time to add several more layers of protection that would—if not stop another gargoyle—at least slow him down.

"They are learning our defensive capabilities," Gregory offered at last. "They may also be waiting until they adjust to this realm's lack of magic before confronting us about Gryton."

She compressed her lips. "That's not a comforting thought."

"No," he agreed.

Private Emerson approached them.

"I hope I'm not interrupting ma'am, but Major Resnick wants me to subtly ask if either of you will have a problem with me keeping Gryton drained until we satisfy Command with the new security measures. Clearly, the ones in place weren't enough to hold him."

Gregory huffed. "I am more than happy to have you keep him depleted."

Lillian elbowed him in the side, and he added, "For now. Until everyone is satisfied."

Erika turned to Gryton and grinned as she stomped over to his cage. "You hear that? You're now a Null's all-you-can-eat buffet."

As humorous as Lillian found the Erika-Gryton dynamic, it still couldn't defuse the tension in the room, which was probably why Gran had left forty minutes ago to whip up something to put everyone in a better mood. Jason had just left to help.

As if her thoughts had summoned her human brother, there was a knock at the door. A moment later, Greenborrow released the ward.

Jason stuck his head in, his gaze seeking her out. "Hey. Found your gargoyles. They're in the kitchen with Gran. Eating cookies." He jerked his thumb to indicate somewhere in the upper levels of the house.

"One of them is the biggest damn gargoyle I've ever seen. Gran is positively crooning over him. Think you might want to come and have a look."

With that, he vanished back out the door. Lillian glanced once at Gregory before they both broke into a run and chased after Jason.

CHAPTER TWENTY-ONE

Gryton

He curled his fingers around the bars of the cage and snarled. There were gargoyles here in the building, and his parents had just left him defenseless against his enemies. He narrowed his eyes as he concluded his sire and dam might just be the worst parents in the universe.

"You," he snapped, directing his attention at the Null. "We need to follow them, find out what the gargoyles are really planning. I doubt it's anything good for the Avatars or myself. And since the humans of this world have already bound themselves to my sire and dam, the Legion gargoyles might see you as the enemy as well."

"Sounds like a good reason to stay away."

But he could see the Null's sharp mind working. She just needed a little nudge.

"You could neutralize a gargoyle as easily as you do me. Capture them and find out what they want."

"And leave you here undefended so you can escape at the first opportunity? Nope."

Gryton frowned at the human, undecided if he hated all humans or just her. He thought it might be just her.

He was still trying to glower a hole in the side of her head when one of the human soldiers approached the cage. "I've radioed the major this newest complication. He's on his way back here with two more units. The rest of my team will stay and watch Gryton. He wants you to come with me and help capture one of these new gargoyles."

"Yes, Captain Stanton. I'll do my best to get close to one and incapacitate it." After she'd addressed her superior, she glanced toward Gryton.

"You behave," the Null whispered for his benefit.

He didn't miss how the Null's brows slanted as she looked over her shoulder at him a moment before she exited the room.

"Not for your asking," he whispered after she'd gone. Grinning, he tested the bars. They gave under his tug.

While the use of his magic would have made his escape easier, he'd still be able to force the bars wide enough apart to grant his passage.

He waited until the guards were talking on the radio. Then with a flex of muscle and a dose of determination, he jerked the bars apart and launched himself from the cage as the wardspells lashed out at him.

Ignoring the vicious spells biting into his back and

sides, he confronted the soldiers swiftly, taking them out before they could do much more than call for backup.

He was still feeling far from mellow, but he allowed the soldiers to live. Once the last one was unconscious at his feet, he sprinted from the room, swiftly climbing the stairs and emerging into the next level of the cottage.

Following the sound of Captain Stanton and the Null's boots as they ran, he spotted the door that led to the kitchen still swinging, telling him which way she'd gone.

He stalked forward and shoved the door aside and nearly ran into the Null. She'd been forced to stop there, not able to venture further into the already crowded kitchen.

Gran stood with three gargoyles arranged around a central table. Another unit of human soldiers blocked the door leading outside, with more men stationed on the veranda. Nearer at hand, Lillian and Gregory stood confronting the three gargoyles. His mother's human brother, Jason, hadn't been lying.

The biggest gargoyle Gryton had ever seen was glowering at him. But that wasn't what made his breath still in his lungs. A female gargoyle stood at the male's shoulder. She was as beautiful and powerful as Gryton remembered her.

"Hello Anna," he said in greeting. "I see you survived."

"Gryton." She tilted her head in acknowledgment.

He noted that Shadowlight had abandoned his plate of cookies and now curled a wing around Anna protectively. Or maybe that was possessively.

She rolled her eyes at Shadowlight and the gargoyle's ears wilted with embarrassment, but he maintained his glower. After a moment, Anna nuzzled Shadowlight affectionately, and Gryton was certain they were speaking mind to mind.

He didn't like the natural intimacy between the two. They felt like a long-established pair, as if they had been fighting side by side for centuries.

A moment later, he was disgruntled to realize he was jealous of a cub. He didn't like the notion or that he wasn't in control enough to snuff out unwanted feelings.

That was unacceptable.

"Hello, cub." Gryton's tone was mocking to cover his own unruly emotions.

But, by the God and Goddess, how had Shadowlight matured so much in so short a time?

Gryton hated surprises.

Unaware, and likely uncaring even if she'd known of Gryton's displeasure, Anna continued forward. No one tried to stop her, he noted.

"I'm told you helped Shadowlight and me escape the Battle Goddess after we fought the blood witch. I remember little after she magically gutted me. Thank you for protecting us long enough for us to escape."

Once again Gryton found himself frozen in surprise, speechless, not knowing what to say. He had expected no thanks.

Anna didn't suffer the same speechlessness he felt, though. And she smiled harshly at him.

"Aiding us that one time doesn't excuse you for everything else you did. Know that I won't kill you out of respect for Lillian and Gregory, but if you step out of line or think to betray their trust, I'll let Obsidian have you."

"I have no plans to betray my sire or dam."

The Null joined them then. The two women sized each other up. Once they had come to some conclusion, the Null directed her comment at Anna. "No worries. He's got a new keeper. I'll make sure Hot Stuff stays out of trouble."

Anna tilted her head, studying the Null curiously. After a moment, she must have concluded the Null wasn't an enemy for her shoulders relaxed, and she lowered her guard. "And you are?" She asked the other woman.

The Null grinned. "Private Erika Emerson."

Another gargoyle came forward. Gryton had been in enough skirmishes with the Legion in his lifetime to know who this was. Adept Thayn was the oldest of the gargoyles and not an opponent one rejoiced in facing in battle.

The gargoyle elder came forward and addressed Anna. "The more important distinction is that she's a Null. And one possessing a very ancient soul."

Erika snorted and muttered under her breath. "First, I'm a Null—a nothing. Now I'm old. Guess that makes me an old nothing. Thanks."

Thayn caught her words and laughed. "There's nothing wrong with being old and wise. While I would gladly discuss the joys of experience, we have a lot to discuss and decisions to be made."

The oldest of the gargoyles glanced over his shoulder at the Avatars, his look thoughtful, or perhaps cunning was a better word.

Gryton felt a touch of unease slide across his soul.

CHAPTER TWENTY-TWO

Obsidian

He held his silence and left Anna and Thayn to do the talking. It allowed him to continue his study of Gryton. It was challenging to think of the commander as family. Regrettably, it was clear by how Lillian referred to Gryton that she embraced him as her son, as someone in need of training and guidance. He also got the impression she planned to lead him further down the path of enlightenment even if she had to drag the fire elemental kicking and screaming.

And it was also clear that Lillian wanted her younger gargoyle brother and her son to make peace. Obsidian grunted. He wasn't ready to make peace yet, but he was attempting to get along with Gryton.

However, if Gryton tried to get any closer to Anna, peaceful coexistence would die a swift death when he grabbed Tin Man by the throat and tossed him out the window.

Anna speared him with a look. *"Calm yourself. I have zero interest in Gryton. Besides, I think he's just trying to get away from the Null."*

Obsidian continued to glare at Gryton, but now that Anna mentioned it, Tin Man did seem to be trying to inch away from the Null.

Private Emerson was having none of it and stayed at Gryton's shoulder like a loyal hound.

Now that he knew that she was a Null and that she'd been sent to this realm by the Divine Ones to help Gryton control his magic, Obsidian counted the human soldier a great ally.

Gryton's disdain for his Null keeper was entertaining. For her part, Private Emerson seemed to take great pleasure in getting under his skin. Obsidian admitted it might be juvenile, but it pleased him that the Divine Ones had created a thorn to repeatedly shove in Gryton's side.

When Adept Thayn had finished explaining about Nulls, Major Resnick had swiftly jumped in and begun the interrogation. Only Gran kept the debriefing civil.

Obsidian had a feeling Thayn was silently laughing at everyone, especially at the little biting exchanges between Gryton and Private Emerson. Eventually, both sides told their stories in full.

Lillian came over and placed her hand on his cheek. "My little brother isn't so little anymore. Goddess, I can't believe it's been almost fourteen years for you. There must be so much more to tell me."

"And I'll tell it all. I promise. Just as soon as we have dealt with more pressing concerns."

"The secret second Legion," Gregory interjected as he padded across the room to join them. "Sly old bastard."

Obsidian wasn't sure if Gregory was referring to Thayn or the Lord of the Underworld.

Before he could ask which, there was a commotion from outside. A guard entered and whispered something in Major Resnick's ear. The major frowned at the interruption but nodded. "Let her pass. She deserves to know Shadow-light is alive."

The soldier straightened, nodded sharply, and then disappeared back outside.

Major Resnick's use of his juvenile name wasn't the first or even the tenth slip of his name. Obsidian supposed he had to expect it. No doubt it would take everyone a few days to come to terms with the fact he was a battle-hardened adult now. Eventually, they would grow accustomed to him and his new name.

The door opened again. This time a dryad accompanied the soldier.

Obsidian stood straighter, his horns rasping on the ceiling. Everyone else faded away as he focused on the dryad.

The longer she looked upon him, the wider her eyes grew. He was becoming accustomed to the initial shock his large size inspired. River recovered quickly. Her gaze running from the tips of his horns all the way to the talons on his toes. She reversed course, meeting his gaze. Recognition reflected back at him.

"Hello, Mother."

She exhaled a shaky breath. Then drew in another before her lips parted. Only a soft, questioning 'Shadowlight' emerged.

"It *is* me." He skirted the kitchen island and bypassed the others in the room. When he was within striking distance, he launched himself at her and wrapped her in his arms.

"My boy. My beautiful boy!" River hugged him back with all the fierce strength in her smaller body.

His mother's tears wet his skin, and he knew at that moment it didn't matter that River had served the Battle Goddess willingly; he couldn't hate her.

"Mother," he whispered into her hair as his words turned into a sob. "I missed you."

"I missed you, too. I can't tell you how relieved I am that you're safe."

She pulled away long enough to wipe at the tears streaking her cheeks. "Look how you've grown. How? What did the Battle Goddess do to you?"

"It wasn't the Lady of Battles." Then he gently began to tell her his story.

When it was over, River was silent for a long time. At last, she turned to Thayn and bowed respectfully. "We might have lived most of our lives as enemies, ancient one, but I thank you most sincerely for looking after my boy. I can see he has grown into a great and powerful man, wise beyond his years. Thank you."

Thayn snorted. "I can't take all the credit. Much of that thanks goes to the Divine Ones for forging two such magnificent young souls to lead the new gargoyle legion."

A throat being cleared drew all eyes in the room back to Major Resnick. "As heartwarming as all this is, I'm needed elsewhere. First priority is getting Gryton back on base. And second, Anna, I still have a lot of questions for you and Obsidian. You'll both accompany me back."

"Yes, sir," Anna barked and then saluted. "I'll shift back to human form for the rest of the debriefing."

"I think that would be best. Your father will be there. He'll..." Resnick just looked at her gargoyle form and shook his head. "It will just be best if you're in human form."

"Yes." Anna swallowed hard.

Obsidian wanted to reach out and pull her into a comforting hug but resisted because he knew how much she hated being coddled. *"My meeting with my mother went well enough. Perhaps yours with your father will go just as well."*

Anna snorted. *"You haven't met my father yet."*

Obsidian shrugged. That was true.

Gran approached them. "Obsidian, we kept your room ready for your return. I'm sure someone can round up a uniform for Anna. Why don't you two go on up while I entertain Adept Thayn and the others?"

Obsidian glanced around. Resnick looked like he wanted to throttle Gran but knew better than to pick a fight with her. As for Thayn, the old gargoyle looked delighted to spend time with Gran.

"They're kindred souls," Anna whispered in his mind.

Obsidian couldn't have agreed more.

"Come." He held his hand out to her. The gesture was innocently made, but he realized everyone in the room was watching and reading more into the gesture than there was.

Anna only grinned at him and then clasped his hand without complaint.

"Let them think what they want," she told him. *"It's none of their business, anyway."*

CHAPTER TWENTY-THREE

Anna

The debriefing was hours in length. In truth, it was more interrogation than debriefing. Eventually, Anna's superiors were satisfied with her answers or at least believed she was telling the truth. It had been a lot to swallow. She couldn't blame them for the doubt she'd seen in their eyes more than once.

Hell, it had been a lot for her to accept and she'd lived it.

To her surprise, she wasn't to be court-martialed or otherwise severely reprimanded. Lillian and Gregory were responsible for that miracle. They'd explained about the powerful compulsion that had controlled Anna and forced her to follow Shadowlight into the Magic Realm after he'd been captured.

Anna wasn't sure it was the magical compulsion. She and Shadowlight had been through a lot together. That formed bonds of camaraderie not easily severed. She thought she would have gone after Obsidian even without the compulsion driving her.

As for the military, they didn't like any part about how she could be compelled to obey Obsidian, but they weren't so foolish to alienate the authority and influence she now had over a powerful faction of the Magic Realm fae. And Obsidian garnered bonus points for having proven to be human-friendly as a child.

Now all she and Obsidian had to do was prove their trustworthiness to Command.

From several new faces around the table, Anna gathered a lot had changed in the months she'd been away Earth time. Before it had only been British, Canadian, and American militaries involved, but now it looked like they'd brought in over half the allied nations into the secret.

Beyond that, she couldn't do more than guess, since no one gave her any information. All information was flowing from her to them. Which was to be expected, she supposed.

"We'll learn everything we need to know later from Lillian, Gregory, and Gran," Obsidian whispered along their link.

"I know." But the debriefing had to finish up before that happened, and it didn't look like the interrogators planned to quit soon.

But they proved her wrong.

The debriefing ended a little over ten minutes later. Anna and Obsidian were ushered under guard to another room in the basement of the town's community center.

"Now what?" Obsidian asked using their mental link.

"I imagine we wait for my father and Major Resnick to arrive."

Obsidian huffed softly. *"That's likely. At one point, I thought your father was going to come over the table and attack the grey-haired man who accused you of turning traitor to humanity."*

Anna winced at the memory. While the debriefing had gone better than she'd thought it might, there had still been more than one rough patch.

"I could scent your father's anxiety over the roomful of other conflicting smells."

Obsidian's words made Anna glad she'd returned to her human form. Her duller senses had probably been a blessing in that roomful of hostility.

The sound of brisk footsteps approaching drew Anna's gaze to the door a moment before it opened suddenly. Beside her, Obsidian shifted, his stance alert and ready for anything, but not overly aggressive.

Good.

Major Resnick stopped a few feet in front of them and frowned.

"Major?" Anna said and acknowledged him with a salute.

"At ease." Major Resnick looked them both over before his gaze settled on Anna. "That meeting might have gone better, but it could have been worse."

She nodded.

"Your father is on his way. He just had to speak with General Tremblay first. There is still some discussion about yours and Obsidian's lodgings."

Anna snorted. "Should I assume some of them wanted us in cages next to Gryton to be overseen by his Null keeper?"

"Yes, until General Williams of the British Armed Forces pointed out that no one wants to see a battalion of angry gargoyles dropping out of the sky to rescue their Rasoren and Kyrsu."

Major Resnick only stumbled over the foreign words a little.

"Wise of them." Obsidian's voice lowered until it was nearly a growl. "Anna may have started out life as a human and still is loyal to her birth race, but if anyone tries to harm or imprison my Kyrsu, it will not go well for them."

"Figured as much. Which is why Brigadier General Mackenzie is still back there reminding everybody what one damned gargoyle is capable of and then multiply that by ten thousand."

"Sounds like dad." Anna rubbed her palms against her thighs. It had been strange sitting in a room while getting questioned and never having her father acknowledge her as his daughter.

Oh, they were both professional. Business always came first, but that didn't mean a kind look would have gone amiss, given they hadn't seen each other in months.

But he hadn't so much is given her a hint of a smile. Now she wondered if he thought of her as changed beyond recognition. Did he believe the daughter he'd known was dead?

Dammit. What was the point of returning to human form at all?

"Your father is happy you've returned." Obsidian

dipped his muzzle and bumped her shoulder affectionately. "Along with his concern, I could also smell the relief that you had returned to him. I think it took him a great deal of inner strength to stop from crossing the room and hugging you."

Perhaps.

She didn't have long to worry. The door banged open, and her father marched in. He halted six feet away and stood there. Just staring.

Then he held his arms open wide. "You going to just stand there blinking at me? Or are you going to give your dad a hug?"

Half laughing and half sobbing, Anna ran to her father and hugged him tightly. His arms enclosed her and the fear that he'd never accept her new nature melted away.

"That's my girl. Always knew you'd come back." His voice was strained with emotion, and when he released her and leaned back, there were tears in his eyes.

"I tried to rescue Shadowlight and escape." She wiped at her own foolish tears. "I always planned to bring him right back, but they captured us before we could escape."

Her father's expression darkened. "The one called Gryton told us some of what occurred. Fuck. I think I grew several gray hairs just listening to that monster's tales."

"It was bad, but I think it would have been much worse without Gryton watching over us. We didn't know he was the Avatars' son. We didn't even know he was protecting us until he helped us escape." Anna just shook her head. Looking back, now that she knew he'd been trying to help, she could see some ways he'd watched over them. "It could have been much worse."

Her father's nostrils flared and his lips compressed. "It was plenty bad enough."

"Yes," she agreed softly.

For the first time, Anna's father turned his attention to Obsidian. "Once I arrived, I talked to every Fae, soldier, and scientist who had contact with you. I read every report. Everything pointed to the fact that you adored my daughter. Which was all fine and good when you were a child."

He paused and looked Obsidian up and down, his frown deepening. "You're no longer a child. I demand to know your intentions toward my daughter."

"Oh, my God! Dad!"

Anna had been expecting a lot of awkward, uncomfortable questions about things she endured while in the Battle Goddess's Kingdom and then later about her time with the Legion. But this line of questioning wasn't one she'd prepared for.

Though, perhaps it shouldn't have come as a surprise. Obsidian was no longer the innocent cub, and Anna was a full-blooded gargoyle now.

Her overprotective father was going to come at Obsidian full throttle.

"It's nothing like that. Obsidian is still Shadowlight. He might have matured and bulked up like a bodybuilder, but he's still my brother."

Her father snorted. "That might be how you think of him, but I assure you, he's male and will have unbrotherly thoughts. You can't trust him."

"You are wrong in that," Obsidian said, joining the conversation. "Anna can trust me always. Yes, I've matured. And the Battle Goddess made many modifications to me that I passed on to Anna when I converted her, but I have known of these changes for many years, and my mentors have trained me well."

Obsidian elaborated further, explaining how his blood, saliva, and seed were all designed to convert others into his slave gargoyle army. He then followed that explanation with another, telling the general how his mentors had seen the signs early and trained him to ignore that part of his nature.

As for the ability to command Anna, his mentors had drilled into him how wrong it was to steal another's will.

"Do you see?" he asked into the heavy silence. "I never have and would never steal Anna's will."

Her father grunted. "But you admit there is a compulsion between you."

"Yes." Obsidian didn't even try to deny it. "And I'll even admit a more than mild attraction to my Kyrsu, but I don't mean to act upon it."

The general still frowned. Anna knew she had to say something.

"Dad, I've been through a lot with him. First as Shadowlight and later as Obsidian. I couldn't ask Fate or the gods for a better partner to have at my back in battle." She paused and gazed upon Obsidian. "Or any other situation either, my Rasoren."

Obsidian made a happy little sound deep in his chest.

Anna grinned at him, then turned back to her father.

"So, you see? We're a matched pair. You're just going to have to deal with it."

Her father still looked unconvinced.

"Let me try," Obsidian said, his thoughts a gentle caress in her mind. *"If I can make him see how I view you, it might convince him that I will always respect his beloved daughter."*

"Knock yourself out."

"Strange human with your even stranger sayings," he whispered as he left her side to walk a circle around her father.

Her Rasoren didn't speak until he had her father's undivided attention. "I'm not a fool. I know the link I share with your daughter disturbs you, but I assure you, my intentions are honorable. Anna has my utmost respect and admiration. I will do nothing to harm or sully the bond we share. You'll see that as you get to know me, but for now, I'd like to tell you about your daughter."

Her father looked brooding for a moment before gesturing for the big gargoyle to continue.

"During our time together in the Battle Goddess's kingdom and later in Haven, Anna overcame obstacles and endured hardships that would crush most others. But she not only conquered them, she grew stronger. Now she leads the Gargoyle Legion as my partner, not because I converted her all those years ago but because she trained and fought and won the honor to lead, impressing even a demigod. I could never steal Anna's will. She wouldn't allow it even if I were weak enough to attempt such an evil thing. And I am not weak. We are both strong. We are a team, and she is the best partner I could ever ask for."

Anna stepped up beside Obsidian and bumped shoulders with him. "Matched pair. Like I said the first time."

Her father huffed. "Fine. If you love him like a brother, I'll welcome another son into my family. Lord knows I already have enough sons to make me grey ten times over as it is. What's one more?"

He turned to open the door and then gestured them out ahead of him. "Let's go somewhere nicer to catch up and figure out what to tell your mother and brothers. The official report is that your team was lost in the forest. Flash flood because of heavy rains this spring. We haven't yet found all the bodies. Local authorities are dragging the lakes. You were presumed dead until you were miraculously found alive in a ravine."

Anna snorted. "Mom will never believe that load of horse shit..."

"No, not likely." Her father snorted. "You know I can't lie to that woman to save my life. She never believed the official report about a flash flood, anyway."

Anna grinned. "Mom only believes half of what you tell her on a good day. She'll think of conspiracies no matter how good the story."

Even as Anna smiled and laughed with her father, she realized Obsidian was falling behind. She glanced over her shoulder as she reached for him with her mind. *"What are you waiting for? Get your big ass up here."*

"I thought you and your father might like some family time together."

"You are family. The sooner he fully understands and accepts that irrefutable fact, the easier everything else will be."

Obsidian merely nodded at her wisdom and joined them. For the first time in hours, the tension between her shoulder blades eased. Perhaps the worst was behind her.

Obsidian snorted with humor at her thought.

"Ah, hell. I don't believe that either," she admitted. *"But maybe we'll get some peace for a time?"*

"Doubtful. I believe there will be too much Gryton in our futures for peaceful anything."

"Meh. You're likely right."

CHAPTER TWENTY-FOUR

The Magic Realm
Vaspara

After half a moon cycle locked in her cell, Vaspara was forgetting what color looked like. As a succubus, she could see in the dark better than some species, but without light, all colors just looked like varying shades of grey or black.

Outside in the hall, a few torches generated a meager light, only enough to outline the door that rarely opened. Sometimes she thought her captors just used the torches to taunt her with the promise of freedom she would never know again.

If Fate was merciful, she'd be left here to starve. If Fate was less kind, she'd be fed to the blood witch.

Her soul was tarnished from long years of serving the

Lady of Battles, that was nothing compared to what the witch would do to her soul before the end.

Vaspara desperately wanted a better end than that. But any chance of being granted a swift death was slim. She noticed during the rare times the guards brought her food that none of them were from her or Sorac's battalions. They weren't even the harpy's soldiers.

Which was unfortunate, since she might have been able to get one of Bervicta's soldiers to kill her swiftly in a botched 'escape' attempt. She knew she had no hope of escape. But if she were dead, Sorac would know it, and he might then fight to break free. Perhaps he'd even escape and go to Anna and Shadowlight to beg them for aid in freeing his draklings. But he wouldn't do any of that while she still lived.

'It would be better if I were dead,' Vaspara mused.

Yet she lacked the means to end her own life. Here she sat. A prisoner with the sole purpose to keep the mighty firedrake a prisoner as well.

As long as Vaspara lived, the Battle Goddess would use her to control Sorac. The only consolation was that she also knew the goddess wouldn't kill or damage the draklings. The deity had waited too long to add more firedrakes to her army. So, the little ones were safe. Well, at least, as safe as anyone could be here.

Footfalls reached her ears, and her senses sharpened. Soon the person approaching turned a corner, and the sound came clearer. Vaspara had grown accustomed to the sentries' individual footfalls. The ones approaching now didn't belong to any of her usual guards. Had a new sentry been assigned?

The mystery resolved a moment later when Bervicta barked at the guards. "Open the door. I need to speak with the prisoner."

"She's not to have visitors by order of the Battle Goddess."

"I'm not a visitor, you fool. I'm here to interrogate her. I need to know everything she knows about the draklings. Sorac isn't very forthcoming. I'm hoping Vaspara will be easier to force to comply."

"I will need to clear it with my Captain."

Bervicta snarled. "I cleared it with Captain Korsha over morning weapons practice. She was still spitting out blood and teeth when I left her in the ring. But by all means, I'm sure I could occupy myself with you while you send a runner to confirm with your captain."

The harpy's menacing tone echoed throughout the corridor, and Vaspara grinned at the chorus of 'that won't be necessaries' that followed.

Bervicta was known for sparring with warriors outside of her own battalion, claiming she hated to cripple her own battalion members, preferring to practice against soldiers under the command of other captains to test their skills.

The harpy was the most powerful and skilled of the captains after Vaspara and Sorac. With the recent upsets in the power structure, Bervicta was now the highest-ranking captain, not counting Blood Witch Taryin.

Even when Vaspara still served the Battle Goddess, she hadn't counted the witch as one of them. The captains had not always gotten along, or even liked each other, but they shared a respect for each other—a kinship.

The witch rose to power through the use of dark magic, not strength, combat skills, and cunning.

But Bervicta was a friend, almost like a younger sister. Family. She might help Vaspara find a quick end.

Then she remembered the present situation. Bervicta couldn't afford to be any of those things, even if the other woman still felt that way about her.

The door's ward spell flared and then dropped away. A moment later it swung open violently, banging against the wall in a way that made her ears throb. The harpy stomped forward, her wings framing her muscular upper body. By her expression, she wished to be elsewhere.

"Don't bother talking unless it is to answer one of my questions," the harpy barked in a confrontational tone.

Vaspara held her silence and Bervicta just glared harder.

"I've been assigned guardianship of Sorac's hatchlings." She paused. A hint of concern crept into her eyes. "The little ones won't eat. They're growing weaker."

"Of course you're failing," Vaspara said. "Though it's no fault of your own. They'll only take food from their parents. But it's more than just that. They need their parents' magic."

Bervicta swore under her breath. "I was afraid you would say that."

The harpy turned to glower over her shoulder at the guards. "I'll need an escort. We're going for a walk."

The guards glanced at each other unhappily, but Bervicta was a captain and could command them.

The senior-most guard cleared her throat. "Captain Bervicta, we recognize your authority. However, we also have strict orders that the prisoner remain here."

The harpy didn't snap back at the woman, merely smiled coldly. "Do you wish me to tell the Battle Goddess that Sorac's hatchlings have all died because you were too afraid to think for yourselves and reason out that Vaspara can save them?"

There was a long pause, and then the sound of a throat being cleared came again. "We'll escort you to the cavern, but Vaspara needs to be back in her cell before shift change."

Bervicta smiled. "This won't take that long."

The guards entered the cell and swiftly unchained Vaspara from the wall. Yanking on the freed length, they dragged her from her cell. She regained her balance and promptly matched the pace set by the harpy and the other guards.

They walked the underground tunnels in silence. Eventually, the floor began to slant upward. Bervicta walked ahead, halting before a sizeable iron-bound door. With a nod to the six guards stationed there, Bervicta silently ordered them to open it.

These guards wasted no time. Shortly the defensive magic had retreated into the frame, and the door was unlatched and shoved open. As the guards entered the room, they formed a wall with their shields.

Vaspara soon discovered the purpose of the shield wall as fourteen screeching, fire-spitting draklings launched themselves at the intruders.

But within moments of Vaspara entering the room, the screeching attack came to a halt as excited squeals of recognition rang throughout the chamber. They must have caught her scent.

"Demon spawn," one guard muttered. As Vaspara shoved her way through the shield wall, Bervicta followed but wisely grabbed a shield from him as she walked by.

"Sorac's hatchlings are vicious little things. They even took down an unwary guard the first day. They didn't eat him, though." The harpy sounded mildly disappointed.

The draklings swarmed Vaspara, jumping up and attempting to climb her all at once. They only managed to knock each other off and nearly took Vaspara to the ground with them under their combined weight.

Laughing and crying and ignoring their claws, she tried to hold them all at once.

"It's all right, I'm here," she crooned warmly to them. Then looking up at Bervicta, she demanded, "Fresh meat. Bring me as much as you can carry."

"Already ahead of you." Bervicta gestured to the guards behind her and one brave soul—the guard the harpy had stolen the shield from—came forward carrying two trays piled high with strips of raw meat.

The draklings hissed at the male, but Vaspara crooned softly to them, and they settled down to wait at her feet.

Bervicta took the tray from the male and crossed the rest of the distance until only two body lengths of space separated them.

"I think I'll just put these down here." She set the two trays on the floor and then backed away. "I like all my fingers and toes."

Vaspara almost laughed at the way the harpy acted. Bervicta was a skilled warrior and could handle any threat, but something about being presented with fourteen hungry firedrakes seemed to put the harpy off her game.

It suited Vaspara. This way, the harpy would continue to look to Vaspara for aid and advice.

Vaspara guided her brood over to the meat and began feeding them small morsels. They grabbed and gobbled them down almost faster than she could toss the next piece, but none of them offered to take the meat from the plate on their own, preferring that she feed them.

On the second round of feeding, Vaspara began pushing some of her magic into the pieces of meat before tossing it into awaiting maws. Soon the trays were empty, fourteen little bellies were full, and Vaspara's magic reserves were less than they'd been when she'd started.

"No wonder they weren't interested in taking meat from us. The little parasites drank a fair bit of your magic."

Vaspara would have been insulted if Bervicta's tone hadn't held pride and a little affection.

"They're strong little monsters." The harpy's expression softened further.

Perhaps Bervicta was more of the mothering type than Vaspara had thought?

Eyes narrowing thoughtfully, Vaspara turned to face the harpy. "You must allow Sorac time with his brood, or they could still die. I'm not sure if my power alone will be enough to keep them alive. I'm not a fire elemental."

Bervicta cursed under her breath. "That will be a logistical nightmare. The Battle Goddess specifically ordered that Sorac never be able to see his young. She fears he'll grab them and run again."

"That may be, but I'm telling you the truth."

Bervicta sighed. "I know."

She huffed again, a long-suffering sound. "I'll speak with the Battle Goddess and explain what I've learned."

"Thank you." Vaspara paused while she debated if she should tell the rest. But if Bervicta wasn't able to convince the Battle Goddess to allow Sorac access to his young, then the djinn's power might be the only thing able to keep the draklings alive. Reaching for the harpy, she opened a private mental link.

"Initially, we stored the djinn's bottle with Sorac's eggs. It was the most protected and warded part of our new territory. The draklings were already feeding on the djinn's power before they hatched. They continued to feed on him afterward. If the Battle Goddess won't allow Sorac—" Vaspara paused, her lover's name hard to speak even in her own thoughts. *"If she won't allow the father to feed his draklings, then perhaps the djinn can provide what is needed. His kind holds mastery over all the elements. He can probably summon up compatible fire magic as needed."*

Bervicta gave her a subtle nod and then continued out loud, "I'll tell the Battle Goddess what I've learned. She's always wanted a battalion of firedrakes. This might be her only chance. If I word it carefully, she may allow Sorac to see his hatchlings long enough to feed them."

Vaspara nodded to her friend. "Thank you."

"Don't thank me. I'm doing this to protect my ass." But Bervicta then added more along their private link. *"It would've been better if you had never been found. You wouldn't have been if not for the tracking spell on the djinn's bottle. That was a stupid mistake. Don't make it again."*

Turning on her heels, the harpy marched from the

chambers, only pausing at the door to glower at the other guards. "What are you waiting for? Bring the prisoner."

One of the female guards stepped forward. "What about the hatchlings, Captain?"

"What about them?" Bervicta snapped, though Vaspara now suspected it was a show for the guards.

The female guard swiftly shut her mouth and ordered the other soldiers under her command to chase off the draklings and secure the prisoner.

Vaspara tensed, ready to fight until she saw that the guards were gentle with the hissing and fire-spitting draklings. All too soon the soldiers had driven off the little ones and had dragged Vaspara from the room.

With a heavy heart, she watched them slam the door shut and renew the wards of protection over it. But even the thick door with its many wards didn't muffle the shrieks of the draklings.

Instinct rose within Vaspara, and before she could stop, she was reaching out to attack the nearest guard. Easily overpowering the surprised warrior, she lunged toward the next closest guard only to be brought up short by Bervicta's sharp words.

"The Battle Goddess will punish Sorac for your transgressions, succubus."

Vaspara froze, the harpy's words returning her to her current reality.

"I'm sorry," Bervicta continued along a private link. *"There is only so much I can do to protect you, Sorac, and your young. And if I'm found out, I'll be killed. Dead, I'll be useless to them and you. Surrender for now, my friend. Fight another day."*

Vaspara straightened from her defensive stance. "I surrender. Don't harm the draklings or Sorac."

Bervicta barked out a short, humorless laugh. "Thought that would get you to behave. Come." She speared the guards with sharp looks of warning. "I need to take what I've learned to the Battle Goddess. Return the prisoner to her cell."

"Yes, Captain!" The senior-most guard replied as she snapped to attention.

After Bervicta had left, and the guards had led Vaspara back to her dark cell, the succubus smiled into the darkness for a long time and began to go over ways to free the draklings and escape. If she was regularly let out of this cell to feed the little ones, the guards might grow complacent, and that might lead to an opportunity to escape with the hatchlings.

Sorac would never act to free himself as long as she and his draklings were vulnerable prisoners.

But if she escaped with the hatchlings?

Vaspara smiled.

Her lover then would be free to torch this fortress-city as he escaped.

CHAPTER TWENTY-FIVE

Anna

In the days following Anna's return and reunion with her father, the tension in the camp was almost thick enough to taste. But Gran worked her magic and miracles and kept the peace. Major Resnick did more than his share of peacekeeping by building bridges to help span the divide between the magic and mortal factions.

As expected, Anna was required to turn herself over to scientists for study. Obsidian went with her, never leaving her side. It was as if he half expected the scientists to steal her away.

Which, Anna reflected, wasn't beyond the realm of possibility.

While they'd been spending quality time with the scientists, Thayn had been reestablishing his friendship with the Avatars. Later she'd learned from Obsidian that Thayn still hadn't told the Avatars the real purpose of their visit.

When Anna challenged the adept, he'd only called her young and impatient, claiming that this peaceful time was the perfect opportunity to learn more about Gryton, his Null keeper, what the Avatars had planned for their son, and how badly they would react when they learned Obsidian and Anna were under orders to bring Gryton and the Avatars back to the Magic Realm to face Lord Draydrak.

Everything Thayn said was logical, but something didn't sit well with her.

"He's setting us up for something," Anna mused, glancing sidelong at Obsidian while they walked toward the maze for their next weapons practice in the glade. Gregory had demanded everyone stay in peak condition, claiming that they might be thrust into battle at any point.

That next battle might come far sooner and from a different direction than Gregory expected.

"Thayn is enamored with Gran." Obsidian huffed with humor and then cleared his throat. "That's why he wants to wait. The longer we're here, the more time he'll have with her."

"I know he's showing interest, but he's too wily. I think there's more going on inside his head than that."

"And yet he's using the excuse of 'peaceful downtime' to accompany Gran everywhere."

"I noticed, but I thought it was just because they were looking to get up to some devilment together."

"But Thayn hasn't been playing his usual tricks and pranks, has he?"

Anna frowned. "Everyone has been so busy. Perhaps he just hasn't had time?"

It was Obsidian's turn to laugh. "When has being busy ever stopped Thayn from playing his games."

"Good point."

"No. Perhaps we should consider it a blessing that someone has caught his attention."

It was Anna's turn to snort. "Well, they'll make an interesting couple."

"Indeed." Obsidian was still laughing when they reached the glade, but soon River came over and called a greeting.

Well, she greeted her son. The dryad still hadn't warmed to her. And Anna was okay with that little detail. She wasn't ready to become friends with the cast-iron bitch anytime soon.

She'd barely finished that thought when Gregory ventured over.

"Do you mind if I steal Obsidian for a round in the practice ring?"

"Knock yourself out." Her eyes slid toward River and then back to Obsidian. *Don't suppose you can convince River to come to watch you and Gregory spar?*

I will try, but it looks like she wants to talk with you. Obsidian turned to the dryad. "Mother, have you come to watch me spar again?"

She smiled up at him, a mother's pride evident in her expression. "Of course! In a few moments. There's something else I need to do first." River looked directly at Anna.

Fuck.

Directing a futile glance at Private Emerson, Anna debated if she had time to get the Null's attention before River dug in for a lengthy conversation. Anna had noted none of the fae species willingly stayed in the Null's vicinity for longer than was necessary.

Anna couldn't blame them. Even when Private Emerson wasn't aggressively absorbing magic, there was often a subtle draining of power. Gregory and Lillian claimed the Null would purify any magic she absorbed and later release it. But as far as Anna could see, the Null wasn't releasing magic, which meant she was likely in a draining mode.

Good.

Anna decided now was as good as time as any to learn more about the soldier's formidable power. And if being near the Null had the added benefit of putting off River, all the better.

"Anna," Obsidian's mother said as she stepped closer. "I'm glad I ran into you. Are you free to talk?"

"I was actually on my way to speak with Private Emerson."

River gave her a pinched look at the mention of the Null. Good.

"In that case, I won't keep you long. I wish to smooth things over. I fear we didn't strike a good accord during our first meeting."

You think? Anna muttered in her head. *I remember something about a human mongrel.*

Aloud, Anna attempted to sound more neutral than she felt. "Happens sometimes."

"It has come to my attention that I was wrong about you, Anna Mackenzie."

Well, fuck me, is this an apology I smell coming? She wondered.

"Shadowlight chose well when he rescued you from the Riven. I didn't see it at first. But then you went after him when he was abducted. No one else did. They said they couldn't risk a war with the Lady of Battles until they were prepared." River nearly spat the last words. "But you went. You disregarded orders and went after my boy."

"I'm just sorry I wasn't able to escape with him and bring him back home."

"That doesn't diminish your bravery in trying." River paused as she glanced toward the new sand ring where Obsidian and Gregory were presently pounding the shit out of each other. She smiled proudly at her son before continuing. "Compulsion might have forced you to follow him, but you survived and prospered. That was entirely your own doing. Obsidian couldn't have found a better second to rule at his side."

"Ah... thank you."

Hearing compliments come from River was throwing Anna off balance, which might be why she didn't see the next subject coming.

"You make him happy. That is what every mother wants for her child."

"Shadowlight was the best little brother I could ever ask for."

River nodded at her words, but Anna could see there was more the dryad wanted to hear.

Anna didn't really know what the other woman wanted, so just continued to ramble. "And he grew into a wonderful partner. He earned the title of Rasoren. It wasn't just given to him."

River nodded again and then arched an eyebrow before looking around, noting where the other stood. She lowered her voice. "I noticed you and my son don't share rooms."

"Well, no," Anna managed after she got over her surprise. "But I don't see what that has to do with anything."

River continued as if unaware of Anna's stricken look. "He is mature, and the bond you share differs from what previous pairs enjoyed."

"Yes. We're aware." Anna said in a neutral tone, giving nothing away.

"But you haven't bonded physically yet?"

Bonded physically? That was a different take on the act.

"That actually..." Is none of your goddamned business. "Wasn't required. Lord Death helped us overcome the last obstacle preventing us from completing the bond."

"Really?" River's gaze sharpened as she speared Anna with a questioning look. "That shouldn't be possible. The bond can only be completed by a physical joining."

Anna snorted. "That isn't entirely accurate. We discovered that a shared trauma could merge our hearts, minds, and souls enough to complete the bond."

"A shared trauma?" River sounded suddenly intrigued.

Anna flashed fang at the dryad. "Yes. Something in my past. Something only my Rasoren will ever experience."

Surprisingly, River looked satisfied at Anna's answer. "As it should be."

"Damn straight."

River laughed. "It's good you are strong-willed. My son should never have to settle for a dull bed partner."

What the actual fuck? Was I just talking to myself?

And just like that, the conversation was no longer in Anna's control and had utterly derailed.

Anna cleared her throat. Time to set the dryad straight. "Obsidian and I don't think of each other in those terms. We're friends. Nothing more."

River laughed in delight. "You're so young and blind. Do you truly not see how my son looks at you? No matter. If Gryton keeps watching you the way he has the last few days, Obsidian will make his claim known."

"I don't know what you're talking about."

"No?" The damn dryad smiled. "I think you do. Besides, you are a mature gargoyle now. If you haven't already experienced your first fertility cycle, you will shortly."

"Obsidian, your mother wants to have a sex talk. I'm out. Finish up your match with Gregory. It's my turn to fight the Avatars!"

Her words made Obsidian stumble. Gregory was swift to use the opportunity, knocking her Rasoren's legs out from under him. Anna's gargoyle partner was too well-trained to land on his ass, but it was a close thing.

"For shame!" Thayn roared from the other side of the ring. Though he was laughing too hard to make his anger convincing. "What was that? You let your Kyrsu distract you!"

How the hell did Thayn know it was her fault? Anna cast a suspicious look at the elder. She'd mastered her shields well enough to keep him out.

The apparent answer hit her a moment later. Frick. Thayn must have been in Obsidian's head, sharing some training tips to help him fight his billion-year-old opponent. He'd heard the entire exchange.

"Sorry," Anna offered.

Obsidian's humor flowed back along the link. *"I'd rather face the Avatars than talk with my mother about mating. You're forgiven."*

While Obsidian was getting teased by Thayn, Anna used the opportunity to escape River and her inappropriate line of questioning.

Anna's father had always taught her when to stay and fight and when to retreat.

River wanting to have a sex talk—retreat!

CHAPTER TWENTY-SIX

Gryton

Gryton watched with interest as Anna fled River, the dryad's probing questions unsettling the human-gargoyle hybrid. He hadn't been trying to overhear the conversation, but his senses were sharper than they had been in days, thanks to the fact that his Null keeper hadn't fed upon him recently.

She seemed to be gaining more control over it.

Though he wasn't sure which of them could be credited for the recent change. Gryton admitted the Null's control in not feeding upon him might have more to do with him regaining mastery over himself. Her ability seemed tied to aggression. His. The more aggressive he became, the swifter and more brutal her response.

But whatever the exact cause, he was enjoying the

restoration of his powers. And his newly sharpened senses had just let him discern something he'd been very curious to know.

Anna and Obsidian were not physically intimate. He'd been as surprised as River by the knowledge. There had to be something substantial that was holding Anna and Obsidian apart.

Gryton mulled over everything Anna had unknowingly revealed.

While Anna had said she loved Obsidian like a little brother, Gryton was good enough at reading people to know a lie when he heard one. And there was a lie buried somewhere in Anna's exchange with River. She might not even realize it yet herself.

However, that Anna and Obsidian weren't yet mates also said a great deal. Gryton would dig until he found what it was. Perhaps Anna truly didn't have feelings for the tactless brute?

Gryton's lips pulled back from his fangs. He'd always admired the human-gargoyle hybrid. If the great muscle-bound oaf hadn't figured out how to woo a woman, that was his loss, wasn't it?

He'd always liked a good challenge. She was certainly worthy of his interest. As Gryton warmed to the idea, he eyed Anna. He'd always admired her tenacity.

"Hey, Hot Stuff," the Null's voice drawled in his ear. "Might want to rethink that entire last five minutes of mental conversation you just had with yourself. The big dude looks like he could break you in two. And while you've been drooling over Anna, I've been studying the big fellow."

Gryton's spine straightened as his elemental fire flared. He both embraced it and fought to hold it in check. Then with his control still at war with his chaotic nature, he turned to the Null, power flickering in his gaze.

"Oops. Hit a nerve, did I?"

"Why are you in my head again?" Threat reverberated in his tone.

"Trust me. If I could stay out, I would. A walk between your ears is mostly the stuff of nightmares. And as much as I don't like you, my job is to keep you out of trouble and maintain the peace. Unless you want me to feed on you again, I'd suggest you not shove your nose in other people's business."

"Jealous?" He asked just to see how she'd react. Though he'd noticed a curious lack of sexual interest from the Null. While he found it refreshing after thousands of years surrounded by succubi and incubi, he also knew humans could be just as promiscuous when it came to mating.

The Null just laughed, her grin huge.

"It wasn't that funny."

After a few more snorts and cackles, the Null eventually got herself under control. "Stop and think about what your comment implies. And then think about if I took you up on your offer."

"I wasn't offering, Mortal."

She snorted again. "Yeah, I know. Still, stop and think about it for a moment."

He just continued to stare.

Rolling her eyes, she pointed at herself. "Null."

After a pause, she pointed at him. "All you can eat buffet."

"Of that, I'm very much aware. However, I still don't see w—"

"Now imagine what a Null would do to you during sex!" She broke out with more hoots and snorts until tears were running down her face.

Gryton's expression shifted to horror before he could smooth it over.

"No worries, Hot Stuff. You're not my type."

He narrowed his eyes, studying her anew. There was truth in her words. Yet somehow that didn't explain her absolute lack of sexual interest. And it wasn't just him. She didn't seem to notice others, either.

Misinterpreting his look, she added. "No, I don't like girls either. No one is my type."

"You're sexless?" Eyes widening, he studied her again, noting her relatively flat chest. "You're not yet mature?"

She looked down at herself and laughed.

"While God didn't give me much in the way of boobs, I am an adult female with all the correct parts. I just don't feel desire for anyone. Some call it being asexual." She shrugged. "I don't care for labels, but that one works as well as any, I suppose."

"Ah." Gryton filed that information away for later. He wasn't sure how to use it yet, but his earlier plan to beguile her just turned to ash.

She smirked at him. "I don't do beguiled. Sorry."

He huffed and mentally cursed for forgetting she could read his every thought when she was close. He hated revealing his plans. Even ones that were now defunct.

He and the Null needed a fresh start, or they would kill each other.

While holding out his right hand in what he knew was a customary way of greeting on this world, he smoothed his expression into something less hostile. "We have become needlessly antagonistic toward each other. I, for one, plan for that to stop now. While we shall never be friends, I think we can behave in a manner befitting our stations and hopefully avoid making each other's existence a complete misery."

Her grin grew huge as she grabbed his hand and pumped it. "I accept your surrender."

It was his turn to laugh. "I never surrender. And in case no one has ever mentioned it, Nulls are as mortal as a human. You will age and die like any other of your kind." He flexed his talons enough that she'd feel their prick. Then he flashed his fangs at her. "Many non-magical means can kill you, such as poison, suffocation, or drowning."

She was still laughing as she squeezed his hand while using her other to smack him affectionately on the shoulder.

"Thanks for the warning, Hot Stuff. I'm eating nothing you make. And I never plan to allow you near enough to try suffocation or drowning."

He matched her smile. "Oh, I doubt I'll need to poison you. I think we can come to some mutually beneficial arrangement in time. But for now, how about we stop trying to drive each other to suicide?"

Her lips still twitched with humor, but her eyes were serious. "I've really gotten under your skin, haven't I?"

Unfortunately, Gryton thought it might be worse than that. She'd stirred his curiosity, which annoyed him no end.

And her snort told him she knew it. That just annoyed him all the more.

"How about we declare a truce for now?" She offered at last.

"A truce is a noble enough solution," he agreed as his eyes slid back to where Anna and Lillian were now crossing swords in the practice area.

His mother and the new Kyrsu were both skilled with the sword, but Anna's skill had advanced to the point she was breathtaking to watch. For a time, he allowed himself to enjoy the rhythm of the two dueling opponents.

"You got it bad, don't you?" the Null stated.

Gryton glowered at her. "Our truce was rather short-lived, don't you think?"

She just shook her head at him. "I plan to uphold my end of the truce, but figured I'd give you a word of advice. Drop your obsession with Anna. Even I can tell she doesn't return your... admiration. And the big fellow? Don't think he feels particularly brotherly toward his Kyrsu."

"You are a great wisdom on the subject of the heart, I see, and not more than a child yourself." He allowed a suitable amount of sarcasm to drip from his words.

She just snorted. "I've got eyes and a big enough brain to figure out what they show me. You could use a little work in that department. Huh? Maybe you need glasses?"

Gryton frowned at her while wrestling back his annoyance, since it just caused her more amusement.

Luckily, Anna and his mother were finishing up in the practice area, and his sire was calling him over.

CHAPTER TWENTY-SEVEN

Erika

Erika rolled her shoulders and stretched, limbering up her muscles. She was growing soft because of this babysitting detail. Once Gryton and Gregory finished up, she planned to take a turn against someone. But just then Erika's strange gift flared to life. She jerked her gaze back to the combatants.

While she still couldn't control her unique superpower to the degree she'd like, she was beginning to understand it. And right this moment, it was preparing for a feast.

Erika stalked closer to the sand ring where Obsidian and Gryton were now circling each other, Gregory having finished his bout with his son earlier.

"This isn't going to end well," she muttered to no one in particular.

Gryton and Obsidian circled each other, both measuring and judging. Their swords connected in a clatter and then the two opponents launched themselves at each other.

The session was breathtaking to behold. They moved with swift grace. It surprised Erika the big gargoyle could move so fast, but he matched Gryton's speed and power.

Of the two, the fire elemental was the prettier fighter, his moves more graceful, his footwork something to be envied.

Yet the big gargoyle wasn't without skills. And his frame looked like it could deliver much more devastating strikes than Gryton's slimmer build.

"You would think so, wouldn't you? But you'd be wrong, Null." The fire elemental glanced sidelong at Erika and grinned at her.

Erika attempted to sound reasonable. *"Come on. Don't be a shithead."*

Gryton disengaged from Obsidian long enough to deliver an elegant bow in Erika's direction, gaining more than one questioning look from the other onlookers. And now that she glanced around, she realized the other fights had stopped to watch this one.

"Seriously! Don't be a total shithead in front of everyone, you twat!"

Gryton continued like he hadn't heard, his attention directed at the gargoyle.

"Shadowlight, I notice you still follow Anna around like a lost pup," Gryton said, his tone inflammatory and his words loud enough to carry.

Erika instantly knew he was trying to anger or otherwise unbalance the big gargoyle. A hostile current flowed between the two opponents. While she didn't know all the details, she knew there was bad blood between them. Now she wished she'd found time to wade through all the reports and briefing materials Major Resnick had dumped on her.

Obsidian didn't fall for Gryton's baiting and continued their bout in silence. He even slammed a fist to Gryton's jaw, the fire elemental failing to dart away in time.

"Well done, Cub." Gryton wiped his hand across his lips. "No one has bloodied me in a fair fight in a long time."

He flicked the blood off his fingers. Where the drops splattered, tiny fires sprung up.

Greenborrow cursed in some foreign language and then stomped out each of the small fires.

While the revelation that Gryton's blood could start a blaze had distracted her, the man in question had landed a blow that sent the gargoyle stumbling back a few steps.

Claw marks now sliced across the gargoyle's chest.

"Want to call a temporary halt to the practice, so Anna can lick your wounds, Cub?"

"There is no magic during the fight." Gran barked out before Obsidian responded.

Gryton tipped his head in acknowledgment of Gran's words. "I'm not using magic. I am magic. I can't control the fire in my blood without using my powers."

"I wasn't talking about the fires!" Gran gave her quarterstaff a shake.

"Ah. The armor? It also helps to contain the fire magic, but I shall cede to your wishes in this since you are correct. It does give me an advantage over a naked gargoyle."

"That's not what I meant either!" Gran's scowl could shrivel balls, but Gryton seemed impervious.

A moment later Gryton's armor was absorbed back into his skin, leaving him in leather pants and boots. His fingers still ended in talons, but they weren't as long or as sharp looking as when his armor grew to cover the ends.

"Fine." Gran waved her quarterstaff threateningly. "But in the future, don't call on magic during practice and don't draw blood. The point of these exercises is to increase your skill enough to battle an opponent and be good enough to defeat them with no need to first maim them."

"As you wish." He gave Gran a surly little bow.

"Keep that up, she'll crack your skull," Erika warned.

Gryton just arched a regal brow at Erika before turning to face his opponent, where he was being doctored by Anna.

After Anna was satisfied Obsidian's injuries were superficial, she gave him a shove back toward the ring. "Give Tin Man an ass-kicking for me."

Erika almost felt pity for Gryton. Everyone hated him.

"Don't waste your pity on me, Null. I couldn't care less about what others think of me."

"No chance of that. As soon as you open your mouth, any pity I feel dies a swift death."

Obsidian came at Gryton, nearly catching the fire elemental off guard.

The two opponents met with a thwack of wooden practice swords and the smack of flesh as they kicked and punched and used whatever body part they could to inflict damage on the other.

For the first time, Gryton's boots began to kick up a

small cloud of dust as he twisted and thrust and lunged. The fight lost much of its earlier elegance.

Their swords came together at an awkward angle, the cross pieces catching together. The two fighters held their positions, muscles flexing in a show of strength. They remained like that, neither giving ground until Gryton leaned close and whispered in Obsidian's ear. Only Erika's link to the fire elemental allowed her to hear what they said.

"I see the Cub is all grown up. Yet, by Anna's dissatisfied look, it's equally clear you don't know how to pleasure a female."

Obsidian growled a warning but kept his composure.

"Dammit, Gryton," Erika warned. *"You will get yourself killed."*

Gryton smirked at her before turning his attention to Anna. Though his words were for Obsidian. "Perhaps I should step in and offer your Kyrsu my services until you figure out the way of things."

As Gryton had planned, the big gargoyle lost his shit in grand fashion. Tossing aside his sword, he dropped to all fours and charged.

Hastily sidestepping, Gryton narrowly avoided getting gored by the gargoyle's horns. Then in a move almost too swift to follow, he used the flat of his sword blade to slap away the gargoyle's blade tip tail.

But none of Gryton's moves slowed the gargoyle. Rearing up to stand on two legs, Obsidian called on his magic. A rushing wave of cold power swirled around Erika's body as it rushed past. In its wake, wickedly sharp shards of darkness coalesced out of thin air.

Erika started forward but instinctively halted when a dome of shimmering power rose up from the ground to encircle the ring, trapping the two opponents within.

Gryton flashed a narrow-lipped smile at the gargoyle. "I thought we weren't supposed to use magic."

"Rules change."

"In that case, let me help strengthen the dome so we'll have more time together." He waved a hand, and a secondary layer of power adhered itself to Obsidian's dome spell.

Anna, Lillian, and Gregory all launched their own magic at the shield within seconds of each other. And Erika witnessed where their combined power was working on chewing through the energy of the barrier, but if she were to guess, the two opponents would still have sufficient time to do serious harm to each other before the dome gave way.

"Hell. As much as I like a good mixed martial arts match, this isn't happening." She stormed forward the last five feet, her natural ability cycling up as it fed on everyone and everything in her immediate vicinity.

When she was within a foot of the shield, her strange talent expanded out from her body, looking like heat waves rising up from her skin. It latched onto the substance of the shield and burrowed in, fine filaments spreading from the point of contact.

At first, there was no discernible change in the shield. At least not to the naked eye. Five seconds crawled by. Ten. Twenty. Thirty. Then like glass fracturing under an impact, a spider-webbing pattern spread across the dome's surface.

Little bits at a time, sections of the shield fell away and vanished into a drifting fog.

Though the magic fog didn't escape. Her superpower drew it toward her, and her body absorbed it. With a little shudder, she stepped into the ring as the shield continued to unravel.

Not wasting any time, she stomped across the distance and latched onto the two startled males. At first, she thought they'd been so focused upon each other they hadn't seen her coming. Then she got a look at Gryton's grimace.

"You have our attention," his words came out in a pained hiss.

"Good. You going to behave now?"

"I doubt we could move a toe out of line even if we wanted to."

She studied them both and then gave Gryton's arm a squeeze. His muscles were tense, locked up tight. "Interesting. Paralysis. Think I just found another side of my superpower. Now, what was that in the ring?"

The fire elemental remained stubbornly silent.

"No? You don't want to talk? How about you have a seat instead?" Responding to her will, her gift reached out and stripped a greater amount of magic from the two males.

To her surprise, she realized the ability was obeying her commands.

She wasn't sure which male was more surprised. Though, to go by his expression, the gargoyle was the more flabbergasted of the two.

"Good. Now stop and think about how stupid you two jackasses just acted. And for what? To impress Anna? She didn't look too impressed as she stormed off. But you've got bigger problems. There are three rather old and powerful godlike beings waiting to have a word with you both."

Erika stepped back and then nodded to Lillian, Gregory, and Thayn. "They're all yours."

The oldest gargoyle flashed her a mouthful of sharp teeth. "Thank you, Null. I shall enjoy having a long talk with them."

"Wait in line," Lillian muttered angrily. "I'm about to have a word with my son."

Gregory's dark laughter echoed through the glade.

Erika would have loved to be a fly on the wall as Gryton and Obsidian got their epic dressing downs. She sighed and glanced toward the hamadryad. Unfortunately, she couldn't stay this close without risking the tree fetus while her superpower was active.

Besides, she was under orders to report any new altercation to Major Resnick. Slumping her shoulders, she trudged toward the nearest maze entrance as the other guards stationed along the wall of the maze moved nearer to take up positions closer to the arguing fae.

When she deemed she was far enough into the maze to be a safe distance from the hamadryad, she stopped and looked around, swiftly realizing she'd taken a wrong turn. A dead-end awaited her ten feet ahead.

"Crazy freaking maze!"

Backtracking, she'd only made it down the lengths of two corridors when the shadows directly ahead shimmered and spat out a gargoyle and a female fae. They made it a few more strides before collapsing in front of Erika.

Or rather, the gargoyle collapsed, and the woman just spilled from his back to land in a crumpled heap at Erika's feet.

"Now what? And what's it with me and mazes and gargoyles?"

CHAPTER TWENTY-EIGHT

Erika

She checked the female fae for a pulse. After a moment, she felt the slow throb. The woman was alive. But something was wrong. Otherwise, there wouldn't be an unconscious gargoyle and his equally unconscious fae companion sprawled on the gravel path.

Since she hadn't met either of them before, she assumed they were new arrivals to this realm. Before she examined them, she radioed in their location. While she waited for backup and the transport helicopter to arrive, she walked a circle around them, looking for weapons. They had what looked like swords and bows.

But they didn't have wounds, so it was unlikely that they'd been injured in a fight.

From Gryton's memories, she learned that new fae

found adjusting to this realm hard. And if they just had the misfortune to meet up with a magic sucking Null within minutes of their arrival?

"That's some welcome to the Mortal Realm."

The gargoyle made a huffing snort at the sound of her voice. Then nothing else for a moment until he issued a second huff as his wings folded tight to his back. He gave himself a shake and then started to rise, but he miscalculated his returning strength and collapsed back to his knees.

"Hey. Take it easy." She hoped he understood English. "I assume you just arrived. It takes some time to grow accustomed to this realm's lack of magic, or so I'm told."

He focused on her, his gaze sharpening.

"I'm Private Erika Emerson. If you wait here, I'll have someone go get the Avatars. Though they probably felt the moment you appeared and are already on their way."

"What are you? What did you do to us?" Suspicion laced his words.

Under the circumstances, she couldn't blame him.

"I'm something called a Null. I absorb all types of magic."

"You feed on magic?" The suspicion in his voice grew tenfold.

Erika held her hands up to show them empty then took several steps away, hoping the distance would slow the drain. "If you believe the Avatars, I don't feed on magic since I don't get any benefit from it. I just absorb it and then release it later."

He slowly came to his feet and checked on the woman while keeping Erika in his line of sight. When he assured himself that the fae was unharmed, he turned his stare back to Erika for several tension-filled minutes.

Then he shrugged and shook himself. "I'm Oath."

"Nice to meet you, Oath."

Just then the woman moaned and rolled over, her hand coming up to shield her eyes from the sun overhead. She spoke a language Erika didn't know.

"What did she say?"

Oath glanced between them before answering. "We come with dire news, Private Erika Emerson. We must speak with the Avatars immediately."

Of course it was dire news.

Fate—the Bitch—never took a day off.

Erika

"Who is she?" Erika asked as the woman blinked up at the sky, still stunned by the combination of being newly arrived and having her magic torn away by a Null. Or maybe it was the hit to the head when she smacked into the ground.

"She's a dryad scout. Recently returned from enemy territory," the gargoyle said as if that should explain everything to Erika.

And it meant something. She glanced back down at the female. As a human, Erika might be new to the whole Magic Realm thing, but she'd already gathered enough to know that anyone recently from the Battle Goddess's kingdom warranted extra scrutiny.

"She carries news of the utmost importance," the gargoyle continued when Erika didn't immediately react.

Frowning down at the fae, Erika gave the woman one last skeptical look and then shrugged. If the fae had been harboring some spell placed on her by the enemy, it was likely gone now after the woman had been drained to the point of unconsciousness. Whatever news she carried might very well be world-changing.

But first Erika had to get the other fae on her feet.

Nodding to the gargoyle, she said, "Help her up. The sooner we get her to the Avatars, the sooner she can share her news."

And the easier it will be to get you both on the transport, Erika muttered in her own head.

While the gargoyle's magic would be useless against her, there also wasn't anything she could do to prevent him from bolting.

But she was lucky. She didn't have to hog-tie a seven-foot-tall gargoyle. He followed her through the twisting corridors of the maze while carrying his barely conscious dryad companion in his arms.

Shortly before they reached the glade, the unit on guard duty joined them and encircled the gargoyle. There had been a couple of tense moments, but the gargoyle soon seemed more curious than concerned.

When they emerged into the meadow at the center of the maze, it was to find the others already waiting. Thayn approached first.

"Oath, Larkwood, what news?" Thayn asked as he helped set the still unsteady dryad on her feet.

Erika stepped back to a safe distance, not wanting to drain the woman any more than she already had.

Anna and Obsidian arrived next, swiftly joined by Lillian and Gregory. Gryton hung back, but still came forward to hear what they had to say. Erika joined Gryton, figuring if they all started talking in dryad or gargoyle or some other language, she could use their mental link to translate.

He glowered at her briefly but was soon focused on the newcomers.

The helicopter carrying Major Resnick and his team arrived before the dryad could complete her tale. A few tense moments ensued when Oath reacted in fear and made to attack the transport. Luckily Obsidian and Anna could calm the gargoyle. During the exchange, Erika learned Oath was actually very young, which explained a few things.

After the initial chaos, things calmed. But another problem soon arose.

"I'm not getting into that sword spinning, monstrous metal death trap," Gryton hissed.

Erika was sure her mouth had just dropped open, but she eyed the still spinning blades of the helicopter in a new light and nearly laughed out loud. "I assure you it is safe to ride in."

"I do not care. I. Am. Not. Getting. In. That. Thing."

"Huh. I really didn't peg you for a coward."

"It's not cowardice; it's survival instincts. Beings, both

divine and otherwise, have been trying to kill me since the moment of my birth." He pointed one long, elegant finger at the helicopter. "That is a death device if ever I have seen one."

"It's not—"

"No."

Gregory stomped over to them and glowered at his son. "You can get in under your own power, or I can shove you in after the Null has drained you. Your choice."

Gryton still looked ready to rebel, but he just nodded a surly 'fine' and then followed Major Resnick onto the helicopter. Erika hastened after him to ensure the fire elemental's good behavior.

Erika had been distracted by Gryton's little drama and had missed some of the dryad scout's news. But to go by the few snippets she'd caught, the emergency had something to do with a djinn. Erika only knew djinn or genies from fairytales and myth. But to go by the concern she'd seen in the female Avatars gaze, Erika knew a djinn was likely more the stuff of nightmares than fairytales.

After Oath and Larkwood climbed in, there was another bit of discussion, but Thayn and Gregory flat out refused to get into the helicopter. None of the other magic users got in, preferring to fly under the cover of shadow magic.

Erika harnessed Gryton in.

"I don't know if I hate you or my sire more," Gryton muttered at last.

He said nothing else, and to her surprise and mild relief—she really was tired of having to drain him every time he overreacted—he didn't bother to fight her either.

They made it back to base without incident.

Though as soon as they touched down, a minor revolt broke out as Oath and Larkwood bolted from the helicopter, knocking their guards aside like the humans were insects. The gargoyle stumbled forward a few steps before doubling over and puking up his last meal. The dryad joined him a moment later.

Gryton stepped off the helicopter and then just stood, looking upon everyone else disdainfully.

When Erika and the rest of the unit circled him, he looked directly at her. *"See? I told you that was a death machine. Nothing capable of bringing a gargoyle to his knees is a benevolent force."*

Erika pursed her lips. Huh. Maybe he was correct? She'd never been fond of riding in the things.

"Move out," Major Resnick barked. The others fell in line, and they were soon through two checkpoints and then safely inside. Though they didn't go to the area with the cells. Gryton, Oath, and Larkwood were all escorted into one of the meeting rooms.

Erika followed behind and was more than a little surprised to see the Avatars and the other gargoyles had already arrived.

How freaking fast can a gargoyle fly?

But, for now, she had other concerns. Her superiors shuffled her and Gryton off to one corner of the large meeting room while the others took their seats. Several of the top brass filed in next, trailed by two of the senior scientists.

Erika and Gryton weren't included in the debriefing, but it soon became apparent why she was here instead of escorting a particular demigod back to his cage. Her superiors didn't trust the gargoyles, new or old. They wanted her here in case there was an issue.

While they didn't trust magic, they'd been quick to utilize Erika's unique ability to neutralize it. If she wasn't so greatly needed, she might have found herself in a cage next to Gryton. That was always an unhappy thought. But if things kept on rolling out as they had been, she probably didn't have to worry about seeing the inside of a cage soon.

From her position by the back wall, she was still close enough to hear the conversation. Understanding it was another matter altogether. As Erika had already discovered upon their first meeting, the dryad didn't speak any of the human languages. Thayn acted as a translator, which meant the humans were in the dark until the gargoyle explained the dryad's words.

As it was, the dryad could have said one thing and Thayn could censor it in any way he wanted.

At least Erika could understand what the other woman was saying because of the soul-link with Gryton.

"It is a handy bit of luck, isn't it?" Gryton said, his tone suggesting something of interest about the otherwise bland comment. *"They could say anything, and your human military wouldn't have a clue. Were I one of your superiors, I'd make learning the other languages my priority."*

"I don't suppose there's some trick I can learn to keep you out of my mind, is there?"

Gryton tilted his head, a tiny smile tugging at the corners of his lips. *"Not in our case. But even if I knew of a way, I would not tell you, not after how you've made me suffer."*

"How have you suffered? Well, besides me having to drain your ass every time you get uppity."

"I'm forced to listen to your endless babble. And even the privacy of my mind isn't a refuge. You're always there, scrounging around for morsels to keep you from becoming bored. You are a leech in every sense of the word."

"And you're an asshole by every definition of the word," she hissed at him. "I told you I couldn't help reading your thoughts. They're just there. Trust me, if I could stop doing it, I'd probably sleep better at night."

He grunted but continued to stare toward the table where the dryad was explaining something.

When he spoke, at last, it came as a surprise. *"Perhaps in time, we will both be able to erect some kind of shield so the other can know peace."*

"Here's to hoping."

He huffed, that annoying little smirk of his back in place. *"In the meantime, you might as well listen in on my thoughts."*

Erika tried to stare a hole in the side of his head as if that would allow her to understand why he was suddenly inviting her into his mind for a look around.

With a shrug, she did just what he suggested, and once again, she experienced the world through his senses. To her surprise, Thayn was relaying precisely what the dryad said.

"Thayn gets points for being honest," Erika muttered softly.

"When it suits him. I imagine he can tell lies better than most. He is ancient. Plenty of time to practice."

"Older than you?"

"Yes."

Major Resnick leaned back in his chair and gave her a stern look.

Hmmm. Time to shut up. But she leaned in closer to Gryton, her lips almost touching his ear. "We will talk more about this later."

"*I don't doubt you'll try,*" he agreed, even his thoughts feeling resigned.

Together she and Gryton focused entirely on the dryad's tale.

The dryad's full title, Erika learned, was Master Larkwood. She was a dryad born of gargoyle stock, the product of a dryad and gargoyle mating. As such, she'd long since mastered the art of concealment and was a skilled scout. Her regular assignments put her inside enemy territory where she routinely spied upon the Battle Goddess's patrols.

On her most recent mission, she'd overheard something that had absolutely terrified her.

One of the enemy, someone called Blood Witch Taryin, had summoned and entrapped a djinn.

From how the other fae reacted, Erika gathered a djinn was terrible news on a good day. But this was somehow worse.

"You know more about all this than I do," she whispered in Gryton's ear again. "Talk."

His snort was his only response.

Unfortunately, while she could read his thoughts, if he wasn't thinking about what she wanted to know, there was no way to force him to. At this exact moment, he was thinking about polishing his armor.

"You're doing it on purpose." Her accusation didn't reap a response from Gryton.

Elbowing him in the side to get his attention, she leaned closer until her breath stirred a few wisps of hair that had escaped his normally well-groomed braids. "Talk or I'll suck you dry first chance I get."

He stared down his nose at her, his eyes narrowing in that familiar way. But with a huff, he answered her. *"A djinn is a very dangerous creature. They normally live in the Spirit Realm, where their energy powers all three realms' growth and expansion."*

"By 'three realms' you mean the Universe, right?"

"Yes."

"Wait!" When Major Resnick gave her another look, she lowered her voice even more. "You're saying their power is like freaking dark matter?"

Gryton gave her a blank look until she explained.

"Yes. Their power fuels the universe's expansion," he agreed as he folded his arms across his chest and leaned against the wall. *"But what makes a normal djinn dangerous to his or her master is that the spirit being has one aim: to get back to the Spirit Realm. And they always get back to their home realm, eventually."*

Erika sensed he was holding something back even if his thoughts didn't outwardly suggest as much. "Keep talking. There's something you aren't telling me."

He snorted. *"There is a great deal I'm not telling you."*

Grinning evilly, she made to grab his bare hand. Skin on skin contact almost always triggered her superpower to feed.

"Wait. I'll tell you the rest." He held up his hand in surren-

der. *"The djinn can be great destructive forces while they are in the magic or mortal realms. Long ago, some masters were foolish to pit djinn against djinn in battle to conquer empires. But sometimes those same djinns would sacrifice themselves in battle. In that instance, their power is absorbed by the remaining djinns but not before it has destroyed a good chunk of whatever realm their masters resided in."*

"Sounds like a cautionary tale why no one should play with the magical equivalent to a thermal nuclear bomb."

Gryton arched a brow again, so she explained. "Weapons of mass destruction. In the wrong hands, they are mutually assured destruction."

"An apt description." Gryton hummed thoughtfully as he switched to speaking out loud now that multiple conversations had broken out at the table. "For the most part, a djinn is only dangerous to his or her master and anyone that master declares an enemy."

Now it was Erika's turn to arch an eyebrow, though it was in doubt of his words, not a question.

Gryton waved his hand dismissively. "Hmmm. Yes, well, sometimes the master's kingdom *gets* vaporized along with the master when the djinn slips his control or outsmarts said master."

"Yep. Djinn sound scary. But I've been in your head. I know what you're capable of. And the Avatars are more powerful than you. Even Anna and Obsidian control great power. If we're honest, you're all the stuff of nightmares."

Gryton grinned, looking almost proud.

"That wasn't a compliment, you dumbass."

He snorted again. "It is if I take it as such."

She rolled her eyes. "Keep talking. You still know more you aren't saying."

Gryton cocked a hip. "We will be here for a couple thousand years if you want me to tell you everything I know."

"I'd be a ghost after the first hundred years, so I'm only interested in the djinns. For now."

To her surprise, he continued without giving her a hard time. "What makes this djinn much more dangerous is that once the blood witch is done, he or she won't be capable of rational thought. The witch's loathsome power will eat away at the djinn's soul until the creature is insane and will attack anything and everything in its path."

Gryton paused and gazed at her.

"Not that what you've revealed isn't scary enough to give me nightmares but keep going."

He nodded, a tiny smile hovering at the corners of his lips. "If my parents can't get to this djinn in time to neutralize the blood witch's work, the djinn may spread the witch's taint to the other djinn in the spirit realm. Do I need to explain how dangerous this could be for the entire universe?"

"Nope. Think I got it. Rabid genies with the ability to control all the dark matter in the universe. No wonder even you look freaked out. We're talking apocalyptic level shit here."

Again, he arched his eyebrow, and she explained.

"That would be an accurate description," he agreed with a smile.

He looked entirely too pleased by this news.

"Why do you look so damn happy about that, Hot Stuff?" She might not know a lot about Gryton yet, but she knew he was a survivor. "Crazed genies running around destroying the universe won't be very conducive to your long-term survival."

"Because, if there is a djinn that needs slaying to save the universe, it likely means that is your real purpose."

"As opposed to what?"

"Killing me." Gryton tilted his head to study her from a new angle. "You see, I was certain the Divine Ones had sent you to assassinate me, and I've been trying to think of a way to kill you that wouldn't get me killed or annoy my sire and dam enough that they would think I was unsalvageable and kill me themselves."

Erika's eyes widened. "I have no wish to murder you in cold blood."

He smiled, a positively wicked look of delight in his eyes. "And I have no wish to get killed trying to kill a Null. Perhaps now I won't need to poison you."

Looking up at the ceiling, she counted to ten. When she looked back at Gryton, he was still grinning. "You know what? I think I really hate magic."

Gryton laughed, a rich, beautiful sound.

She hated that, too, she decided. And everything else about the overconfident little prick.

CHAPTER THIRTY

Gregory

After the dryad had told her tale and the meeting had ended, Gregory had convinced his Lady to come for a run with him. Now they stood in the forest outside the military's temporary camp. The fumes of their machines still burned his nose, and he wanted nothing more than to run off into the woods and hunt with his Sorceress at his side or on his back.

But there was no time for anything more than a quick run.

"We have to return to the Magic Realm," Gregory said into the silence, his heart heavy. A few months ago, he'd wanted nothing more than to return home with her.

"I know." Lillian reached out for his hand.

"Our allies aren't ready yet."

"I know that, too." She sighed. "But we don't have a choice. We must bring the war to the Lady of Battles before the blood witch drives the djinn insane."

"Or she uses him to summon more."

"That, too." Lillian gave his hand a tug and started to walk. "There is one blessing in all this."

Gregory flicked an ear in question.

"From what Gryton has told us, there is only one blood witch, and she is self-taught. The Battle Goddess isn't so foolish to allow her to take an apprentice. It's unlikely the witch will summon a second djinn. She's too smart to attempt something so foolish. No master can hope to control two djinns and survive more than a short time."

"We can only hope our son is correct in his assessment of the witch's intelligence," Gregory said, knowing he sounded doubtful.

"He watched her develop. Gryton wouldn't have maintained his position as commander for as long as he did without learning how to read people. He knows her. If he claims she isn't so foolish as to bind a second djinn, she won't. And as long as the Lady of Battles forbids her from taking an apprentice, the Magic and Mortal Realms should be safe from a second djinn."

Gregory huffed. "One djinn is bad enough. Especially if it is who I think it is."

"You think it is Naharnin?" His Sorceress questioned, her voice a soft whisper.

"Naharnin always frets when we leave the Spirit Realm to be born as flesh and blood beings. He would know all that has befallen us in this life. If he felt a djinn being summoned, he would be the one to answer it to come to our aid."

"Thick headed male."

Gregory laughed. "I would do the same in his place."

"My point exactly." Lillian's expression turned serious. "If it is our ancient companion, then he will hold out longer against the blood witch's magic than another djinn would. That is a blessing. I would rather battle a sane djinn than an insane one."

"And I would rather not battle a djinn at all, especially not Naharnin." When he felt his throat tighten with emotion, he cleared it and continued on like his voice hadn't just trembled. "The destruction will be vast."

"Yes, but only if we fail. I don't plan on failing him. We will rescue Naharnin and make the witch pay." Stepping up to him, Lillian rested her cheek against his chest. Sighing happily, he folded his wings around them both and nuzzled her hair. She relaxed into him, her weight and warmth pleasant against his skin.

"I could stay like this forever," she purred. "Regrettably, we must make plans and ready our human and fae allies to journey to the Magic Realm within the next few days."

With a final nuzzle to her hair, he let her step back. "I will go tell Thayn that we are ready to face Lord Draydrak and then we must convince the humans to allow the new legion to travel from Haven to the Mortal Realm."

Lillian laughed. "I'll recruit Gran to help with that. We might need her and her art of persuasion to accomplish that miracle."

"There is someone else we must try to wake first."

"My father." His Sorceress tilted her head back, her

gaze meeting his. Pain shimmered in their depths. "It could be dangerous for him."

"Yes. But it will be more dangerous if we don't wake him. Stalks the Darkness lived in the Battle Goddess's kingdom for years. We need his knowledge. If we can heal and wake him, I want him as one of our captains. We finally have enough gargoyles here to attempt a healing. Even Gryton and his Null may be able to aid us." Gregory's wings twitched with the need to encircle her again. "But it is your choice; you and your family's."

Lillian reached up and cupped his face, her thumb stroking along his cheek. "He's a gargoyle. I already know what he would want—to fight. I'm sure my mother and brother will agree when we ask them."

He nodded, but his mind was focused on the feel of his Sorceress's fingers stroking his skin. Reaching down, he grabbed her hand and placed a kiss upon her knuckles.

"Then in the morning, we will go find your mother and brother, and we will heal your father enough to ask him if he wishes to risk being fully awakened."

"I would like that."

CHAPTER THIRTY-ONE

Obsidian

He stomped up the stairs with no actual heading in mind. Realizing as much, he huffed in annoyance. Obsidian supposed his room would do. His lonely room, which separated him from his Kyrsu by a stout wall.

But he wanted solitude, didn't he? He wanted a place where he could rest and recover. A place to hide more like it. His lips pulled back from his teeth in a bitter grimace.

While the arrival of the dryad had been a distraction and allowed him to pretend for a time that he was still a worthy leader of the Legion, once the meeting was over, he was again faced with his earlier failures.

It hadn't helped that the Avatars had released him with the order to go rest and recover from getting drained by the Null. In their defense, they likely hadn't meant for it to sound like a parent shooing off an overtired cub, but he couldn't help but make the comparison. Because he had acted just like the old Shadowlight at Gryton's first taunt about Anna.

He wasn't sure which was worse. Humiliating himself in front of Anna or Thayn.

The longer he thought about it, he decided it was worse to embarrass himself in front of Anna. He'd worked so hard to be worthy of her.

"Oh, stop your stewing."

Anna's voice chased him up the stairs and his wings quivered with tension.

"I'm not stewing," he said in a surly tone. But really all he wanted was to turn to her and beg her forgiveness for being so foolish. But also, for not beating Gryton soundly like she'd asked. But he wouldn't show any greater weakness than he already had. Anna deserved a strong Rasoren, one capable of being her partner and her equal.

Back when they were still trapped in the Battle Goddess's kingdom, he'd known Gryton had shown an interest in Anna. But now, as an adult, Obsidian was only beginning to realize to what lengths she would have gone to protect his younger self.

Even with the trauma Anna had suffered at the hands of other males, she would have placed herself in Gryton's bed if she thought it was the only way to protect Shadowlight. It hadn't come to that, but that didn't lessen the stress she must have suffered.

While there was nothing Obsidian could do to change anything from that time, he very much wanted to put

Gryton in his place and show Anna that her Rasoren could protect her now.

But he'd failed miserably.

"Sulking isn't pretty, my Rasoren." Anna's voice was tinted with humor.

In the next moment, he knew why as she grabbed his tail and gave it a firm tug. "Wait up for your poor Kyrsu. I'm still in human form, and my legs are shorter than yours, if you hadn't noticed."

She gave his tail another tug, and he stopped outside her room.

"Come in. I want to talk."

Obsidian gently tugged his tail out of her grasp. "I should go and rest. We can talk in the morning."

Anna chuckled. "You will sleep in my room tonight. No way am I leaving your side after what the Null did to you. I felt our link vanish for a moment. It was the most terrifying thing I've felt in a while."

He glanced at her for the first time. "I'm fine. The Null only drains a fae. She doesn't cause permanent damage."

"That we've been told. Get in here. You're sleeping with me tonight. I'll accept no argument."

What must be blatant astonishment on his face made her laugh. And as much as his pride was still stinging from earlier, and her laugh just now didn't improve his mood, this was what he'd desperately wanted but had been too much of a coward to admit, even to himself.

Anna's expression softened. "We're linked. I felt your loneliness."

Feeling even more foolish than he had earlier, he looked down at his talon-tip toes as if they were fascinating.

"I miss sharing a room. I miss sleeping with your arms wrapped around me, holding me close."

He glanced up in surprise. Looking at her, seeing the love in her eyes, he understood for the first time how fortunate he was.

"My Anna." He stepped into her and wrapped his arms and wings around her. "The Divine Ones couldn't have bonded me to a more perfect soul."

Anna snorted with humor, and then pressed a kiss to the skin over his heart. As far as showings of affection went, it was relatively small and innocent, but it meant the world to him. He nuzzled her collar bone and purred his happiness as the last of the tension flowed out of her body. His turbulent emotions soon calmed.

"Come on," Anna said as she stepped away from him. "We should make a place to bed down for the night. There's no way we're both going to fit on that narrow bed, and dawn will be here before we know it."

While Anna raided the closet for more bedding, he stripped the bed and arranged the blankets and the two pillows on the floor. He gave the pillows an extra fluff, but if he knew Anna at all, he'd likely be her pillow, which suited him just fine.

Soon Anna returned with more blankets to make their nest softer and then after disappearing down the hall for what seemed far too long, she returned smelling of soap and damp skin and only wearing a towel.

"Figured I should shower instead of inflicting sweaty-smelling human on you all night."

He gave himself an inquisitive sniff.

Anna grinned. "Don't worry, you smell good. You always

smell good. I don't know what it is about gargoyle physiology, but if someone could figure out how to bottle that scent, they'd make a fortune within a month. I almost shifted to gargoyle form for that very reason but didn't think we could fit two gargoyles into the space between the bed and the wall."

He would have made it work. He was happy to have Anna sleep next to him in whatever form she wanted. Their new link made it a craving he didn't want to fight.

Watching as she dug around in a drawer, he noted she pulled out a long shirt made of some soft material and what she called panties.

He found himself much more interested in human attire than he'd been as a child.

"Mind turning around?" She called over her shoulder.

He did as she asked, but it wasn't until he was facing the mirror that he realized her miscalculation. But she dropped the towel just as he was going to speak, and he suddenly found his tongue stuck to the roof of his mouth.

Unable to stop himself, he watched her shimmy into the simple undergarment, fascinated by the flex of her muscles as her firm backside was covered by the blue panties.

She turned then to grab the top from where she'd tossed it, drawing his gaze back to her, and he could look his fill at her other curves. This wasn't the first time he'd seen her. Gargoyles were communal bathers mostly, and she'd bathed with him before, but those times he'd always been careful to keep his gaze averted so he wouldn't embarrass himself with a sudden and savage bout of arousal.

But this time he'd been too weak-willed by the temptation the mirror represented to look away. His body slipped his control, responding eagerly to the sight of hers.

He flushed with shame and glanced down, then swiftly hooked one pillow with his tail. Hastily he positioned it to hide the evidence of his weakness and hoped his stance looked casual enough.

Glancing back up into the mirror, his gaze locked on Anna's eyes.

"Busted." She stood with her arms crossed and one eyebrow arched.

"Anna, I'm sorry. I didn't mean—"

"Relax." She walked closer and halted directly in front of him. "I think we both knew this was going to happen from time to time."

"It shouldn't have. You're not in heat. I shouldn't have been so weak."

She snorted again. "You might be a gargoyle with impressive discipline, but you're also a young, healthy male. I doubt you're the first to have a similar... problem among your classmates."

"Yes, but with your..." He fell silent, not wanting to talk about it and bring up painful memories.

"With my history?" She reached up and cupped his face. "You shared in all those horrific memories. You know what it's like. You didn't turn away from me because of my... damage."

"You're not damaged," he soothed. "I'll never turn my back on you. But I also don't want you to feel trapped or fearful of me. Ever."

"And I never will. I know I'm safe with you, my

Rasoren." She stretched up and rested one hand on his shoulder. "That knowledge likely makes me act a little selfish. I know I can enjoy small intimacies with you that I couldn't with another male. I want you to enjoy them, too. I know it will be a long time before either of us is ready to take that final step. But I don't want you to ignore your own needs in some misguided assumption you're protecting me."

The hand not on his shoulder moved down his chest, her caressing fingers drifting lower and lower as they ran along his tensed abdominal muscles. His breath escaped in a hiss when she cupped him through his loincloth. "I could help you so you can sleep more comfortably."

The temptation to accept what she was offering was powerful. Yet there was something more, something she was trying to hide from herself.

He captured her hand, curling his fingers around hers, and then he gently dislodged it and brought her hand up to his muzzle where he kissed her palm. "As much as I would enjoy that, the tension in your arm and the cold sweat along your sides tells me you aren't ready for that yet. I care for you too much to ruin this between us."

Anna glanced down, breaking eye contact and exhaling loudly. "I'm sorry. I thought I could handle this, but I'm still a mess."

"You're not a mess. You are brave and resilient. If you weren't, you wouldn't have survived everything that you've suffered. In time you will be ready. We both will be ready. And it will be a most magnificent joining."

"Thank you for your patience and understanding." She stretched up on her toes and pressed a kiss to the side of his muzzle. "I'll try not to make this any harder for you than it need be."

Obsidian reached up and touched where her lips had so recently brushed against his skin in a kiss. His first kiss.

"You kissed me."

"Yes, I did."

"That is worth far more to me than any trivial ache I might suffer."

"You're such a romantic." She rolled her eyes. "And if I blush any harder, I will combust."

Her words made him laugh, and just like that the tension between them vanished. He leaned down and pressed his forehead against hers. "I love you, my Kyrsu."

"Love you, too." She straightened and cleared her throat. "Now go deal with that," she waved her hand in the general direction of his nether regions without glancing down. "Or that's all I will think about all night, and I'm pretty damned sure it won't be fear I'm experiencing when I do."

Obsidian snorted with laughter. "I'll go take a cold shower."

But as he was walking from the room, he was thinking about how much he liked the idea that the state of his body distracted her. He liked the idea that she wouldn't be able to focus on anything else.

It felt more than a little deviant, and he liked it.

CHAPTER THIRTY-TWO

The Magic Realm
Bervicta

The soft rattle of chains announced the Battle Goddess's approach. Bervicta shifted, her newly healed wing tremored slightly. It would take another moon cycle until she built up the muscle again to what it was before the incident where the Avatars had rescued Gryton. For now, she was limited to short, unpleasant flights. Despite that weakness, she'd rather have been winging her way up the side of a mountain instead of facing the Battle Goddess.

But she had to convey everything she'd learned from Vaspara without seeming like she was the succubus's ally. If she failed, the draklings would die, and Sorac would rage until he was dead and had taken a chunk of the fortress with him. Then Vaspara would be killed since she'd no longer be needed to control the firedrake. Bervicta wasn't willing to wager on her own chance of survival after that.

The rattling of chains grew louder, and then the Lady of Battles appeared at the top landing where she overlooked the great hall spreading out below them.

Bervicta bowed, head bent in silent supplication as she stared at her own ghostly reflection on the highly polished stairs.

"Rise, my captain. What news do you have to report about my new draklings?"

The pride in the Battle Goddess's tone was a good sign. She needed the demigoddess to desire the little ones' survival more than her need for revenge.

"My Goddess, I have discovered something concerning. The hatchlings wouldn't take any of the food I offered. Nothing I gave them interested them, so I went to Vaspara and asked for aid. Before you strike, know I didn't have a choice. The draklings would have died, your dreams of a winged battalion dying with them."

"Go on," the Battle Goddess urged, her voice outwardly calm, but Bervicta had known the goddess long enough to sense the tension flowing below the surface.

"I spoke with Vaspara to learn about the care of draklings. She told me they will only feed on kills provided by their parents. Worse, they also feed on their parents' magic. She claimed without her and Sorac to oversee their care and feeding, the draklings would die." Bervicta paused and then just forged on. "I tested the truth of Vaspara's words before I brought the news to you."

The Lady of Battles narrowed her eyes as she leaned

down to spear Bervicta with a hard look. "And what did you learn?"

"What Vaspara told me proved true. The draklings immediately devoured everything that came from her hand. I also witnessed her feeding them her magic. It sated them, for now, but she fears her power alone won't be enough to keep them strong, that they'll need Sorac's fire magic as well since they're already accustomed to it." Bervicta paused and picked her next words with care. "While I suspect Vaspara and Sorac very capable of a second betrayal if they think it will save the young, I didn't detect any lie in what she told me."

"I shall be the judge of that."

"Of course." Bervicta bowed again. "If I see any decline in the draklings, I'll notify you at once."

"Good. Is there anything else you learned?"

Bervicta straightened from her bow. "I have another concern that I can't in good conscience keep quiet."

The Battle Goddess arched a brow. "Go on."

"If Vaspara's power isn't enough to keep the draklings alive, Sorac will go insane at their deaths. He'll rage. Unafraid of death, Sorac may even overcome the spells Taryin has placed on him. He could wreak great havoc in the time it takes the other captains to rally and kill him. Worse, he is still so closely tied to his battalion. They may join him."

Bervicta paused and cautiously eyed the Battle Goddess, but no deadly lance of magic pierced her breast, so she continued. "I believe Vaspara's soldiers are just as loyal to her. I fear they don't see Sorac and Vaspara's defections as unjust. Both were sent on a suicide mission because they angered you in their questioning of Taryin's methods."

"You speak what no others would. I don't know if that makes you brave or foolish, Harpy."

"It makes me loyal to you. I have no ambition to see you overthrown by your brother. If you fall, so do we all. I'm not so foolish to think his Gargoyle Legion will take prisoners. It would be in your best interest to continue to allow Sorac and Vaspara to live even after the draklings are weaned."

"You speak treason."

"I speak the truth. And Sorac and Vaspara aren't the only captains uncomfortable with the witch's methods."

"What other captains! Tell me."

"All of us. All of our seconds in command and so on down the line. Everyone wonders if they will be the next to be sacrificed to feed Taryin's spells."

The Lady of Battles scoffed. "Taryin knows her place. She won't act unless it is on my behest."

"And yet she summoned a djinn from the Spirit Realm."

"Tread carefully, Harpy."

"I know Taryin is needed. Even more so now after the defection of River and Stalks the Darkness and then the loss of Anna, Shadowlight, and Gryton. But there is a way to prevent further losses." Or Divine Ones forbid, a civil war.

The Battle Goddess's rage nearly vibrated in the air, she was so livid. But her tone was icy cold when she spoke. "I understand your reasoning." She tilted her head and glowered at Bervicta. "I assume you have a plan that will prevent a rebellion and just happens to save your two friends."

Bervicta bowed again. There was no escaping her relationship with either Vaspara or Sorac. "My Goddess, I am loyal. However, I understand that I must now prove my loyalty. And I will. Both Sorac and Vaspara were my mentors. I know them. I know how they think. I truly believe their loyalty can be forced as long as we treat the draklings well. After all, where else can a firedrake and a succubus go where the light won't hunt them down? They only defected because Sorac feared Taryin would use his brood to fuel her spells."

"Vaspara told you this?"

"She didn't have to tell me. It was all over her face. She loves the firedrake and his little ones. She acted to protect them. You can use that to your advantage."

"I never would have allowed harm to come to the draklings. They are too valuable."

"But Taryin has proven she can't be trusted, that if she thinks she can serve you better, she'll go ahead and do it. Sorac knew this, and his firedrake's instincts were too powerful to ignore."

"I can see your way of thinking," The Battle Goddess admitted. "But he and Vaspara were duty-bound to come to me and tell me these things themselves."

"They would never question you openly. Not after River's betrayal and then how Gryton aided Anna and Shadowlight. Both captains feared you would assume they harbored the same traitorous thoughts and have them killed."

The Battle Goddess's expression darkened. "I do not

forgive them, and if they make so much as one misstep, I'll kill them both and their draklings, too."

"You could set the djinn to guard the draklings when I'm needed elsewhere and Taryin isn't using him for one of her spells. As long as you control the draklings, you control their parents. And the djinn would be more than capable of preventing either of the parents from escaping with the little ones."

The Lady of Battles nodded, deep in thought, her gaze unfocused. "You can tell your mentors the good news while I speak with Taryin about what we shall use to ensure Vaspara and Sorac's future loyalty."

"Of course. What other rules do you wish to enact?"

"They are never to be allowed outside with the draklings. Only one parent at a time can be with them. Sorac and Vaspara are never to see each other again. I'll leave you to oversee those details. And if either of the traitors escapes with their draklings, it will be you I kill very, very slowly."

"And rightly so for such a failure, my Goddess." Bervicta bowed deeply a second time.

After she was dismissed, she marched away to see to the Lady's orders. It didn't occur until later that she hadn't mentioned one highly important detail. She hadn't said that the Djinn could likely feed and raise the draklings all on his own.

And the Battle Goddess hadn't detected the omission.

Bervicta decided the Divine Ones must have smiled upon her for the first time in her existence.

CHAPTER THIRTY-THREE

Erika

The next morning Erika was up early, hoping to get a little extra time in the mess before going on duty, when Sergeant Maracle appeared at her shoulder. She was learning the names and histories of the other members of the units tasked with babysitting Gryton. The close-mouthed sniper had a dry wit that she liked.

"The Avatars need you."

Looking down at her uneaten breakfast and the full cup of coffee, she muttered darkly, "Of course they do."

"I didn't catch that?" But his smirk told her otherwise.

"Just said I'd come at once."

"Good. We're to meet up with the rest of the team and go collect the prisoner and then report back to the maze."

Erika followed Sergeant Maracle until they reached Gryton's location.

As usual, the fire elemental looked relaxed and unconcerned with being imprisoned in his clear-walled cage. Though she knew inwardly, he wasn't as calm as he pretended. To judge by his current emotional feedback, she gathered he would have been pacing while he waited for her to arrive if there had been room in his cage.

"Took you long enough," he drawled when she walked over.

He unfolded himself with a show of masculine grace. Today he was again wearing the fae style of clothing, his lower half covered by the flowing silk-like pants the sidhe had given him, though he hadn't yet donned the long tunic.

He glanced behind her, his gaze tracking through the still-open door and out into the hall. After a slight hesitation, he reached down and pulled on the tunic. He was still belting it in place when she grinned suddenly.

"Ah. The sexiness was totally for Anna. Lucky for you, we're meeting them in the glade. Otherwise, big nasty would likely have tried to take another swing at you. Then I'd have sucked you both dry, and it would be nothing but bruised pride and bleeding egos for the next twenty-four hours. Aren't you lucky it was just me?"

"The luckiest."

His dry tone had her laughing before she could stop herself.

"You know what this is about, Tin Man?"

"Don't call me that."

"Oh, you prefer Hot Stuff. Works for me."

He glowered and she ignored. "Oh, come on. Did

anyone mention what this morning's early roll-call is about?"

"No one ever talks to me."

She arched a brow.

"No one but you," he clarified. "I'm unaware what today's training may be."

"Well, let's go find out."

She nodded at the leshii and the three guards positioned inside the chamber. Soon Gryton was unchained, and she was escorting him out of HQ.

A little over an hour later, Erika found herself back in the glade, standing with the others looking at the statue of a gargoyle. She'd been told this was River's mate and Obsidian and Lillian's father.

"I shouldn't be here," Gryton said, his tone guarded.

"Why? Because you nearly killed him and if they wake him, he will probably try to return the favor?"

Gryton snorted. "I'm not afraid of him. But if he attacks me, I will defend myself. And if I kill him, what then? My mother and Obsidian will be furious and out for my blood. And then Anna and Gregory will join in their partner's causes."

"Think you forgot about River. She seems pretty badass for a dryad."

He just continued to glower at her.

"Oh, don't worry. If it turns into open season on Gryton, I'll make sure you aren't killed. I hear that will be terrible for Earth."

"I don't need your protection."

"What you think has zero influence on me fulfilling my assignment."

Gryton continued to look unimpressed, but Erika didn't care.

She cleared her throat. "Were I you, I wouldn't worry about Stalks the Darkness. It's my understanding that this is a stretch, anyway. He might be too weak and need years more of rest before he'll wake. At least that's what I read in the file on the way over here."

"With the Avatars, Thayn, and the new Rasoren and Kyrsu combining their magic, the impossible is going to become much more possible."

Over the next hour, Gryton's words looked more and more like the truth.

It just didn't happen as Erika had envisioned. Instead of feeding the magic to Darkness directly, they wanted to funnel all magic through her first.

At her skeptical look, Lillian clarified. "The magic each of us gives off is different. Think of it like the variances that cause different blood types. As the Avatars of the Divine Ones, Gregory and I can call upon and wield all forms of magic. But with other fae races, their magic is most often dictated by what element their species is strong in. Gargoyles and dryads sired by gargoyles have compatible magic because they're genetically related and can both control the elements of earth and air."

Erika understood the basics and nodded for Lillian to continue.

"Because Nulls absorb all types of magic and then later purify and release it, we can filter our various types of magic through you. What you give off is a neutral, or universal, type of power. That will make it easier for Darkness to consume the magic and heal. His body won't have to first convert it into something useable."

"I'll just take you at your word. Tell me what you want me to do." Erika glanced to the side where Major Resnick was standing. The rest of his team was spread out around the glade accompanied by several scientists.

He nodded even though he'd already instructed her to aid the magic wielders in whatever way they needed.

Lillian gestured everyone closer to Stalks the Darkness. "All you have to do is stand there close to him. We will feed you power one at a time, and once your body has processed enough of it, you will naturally radiate the purified magic back into this world."

On a scale of one to ten, trying to wake a statue was only about a two on the scale of weird shit she'd seen since arriving, so she just stood there as Lillian closed her eyes and summoned a wave of power.

Like all magic, it rushed into Erika but generated only a tingle in response. Once the Sorceress was satisfied that she'd shared enough power, Gregory stepped up and did the same, followed by River, Thayn, and then Anna and Obsidian.

They all donated a great deal of magic. But she was certain River had donated more than she could safely give because the dryad woman was nearly swaying on her feet afterward. The others noticed, and Obsidian supported his mother gently.

As each of the other gargoyles surrendered their magic to Erika, they then went over to Darkness and began painting symbols upon his stone skin with their own blood. Watching intently, Erika spotted the exact moment some of the purified magic reached the statue, causing the symbols to flare up and glow.

A shadow fell across Erika, and she looked up to see Gryton standing before her.

"I might not be a gargoyle, but my magic is second only to the Avatars' in strength, and they say my magic will aid them in healing Darkness."

He'd barely finished the last word when fire burst to life above his palms. Even his eyes shimmered with a molten glow as he watched her. Then he made a violent motion like he was pitching a ball and launched the first volley of his fiery power at her.

She instinctively winced even though his power did no more harm than the other magics she'd absorbed.

"You totally don't care about helping Darkness. You just wanted an excuse to toss fireballs at me, you jerk."

He gave her a secretive little smile and launched an even bigger fireball at her.

She gave Gryton the finger when Major Resnick wasn't looking. However, Thayn didn't miss any of the exchange and stalked over to stand off to one side. He glanced first at Erika and then Gryton and then back again before breaking out in laughter.

"Keep that up younglings, and we'll have enough magic to wake Darkness ten times over."

Thayn's words caught Gregory's attention, and he growled something low at Gryton.

The fire elemental just shrugged and then asked in the most placid of tones, "Am I not doing as I was instructed?"

Gregory hissed, "You're not supposed to enjoy it!"

Gryton shrugged and made a dismissive grunt that sounded suspiciously like his gargoyle father.

"I think I'm seeing some family traits," Erika offered, only to have both males turn their glowers at her.

Erika ignored them and watched as Lillian finished up the healing spell she'd been performing on Darkness. After a moment, she stepped away from the statue. "Now, we wait."

River stepped in closer to the statue until she could rest her hands upon his shoulders. After a minute like that, she leaned her full weight against the statue and pressed her face into his stone neck.

Erika wasn't sure if the other woman was crying, but she was certain that River was trying to reach her mate along a mental link. While she didn't know the gargoyle at all and knew River only slightly better, she felt sorry for the pair. It was clear the ordinarily cold and distant dryad loved the gargoyle.

When the Sorceress came to stand next to her, Erika decided now was as good a time as any to ask one question that had been bothering her. "Earlier, when you were talking about the various elemental magics and the species aligned with those elements, I noticed you didn't mention Gryton. He's a fire elemental, obviously. But what species is he? It wasn't mentioned in any of the reports. And I haven't been able to find a reference to it in any of Gryton's memories."

Lillian looked over at Gregory, and a wordless conversation ensued for some moments. Then, at last, she turned back to Erika. "Gregory and I don't remember our last life together, but Gryton is an elemental dragon and from snip-pets of his memories, we know we both wore dragon forms when we begot him."

Lillian circled Gryton, her head tilted to study him. Gryton didn't twitch under the scrutiny. If anything, he looked bored now that he wasn't tossing fireballs.

There was another gruff gargoyle huff, and then Gregory joined the conversation. "Gryton is still develop-ing. No one yet knows what he will become when he reaches his full potential."

"Speak for yourself," Gryton snapped and then turned on his heels and walked over to gaze upon Darkness.

Gregory leaned down until his muzzle was nearly brushing Erika's ear. "He's only touchy because what I say is true. Only the Divine Ones know what he will become and what his purpose is."

"But you have a theory, don't you?"

Gregory gave her a big gargoyle grin. "Perhaps."

"Perhaps? What kind of answer is that? It was a yes or no question!"

He just shrugged again and then joined Gryton by the statue.

Which, Erika was just noticing, was darkening from a grey tone to a rich ebony shade. Others had already seen the change and were moving closer to help.

She moved back to a safer distance but remained close enough to monitor Gryton.

But for once, he followed her lead, putting some distance between himself and the rest of the group clus-tered around the statue. He didn't join her though, instead standing off to one side being his usual aloof-ass-self.

Not long after Gryton had taken up his new position, there was a pained groan from the direction of the rest of the group. A moment later, the gargoyle started sliding sideways off the pedestal he'd been perching on. Gregory and Obsidian caught him before he toppled off onto the ground.

"What happened?" He glanced around, his gaze landing on Thayn and widening before sliding to Lillian and Gregory next. A moment later he took in Anna in her gargoyle form and jerked in surprise. Next, his gaze traveled to Obsidian.

Erika didn't know if recognition would have shown in his expression or not, because his gaze traveled beyond Obsidian to land on Gryton, catching and holding Darkness's full attention.

"You!" Darkness's snarl pierced the glade's calm and birds erupted out of the hamadryad. The gargoyle continued to growl as he leaped into motion, shoving several of the others aside as he called upon his shadow magic.

Erika knew she couldn't drain Darkness without setting back his recovery. But she couldn't let him attack Gryton either.

Darting between the two, she hoped her Null's abilities would absorb whatever opposing magics the two tossed at each other without actively beginning to feed.

She braced for the attack, but it didn't come. Lillian and Obsidian had placed restraining hands on Darkness's arms.

"Easy," Lillian said in a soothing tone.

"Father," Obsidian added. "Much has happened since

you were last awake. And as much as it pains me to say it, Gryton is now an ally, that is the truth."

Darkness looked absolutely shocked. Not that she could blame him. She'd likely react the same under the circumstances.

Gryton cleared his throat and directed his words at Darkness. "You will be pleased to know that even though I am an ally, I am also a prisoner until I can prove my trust-worthiness. It seems our situations are now reversed."

Darkness snorted, his lips curling away from his teeth. "If what you say is true, you at least will have been treated better than I ever was."

"You'd be surprised." Gryton's droll comment only earned another soft growl from Darkness.

"My beloved, listen to your children." River stepped in and hugged her mate. "They speak the truth. So much has happened." She looked at Obsidian. "Our son is all grown up and is the Rasoren of the Gargoyle Legion."

That news shocked the gargoyle, for he twisted to gaze upon his son again. "Truly?"

"Yes, father."

"How long have I been out?"

"Only a few weeks here in this realm, but for me, it has been almost fourteen years. There is much to tell."

"But Gryton?" His gaze narrowed again on the fire elemental.

"The Null keeps Gryton under her watchful gaze," River soothed.

Erika nodded at Darkness. And while she wouldn't have minded sticking around for the reunion to learn more of this strange family's dynamic, Major Resnick was approaching.

"You're to report with the prisoner to the labs for your medicals."

"Our medicals, sir?"

"Yes. They've been badgering me all week. I told them this afternoon is as good a time as any. Take Gryton and his security detail and report there at thirteen hundred hours. You should still have time to grab some grub first if you hurry."

"Yes, sir!" She snapped to attention and then turned to carry out his orders.

Marching up to Gryton, she shoved him in the back.

"Come on. You get to tour the mess. Can you do that glamour thing your mother mentioned before?" she waved her hands at his fae clothing, "To magically blend in or do we have to stop somewhere and force you into some fatigues first?"

He made a disdainful expression. "I can adapt my clothing to look like anything."

"Perfect!" She gave him another friendly shove to get him moving. "I'm starved. Let's go."

CHAPTER THIRTY-FOUR

The Magic Realm
Vaspara

The first days after her capture, Vaspara never knew when death would come for her. But as each day passed, and she still drew breath, she began to think the harpy was capable of real miracles. Then twelve days in, the Battle Goddess named Bervicta as the new Commander, enraging Taryin beyond words, or so Bervicta told her.

The harpy also convinced the Lady of Battles to allow Vaspara to feed the draklings and even visit with them for short times. She'd heard that Sorac was allowed to bring them kills he'd laced with his own magic. She allowed herself to hope she and Sorac might one day be able to appease the Battle Goddess and earn forgiveness.

That hope only lasted until Taryin came on the Battle Goddess's order to bind Vaspara's soul with darkest magic.

During the ritual, Vaspara had prayed to the Divine Ones for death, but they didn't grant it. Instead, a cool, almost oily power now shifted and crawled under her skin, burrowing through her chest and up along her spine and into her mind. She was still herself and yet not. Something fundamental was being stolen away day by day.

But she was now regularly granted time out of her cell to feed and care for the draklings. They even restored her title of captain, and they allowed her to continue training her troops. Sorac was granted all these things as well. And yet Vaspara couldn't feel near the amount of joy such change should have brought.

The only thing that might have pierced the blood witch's spell—seeing Sorac and feeling his love for her and his draklings—was far beyond her reach, the Goddess having ordered that Vaspara and Sorac never see each other ever again.

She'd had to content herself with his fading scent each time she visited the draklings after he'd already been and gone. Then one day Sorac had started leaving her letters in the draklings cavern. Reading his words of love had finally sparked joy like she'd once felt, and that hope helped her to endure the witch's spell.

And since nothing in Taryin's orders had forbidden communicating through letters, Vaspara had written back. They'd both been cautious not to reveal that small bit of contact for fear a new order would stop them from sharing in even that bit of solace.

After reading each one, she committed it to memory

and then swiftly burned the letter, fearing to leave evidence for others to find.

Vaspara was just thinking of ways she and Sorac might steal a few moments together here and there when her cell door rattled as the latch was pulled back. A moment later, two figures blocked some of the light.

"We discovered your little secret, Succubus," Taryin hissed.

Bervicta marched into the cell. "I put my life and career on the line for you!"

What? What had they discovered that she hadn't already told the harpy? Sorac's letters? Neither of them would be this enraged over that. A simple order would swiftly put an end to it.

With no idea what they were referring to, Vaspara just came to her feet and stood defiantly, maintaining her silence.

"The djinn," Bervicta shouted, but her eyes were calm and trying to convey something. "He finally slipped up when Taryin and I were bringing him into the draklings' chamber for guard duty. The little ones were awake and hungry. We both witnessed how swiftly the little ones latched on and began feeding from his power."

Taryin smiled. "He couldn't resist my questioning. That wasn't the first time he's fed them either. He admitted to providing what they needed regularly back on the island when you and Sorac were off building a village."

In sudden understanding, Vaspara realized Bervicta had never told the Battle Goddess of the djinn's ability to feed the draklings. Now it made sense why Vaspara and Sorac had been granted so much time with the little ones.

Vaspara knew she owed the harpy for that gift, and it was time to repay the debt.

She sneered at the two women. "Of course I withheld information that would cause my death. And since you didn't directly question me about if the djinn could feed the draklings, I never had to answer you."

"We know your secret now, and I've already shared it with the Battle Goddess." Taryin smiled, the look predatory. "I've been ordered to reassign you to a new task now that you're expendable."

CHAPTER THIRTY-FIVE

Gryton

In the days after Stalks the Darkness was returned to life, Gryton fell into a routine of training, interrogations, testing by the scientists, and then more training. The only glimmer of enjoyment he took from the entire experience was that the Null had to suffer through the same things.

But at least there was an end in sight.

All the misery would culminate in a week's time when the Avatars and Major Resnick would lead a mixed company of human, fae, and gargoyles into the Magic Realm to meet with the Lord of the Underworld. If all went well, then they would continue on to Haven where the new legion would meet their equally new allies.

It all sounded well and good, but Gryton didn't trust any of it.

Besides the obvious trap where Anna, Obsidian, and Thayn might be doing all this to lead him into Lord Draydrak's reach, something else was off. Gryton experienced a tingle of warning every time he looked upon Thayn. Gryton's instincts were telling him the oldest gargoyle wasn't being truthful with the Avatars.

Oh, not even the ancient one could lie to the Avatars and not be discovered. But withhold the full truth as to his purpose here? That was entirely within a gargoyle's ability to hide without triggering an alarm in others, even Gryton's sire and dam.

But Gryton had been born suspicious. It was the only reason he was still alive.

And all his finely-honed instincts said this was all an elaborate trap for someone. The most likely targets would be him or his parents for begetting him.

He would have spoken about this to his mother except he was never alone with her. And he couldn't mention it in front of his father. Thayn was one of Gregory's oldest friends. He wouldn't believe the ancient gargoyle capable of deception until he buried a blade in the Avatar's heart and sent Gregory back to the Divine Ones.

If he could trust the Null, he might have confided in her since even with all her faults, she was a shrewd one. He snorted to himself. She was in his head enough she may already have seen some of his concerns and reported them to her masters.

But if she hadn't already discovered his worries, he wasn't about to betray them to her so she could spread the word. Stealth and secrecy might be the only weapons he had to use against Thayn's plans.

Presently the Null was talking to Anna. The two women had struck up an odd friendship. They took great pleasure in trying to surpass each other in annoying him. They'd already tried so many 'nicknames' on him he was immune to their jokes and insults, but that hadn't stopped them from laughing and jesting with each other.

As for Anna's partner, Obsidian looked almost as perplexed as Gryton felt. As if thinking of him summoned the massive wall of muscle, Obsidian appeared in Gryton's line of vision.

"You. Practice ring. Now."

Gryton snorted and snatched up one of the practice swords from a bench as he walked past. After his and Obsidian's first disastrous match in the ring, no one trusted either of them. They'd both been ordered to wear temporary control collars Gregory had made for them to stop them from using magic in the ring.

They were almost at the practice sands when Anna called out. "Hey, wait you two. Major Resnick wants the soldiers to learn some basic sword skills to add to their combat skills."

"If we're down to swords and crossbows," the Null muttered to herself, "we're so fucked it won't matter."

"What was that, Erika?" Gran shouted from the other side of the ring while spinning her quarterstaff lazily. "I don't think I caught all of that."

"Nothing. Just talking to myself," she shouted and then added in a whisper once she'd moved safely behind Obsidian's concealing wings, "You crazy old witch."

Gryton's gaze followed the Null. He grinned and directed his question at Anna. "You wish me to train the Null?"

Anna snorted. "No. I want Obsidian to train her. I'm not giving you a chance to kill her, she's too good at needling you. I'm not risking losing such a remarkable ally."

"How disappointing," Gryton said, fighting back a rare genuine smile. "Guess that leaves you and me for the next matchup."

Obsidian stomped forward, his voice more growl than words. "If you think I'm letting you anywhere near my Kyrsu..."

"Nope. So not happening," the Null barked out as she scooped up a practice sword and prodded Gryton in the chest with its tip. "No way am I letting you draw Obsidian into another fight. Not on my watch. If you've got such a hard-on to cross swords with a woman, you can cross swords with me."

"You're female?" He challenged with a laugh. "You're sure?"

She waved her other hand at him, the middle finger raised in a lonely salute.

He snorted, having gathered the meaning a while ago. "I'd really rather not fornicate with you."

"Missed something in the translation. Get your ass in the ring, Hot Stuff."

Not one to turn down a challenge, he joined her in the ring and was as surprised as everyone else that she possessed some basic skills. Her defeat was still easy. He didn't even have to work that hard to disarm her the first time, but he still found himself fascinated why and how she possessed the basics of swordsmanship.

"Where did you learn to hold a sword? I wasn't aware humans of this world trained in edged weapons, preferring to put all your faith in the less reliable gun."

"I told you about my weird siblings. The oldest two try drilling some basic moves into me at every family get together. Most competitive family on the planet. I swear."

Anna chuckled as she joined them. "You haven't met my brothers yet. Five of them. Only one isn't military. Competitive doesn't even describe what happens on the rare occasion they all manage to get together."

There was a soft tone in her words at the mention of her brothers. It was clear she missed them. The Null was drawing breath to commiserate when Gryton snapped his sword out, striking hers and nearly knocking it out of her hand.

"Less talk," Gryton said as he attacked, "more swordplay. Unless you want to be killed by the first sword you meet on the battlefield?"

The Null wasn't put off by his abrasiveness. "Ah. I think he cares. What do you think, Anna?"

"Tin Man doesn't have a heart." Anna's grin was huge, her words spoken in jest, but she'd hit upon the truth.

He didn't have a heart. He didn't feel compassion or other weak emotions that could get him killed. His motives had changed when he'd learned her purpose was probably to neutralize the djinn and not assassinate him, but his purpose was no less selfish. The longer he could keep the Null alive, the better his own chances of survival became. He just had to bend her to his will, and then he could use her to kill his enemies.

After all, even demigods weren't immune to Nulls. If he could win this Null's loyalty, he might be able to use her to kill Lord Draydrak and the Lady of Battles. Leaving only the Avatars as a threat to his existence. And as far as their relationship with him went, he was sure he was winning his mother's affection.

His sire? Hmmm. That was another thing entirely. But if he could win one half of the Avatars, the other half would eventually come around. Their shared nature was a weakness in such a situation, a weakness he had no issue with exploiting.

Their weakness also reminded him why he preferred to be singular for all eternity.

"If that's true, why do you want to get in Anna's pants so bad?"

He'd thought he was keeping the Null too busy to peer into his head. Apparently, he needed to keep her busier if he wanted privacy. Lunging toward her, he brought his sword down upon hers with bone-breaking force. As he'd expected, her ability absorbed most of the impact, but not all of it. She stumbled back three steps.

"Ooh! Testy. Hit a nerve." She chuckled but had to retreat from him, her clumsy parries and thrusts no match for his more skilled strikes.

She might be no match for him, but he allowed her to stay on her feet. He was just warming up.

"A human term 'to scratch an itch' describes it best."

He planned to enjoy this little helping of revenge for all the times she'd fed from him.

The Null was soon sweating and panting, but her mouth never stopped. "I'm curious. You say scratch an itch, but as a fire elemental are you even really male? As in with the biological drive to reproduce and all?"

He arched a brow.

"I mean, I've been in your head enough times that I've seen things. When you were... er... new, you didn't even have a body, let alone a gender. You were just," her face screwed up as she looked for a way to describe what she'd seen.

"A sentient ball of molten power and fiery rage," he offered helpfully. "One with an insatiable curiosity to learn what I was and where I came from mixed in with all the fury?"

"Yep." She cleared her throat and continued in more serious tones, "I can understand that need to know things, to understand. I've always been fascinated by what makes a person tick."

"And I'm a curiosity you can't figure out?"

"Yeah. But I think I understand you better now."

That was doubtful, but he'd toss her a bone. "Go on. Ask your question."

"What made you first decide you wanted a flesh and blood body? Your first form was much more impervious to attack. And why male?"

"I wished to experience other sensations, other situations, to interact with the world without reducing everything I touched to ash. And to clarify, I tried a female form first." He laughed at her surprised expression.

"Okay. I totally didn't see that one coming." She tilted her head one way and then another as if trying to imagine him with a female form. In the end, she just nodded. "I've been inside your head. I just can't imagine you as a girl."

"Since the Lady of Battles was the only being in the universe to offer me protection from her Twin's army, I wished to honor her by emulating her, so I adapted my form into that of flesh and blood and female."

"And...?" She gestured at his body.

"Being female never felt right. I decided there was something fundamentally male about my nature and took on this shape. I've worn this form for close to six thousand years."

She pressed her lips together and nodded. "Yep. I stand corrected. You've been male longer than almost any male alive. Shutting my mouth now."

Then she came at him, their wooden swords clashing in dull thwacks before she spun away from him to slash at his back. He darted forward and circled her in a swift, deadly dance, allowing none of her strikes to land.

In a momentary pause in the fighting, Thayn interjected, "Well, I think I've learned more about Gryton in an afternoon than I could ever gather with thousands of years of spying."

Gryton and the Null continued their fight, but they both glanced at the old gargoyle when a pause in their bout allowed. He noted that the gargoyle was staring at the human while rubbing his muzzle thoughtfully.

"Avatars, help spark an old fellow's memory, would you?" Thayn shouted over the cracks of wooden swords.

Gryton's sire and dam broke off their own practice with two of the human soldiers and wandered over to watch.

Thayn pointed at the Null. "What soul is that. In this

magic deprived realm, I can't see past the flesh to see the soul beyond." His tone hinted that he'd been frustrated by that for a few days now.

Gregory approached the practice ring. "Lillian and I have been discussing this. But in this Realm, we are limited in the same way. Though we recognize a first wave soul when we see one."

Gryton saw when his keeper's eyes widened. "I'm not sure I really want to know what y'all are talking about, but you can't just say something like that and stop there."

Lillian laughed. "No. That wouldn't hardly be fair. We know you're an old soul. One of the first ones created after us and the djinns. You're older than Gryton, the Twins, even Thayn. Though until we travel to the Magic Realm, we won't be able to say for certain which soul is housed in your flesh and blood body."

"Fine. Now I know y'all just pulling my leg. I'd know if I was a gazillion years old."

Thayn huffed with sudden humor. "Gryton, you should be flattered. One of the first wave found you intriguing enough to suffer being born again. There may even have been a fight to see just which of the elder souls got to be reborn to become the keeper of the Avatar's son. Your birth is likely the most interesting thing to happen in the universe since the Twins' creation."

Gryton's mother just rolled her eyes at Thayn's comment and continued to explain the way of things to the Null. "Most souls don't remember their previous lives. The older the soul, the more knowledge and memories they possess. It's too much for most mortal brains to withstand, so while the soul remembers everything it ever experienced, the mortal mind only remembers what it experiences in the current lifetime."

The Null's mouth opened and then snapped closed, speechless for the first time. Gryton hadn't thought that was possible.

"Some of the elder races are more highly evolved, their minds can process more. That's why some, like gargoyles and the sidhe, will have some recall of previous lifetimes. Gargoyles are likely the most adapted to this since they have genetic memory passed down from father to son."

As Gryton watched, the Null's eyebrows scrunched over her nose. "Some humans claim to remember previous lives. Is that possible or just bullshit?"

"It is possible. In those cases, the soul and the mortal mind overlap during dreams. The 'true dreaming' happens when the soul's memories bleed across during dreams. It isn't enough to overtax the mortal mind, and often upon waking, they will just think it was an odd dream."

"For the record, the whole 'rebirth' thing sounds kind of shitty. What's the point if you have to relearn everything every freaking time?"

"It allows the soul to continue to learn," Lillian said, then added with a hint of humor. "Or to fix things that went wrong in a previous life."

"Still sounds about as much fun as a root canal."

Lillian's lips twisted with suppressed humor, but she merely nodded. "An old soul has often already seen and heard and experienced everything. They normally aren't eager to embrace a new life. And we rarely see one of the First Wave reborn. They normally prefer to experience the wonders of the universe in a non-corporeal form."

Even with what his sire and dam had just revealed, he still couldn't see the Null as anything other than the talkative mortal who enjoyed picking away at his mental armor or crawling around inside his head looking for interesting tidbits.

He just couldn't see her as older and wiser than him.

"Being picked for the role of a Null is a great honor," Lillian continued. "The Divine Ones only ever pick an ancient soul they've known for a very long time. They never trust that kind of power to a less tested spirit."

"Well, guess I couldn't have asked for a more interesting destiny." The Null turned her gaze back to him. "Buck up. Maybe this lifetime will be a grand adventure. Think of all the fun we'll have. A girl and her dragon."

"Mortal, I am not your dragon. And once we engage with the Battle Goddess's army, there will be more 'fun' than you know what to do with. I mentored the captains and oversaw the training of all those under their command. Fighting them will not be fun. It will be a 'world of pain' that you'll be facing."

"World of pain?" She smirked. "Now who has been poking around in other peoples' heads?"

He grinned, his lips stretching wide to show his fangs. "I admit guilt in this instance."

The Null was watching him with renewed interest. "I still like the Divine Ones and their 'girl and dragon' idea."

"I. Am. Not. Your. Dragon."

"We'll see." Her smirk was back in place. "By the way, if you're a dragon, like your parents say, why don't you ever shift to dragon form?"

Her grin faltered suddenly, and he knew she'd seen the

stricken look that had flashed across his features before he could regain control. He stared her down, not wanting to talk about it.

She glanced around and then lowered her voice. "I'm sorry if my thoughtless words upset you. It's none of my business why you don't shapeshift."

Had the Null just apologized to him? He couldn't have been more surprised if his gargoyle father had told him he loved him.

But then he surprised himself more by reaching out for their soul-link and telling her something he'd never told another soul. *"I don't dare shift. My dragon is too powerful. Too chaotic. If I ever shifted to my natural form, I would lose everything I've fought so hard to gain. My hard-won control. Mastery over myself. Everything I am would be gone."*

She reached out to him and rested her hands on his shoulders, her gaze as serious as he'd ever seen it. "Then I'll do everything in my power as a Null to make sure the dragon never gets the upper hand."

His lips parted, a 'thank you' on the tip of his tongue, but he closed his mouth before the new weakness had him uttering the words.

"You're welcome anyway, you prickly bastard." Then she grinned and thumped his back. "Oh, look. I think your dad wants to try kicking your ass in the practice ring again."

Glancing over his shoulder, he saw that the Null wasn't wrong. Gregory was approaching with a huge gargoyle grin and a wooden practice sword.

CHAPTER THIRTY-SIX

Vaspara

"This is madness," Bervicta hissed as they carefully picked their way through one of the forests of this world in the Mortal Realm. Vaspara couldn't disagree with her harpy friend. It was more like a suicide mission than madness, but she didn't correct her companion.

"No matter the outcome, it will be a win as far as the Battle Goddess is concerned." Vaspara skirted a large tree trunk and surveyed the land again. They had only run into one patrol of human soldiers. They'd kept clear because they weren't sure what the humans of this world were capable of, but they remembered Gryton's tales from his time here.

If the humans could do him harm, Bervicta and Vaspara

didn't want to risk getting discovered yet. They'd be fighting humans soon enough, anyway.

"How so?" Bervicta asked. "You're much more likely to die than kill Gryton. Hence my 'this plan is madness' argument. A suicide mission at least has a hope of success before death. I don't know what the Battle Goddess was thinking."

Vaspara snorted wryly.

"I'm not insulting your skills. But Gryton is a force of nature and has somehow aligned himself with the Avatars."

"He could talk the skin off a wolf," Vaspara agreed, but after a moment her smile slowly died. "The Battle Goddess's plan is actually rather brilliant. If I assassinate Gryton with the djinn's spell, his death throes will consume this planet. If I fail, I'll die. Yet my death won't be by Taryin or the Battle Goddess's hand. I'll have died as many other captains before have died, perishing in an attempt to increase our goddess's glory. They will revere my name." Bitterness bled across her words. "Sorac will never know the truth."

"Glory." The harpy scoffed. "A slave to Taryin and the djinn more like."

"No one else knows that."

"Besides me. Which is likely why I'm here. If I die 'gloriously' all the better."

Vaspara sobered further. "I'm sorry you got pulled into this death's mission."

"Ah well, I've lived a long time. Better to die a clean death at the hands of our enemies than be devoured by the blood witch." The harpy unfurled her wings and gave them a little shake as she stretched. "And just what is

Gryton, exactly, that he'll transform into a bleeding sun at his death! You think he was sired by one of the ancient demons from the void? But he can't be that. The Avatars would have killed him already if he was one of them. While the Avatars mostly ignore minor demons like incubi and succubi, they never turn a blind eye to soul eaters."

"Gryton wasn't sired by a demon from the void. It's worse than that. Or better. Depends what side of the fight you're on."

"How do you know?"

"The djinn told Sorac and me." Vaspara scanned the land around them as she walked. When she was sure no patrols were within sight, she answered the harpy's question. "Gryton is the son of the Avatars."

"What?! Another demigod like the Twins?"

"No. Not like the twins. He wasn't born of Divine will. The Avatars slipped up and broke their big vow. Though I think Gryton is powerful enough to still be called a demigod."

The harpy was silent for a long time. After a while, she shook her head. "I'm speechless."

"Sorac and I were as well when we first learned about Gryton's parentage."

"Don't suppose we'll live long enough to see him and ask how he hid that for all these years."

"No, not likely." Vaspara's throat tightened. It wasn't the thought of death that made her want to cry. She'd known she'd die in battle one day. But she'd always envisioned that death would occur with Sorac beside her.

But then they'd escaped with his clutch, and she'd

allowed herself to hope for something more, to admit her love for the big drake and even embrace his love.

Now she was walking toward death without Sorac. She'd never see him or their draklings again. Worse was knowing the pain he'd experience when he'd learned the Battle Goddess had created a portal spell and spirited her off to this mortal world on a suicide mission.

She'd never have the chance to tell him goodbye, and that she didn't regret loving him.

"Patrol ahead," Bervicta warned, drawing Vaspara out of her despair.

Vaspara nodded and then vowed to get her head in the battle to come.

Soon the number of human patrols increased, making Vaspara and Bervicta work harder to keep themselves hidden.

Eventually, they arrived at a tree-covered rise overlooking a town. More forest encircled the town, surrounding it on three sides. There were many of the strange, perfectly smooth roads leading in and out. Horseless carriages moved up and down them in both directions.

"We should stay clear of the roads," the harpy suggested. "Too much traffic. We might not hear the patrols until too late."

"Agreed." Together they made their way deeper into enemy territory, led by the assassin spell the djinn had implanted in Vaspara. It allowed her to sense Gryton's location. Though sometimes he seemed to just drop out of existence altogether, only to return a few hours later like he'd just reappeared.

"It's strange. He keeps vanishing, but I'm not sensing

any kind of portal spell that would suggest he's gone back to the Magic Realm. Then, a while later, he reappears. That's the third time it has happened."

"No one has enough magic to waste building that many portal spells. It must be something else about this world. There's a lot of death metal deep below our feet, and it's even built into their dwellings. Perhaps they've imprisoned Gryton in some kind of cage made from that iron."

Vaspara shrugged. It was a more plausible explanation than Gryton popping into the Magic Realm randomly. "I still don't like it."

"I like nothing about this mission. Too bad no one asked me."

Vaspara glanced sideways and smiled at the other woman. "You are a good friend, thank you."

"Friend? I don't have friends. Friendship is a luxury no captain can afford. Falling in love has softened more than just your heart if you ask me."

Vaspara snorted again but just shook her head and continued through the forest until they came to the edge of the town.

"You should stay here. It will be easy to see from here if I succeed. And if I fail, you'll still be far enough away from all the action to escape back to the Magic Realm and report my failure."

"Yeah. Because that will be good for my continued longevity."

Vaspara clapped her hands to her friend's shoulders. "But you'll survive a little longer, maybe blame Taryin for not being able to control her pet djinn well enough to force him to build a reliable assassin spell."

"Worth a try."

"And... and perhaps if you see Sorac again, you can tell him I met a quick, clean death at the hands of Gryton or the Avatars."

"Of course."

"And tell him I love him."

The harpy snorted. "He already knows that. Has known it far longer than you, I'd bet. But I'll tell him for you."

"Thank you." Vaspara sniffed and firmed her spine. "Don't stick around once you know if I succeeded or failed. If I succeed, you might have a chance to escape depending on how long the Avatars can contain Gryton. Perhaps you'll even make it back through the portal spell before he destroys this world. Goodbye, Bervicta."

"See you in the next life, Old Friend." Bervicta's words were so soft Vaspara barely heard them, but she did, and they somehow gladdened her heart.

CHAPTER THIRTY-SEVEN

Erika

Tension lay thick in the air. Or perhaps that was just late-season humidity, Erika mused. Neither one was particularly welcome, but she couldn't do much about either. The Avatars were making final preparations for their journey back to the Magic Realm to face a demigod and determine if he was friend or foe. Hence the tension in the military camp.

Erika was still foggy on some details but got the gist. The Avatars had been very naughty, and Gryton was the forbidden fruit of the union. Now the death god was after Gryton because of orders from the Divine Ones.

Hmmm. Nothing like walking into a trap. But it had to be done. They needed to know where the demigod and the Avatars stood. As for Thayn, Anna, and Obsidian, they seemed fine. But then again, she'd known them only a few days. Not exactly enough time to really get to know a person's true motives.

"Are you recovered enough from yesterday for another lesson in swordplay, Null?"

She stepped into the ring and saluted him with her wooden sword. "I'm always ready for anything, Hot Stuff."

While she didn't know the motives of the others, Gryton was another matter. His motivation was only too clear: survive at any cost.

While his headspace was the stuff of nightmares and he'd taken part in horrific things, he hadn't had a lot of choice in his... career path. He'd had to align himself with the Lady of Battles or die. And his will to survive was too strong to surrender himself to Lord Death.

If she was honest with herself, she felt pity for Gryton. Most of his actions were not those of an evil man. He didn't glory in death and pain and destruction. And while ambition drove him, it was more to prove he was the master of himself. No little feat considering what he'd started out as.

And then there were the other memories, those where he'd mentored and sheltered those under him, even taking punishments onto himself. Many times, he'd acted as a buffer between an insane demigoddess's rage and those he commanded. In no way could that have been an easy life.

In fact, the more she thought about it, the more she realized what a lonely life he'd led. From the moment of his birth, he'd been an outcast, an abomination, hunted by all, loved by none.

He had no friends, no trusted ally he could unburden

his soul to. There had been a few captains who likely would have made good friends and companions if he'd ever allowed anyone into his heart. But he viewed such emotions as a threat to his defenses, a weakness to be hunted and eradicated.

Anna and Obsidian called him Tin Man. That was more accurate than they might realize.

"If you only had a heart, Tin Man."

"What are you yammering on about?" Gryton growled.

"I said, if you only had a heart, Tin Man, I'd put this sword through it."

"And I'd burn that practice sword to ash long before you found my heart." Humor flashed in his eyes. "Besides, you'd first have to actually be able to land a strike, Null."

She flipped him the bird with her left hand, while her right thrust the point of her wooden sword toward his belly. He'd relinquished his scaled armor this morning and was wearing army fatigues, willingly of all things. It gave her something other than impenetrable armor to hit.

Which was easier said than done. The jackass was lighter on his feet than a dancer or martial artist. Yesterday he'd just been playing with her, allowing her to block a few of his strikes. Today he'd already walloped her at least five times.

"I'll be black and blue by the time you're bored with this whoopin' session," she accused.

"No, you won't. You're a Null. Your body is absorbing most of the energy of my strikes before it can damage your flesh, just like it would with magic."

"Bullshit. The strikes still hurt."

"I said most of the energy. Not all." He grinned and

caught her across the shoulder with the flat of his sword this time. "The pain is good. It will motivate you to move faster. And the reflexes you hone here today might save your life in the future."

"You just enjoy beating on me."

"I won't deny that."

He suddenly flashed his fangs at her, which was never a good sign. "Now let's start."

"Start? What the heck was the last ten minutes?"

"Warm-up."

He then showed her the difference. Erika only kept her feet because she ran away from more than one of his attacks.

"The point of the practice ring is that you're supposed to stay within a defined space until you're good enough to take your skills out into the real world where other obstacles and adversaries are waiting to trip you up and dispatch your sorry hide."

Erika grunted in surprise as she backed into one of the standing stones that circled the hamadryad, proving his point most eloquently. The tip of his wooden sword pressed against her throat.

Cursing, she glared at him and then spat out, "You waited to time that just right, didn't you?"

"Yes."

She met his next two strikes and then darted away, jogging backward across the long grass to get away from him and give her arm a rest. Crossing swords with him was like dueling with a plane's propeller, his blade whirling fast enough to seem like three.

"You need to pay more attention to your surroundings,"

he offered helpfully just as she backed into one of the maze's green walls.

She rolled out of the way a moment before Gryton's wooden sword slashed deep into the green walls. When he extracted it, a portion of the greenery fell to the ground.

"Shit! Were you trying to take my head with that last one?"

"No, this is just a little bit of—" Gryton bit off his last word as his gaze darted to something behind her.

She almost fell for it too. "Oh. Not this time, Hot Stuff."

Bringing her sword up, she leaped forward. Gryton moved faster, shoving her behind him even as his scaled armor flowed across his body, covering every bit of his exposed skin. A moment later the wooden sword he'd held burned to ash and two swords made of fire appeared in his hands.

He and his new opponent—an adversary Erika hadn't seen coming—came together in a rush of sparks and flame.

Erika scrambled to her feet and looked for a real weapon, but everything was over on the table by the practice ring. The rest of Gryton's detail rushed forward, guns raised, but Gryton and the newcomer—a blonde female— moved too fast, twisting and lunging and circling each other, magic rising from the ground to partially obscure them, never giving the soldiers a clean shot at the blonde intruder.

"Get down!" Erika bellowed at Gryton even as she sprinted for her gun. But it was clear he couldn't stop moving long enough to allow any of the unit to get a shot off.

Erika once again found herself in Gryton's mind and suddenly had a better understanding of what was happening. The newcomer was one of the Battle Goddess's captains. She'd once been one of the few he'd counted as an ally.

While she was no longer his ally, Gryton had already spotted one reason why. Seeing through his eyes, Erika witnessed the coiling, leech-like magic crawling across the woman's body. The way the magic shifted and moved it was almost like…

"Like she's being controlled?" Gryton's voice was suddenly in her head. *"Because she is. That is blood magic."*

"Fuck. It's ugly."

"Indeed. It is."

Gryton might have said more, but just then he had to leap to the side and dart away from a snaking tendril of shimmering gold magic that had erupted out of the woman's chest. She hissed in pain as the reddish-black energy slithered away from the gold.

It looked almost like the two powers were at war. But that made no sense either.

"They are not at war in the sense you mean. But they are anathema to each other. I'm fairly certain that other power belongs to the djinn. The two spells are unrelated and serve different purposes."

"You can tell all that by just looking?"

"Yes."

Gryton leaped back a second time as another golden tendril emerged from the woman. The stranger screamed and half-collapsed as another wave of the golden power pulled itself free from where it had been entrapped inside her.

"If the reddish-black coiling crap is used to control her, what the fuck is the golden shit doing?"

"That," Gryton sent along their link as he slashed out with one of his fire swords only to have it lose form and substance as it touched the magic, *"Is a very, very powerful assassin spell."*

The magic in his fire-sword expanded out, doubling in size. He leaped away from the raging ball of fire that had once been his fire-sword, and then he kept on retreating across the meadow. But she'd already caught his thought. The assassin spell was specifically designed for him. One he had no way to fight to judge by the destabilized fire-sword. From looking in his mind, she knew it was about to explode.

"Down! Down! Down!"

She and the rest of the team hit the ground moments before the ball of fire detonated like a bomb. The shockwave raced over her head, a wave of super-heated air displacing dust and debris.

"Shit," she whispered once it had rolled past, leaving still hot, but breathable, air in its wake.

Looking around, she saw that the picnic table that once had held all the practice weapons and other gear—her gun included—was now aflame and half-buried in one of the maze walls, the contents that once sat on it now scattered everywhere. Unfortunately, she didn't see her gun or any other useful weapon.

By the time she'd leaped back to her feet, the golden spell had continued to extract itself from the prone female.

Now eight long tendrils were writhing in the air above her. The woman's body convulsed, back arching as she screamed.

Erika's own gift was already responding to the threat, but as fast as she drew magic away from the spell, it replenished itself from somewhere else. She glanced at the woman but was confident it wasn't coming from her. Erika's gift sensed something else far off, like an open door that allowed magic to flow through from another location.

She was sure that other location was the Magic Realm.

Sergeant Maracle came over and squatted in the grass next to her. He handed her gun to her. "What's wrong? Why haven't you drained that thing yet?"

"I'm trying. But it replenishes itself as fast as I'm drawing power away."

Captain Stanton dropped down next to them, using the standing stone to Erika's right as cover in case of another firebomb. "Can you fight that thing or not?"

"I think so, sir. We need to get closer."

"Of course we do." There was a hint of reluctant acceptance in his tone. Stanton raised his arm and gestured the others forward. "Focus fire on the spider!"

Erika glanced back at the spell and realized it really did resemble a spider now that the eight legs were levering a rounded body from the chest of the female. With one more strong pull, the assassin spell heaved itself free and then darted forward, racing toward Gryton.

"Fuck! It can't reach Gryton, or we're all going to die!" She directed her fire to the spider's legs, hoping the magic there might be less dense and that the metal of the bullets slicing through it might disrupt the spell enough to sever a limb or at least slow the beast.

Apparently, Captain Stanton had deduced the same thing for he and the rest of the team were firing on its other legs.

The hail of bullets sliced through the magic composing the spider's leg, tearing pieces from the spell and scattering them in a flurry of bright sparks. But it didn't slow the monster like she'd hoped. It still raced toward Gryton, who was presently hoofing it toward her position.

He ignored the rain of bullets and leaped over Erika and the other soldiers to land gracefully behind her. "You need to keep that thing off my back for a bit longer until I've had a chance to study the spell holding it together. If it manages to wrap itself around me, I'm not sure if I'll be able to hold cohesion."

"Understood. Spider gets to you; you go supernova all over the place."

"Something like that," he agreed.

Erika, Maracle, Stanton, and the rest of the unit all concentrated fire upon the spider's front right leg. This time their combined firepower sheared through the appendage.

"Hell yeah!"

But as she was picking out her next target, the spider only paused as a shudder raced over its body. A moment later a new leg emerged from the stump.

"Fuck," Stanton yelled and then lobbed a grenade at the creature. The explosion knocked the spider off its feet, but it was back up a second later.

When it was ten feet from them, it leaped high in the

air. Erika stood in front of Gryton screaming at the monster as it came.

Only it didn't reach her.

Blinking in surprise, she watched as a wall of fire magic sprang up in front of the golden spider. As had happened before, as soon as the spider touched Gryton's power, his fire magic destabilized, the wall reacting with explosive force.

Everyone dived for the ground a second time. When the smoke and fire had cleared, Erika spotted the spider on the other side of the glade, half-buried in one of the maze's green walls. But the spider wasn't harmed and was soon scrambling toward Gryton with single-minded purpose.

"We need to get the prisoner out of here," Captain Stanton yelled.

"No," Gryton shouted back. "it will just follow. We must kill it now before it grows stronger. It's feeding off magic and the energy your weapons create."

Stanton cursed.

But if something could draw the magic out of the spell faster than it could intake it, then the spell would unravel like any other exposed to her too long. And without the spell's will transforming the power supplied from the Magic Realm into a weapon, then it would just be harmless energy. She straightened and studied the terrain. If she circled around and came at it from the west, she should be able to avoid the worst of the crossfire and magic fireballs.

"Wait." Gryton grabbed her arm. "You're not indestructible, and you don't know what else that thing has in the way of defenses."

"But it's magic, so—"

"It's djinn magic. And we haven't yet discovered your upper limit. On the battlefield isn't the place to find out."

"Not sure if that thing will give us a choice."

"It triggered all the protections within the maze. The Avatars are aware and coming." He pointed off to the north side of the glade. A shimmering in the air soon coalesced into silvery ropes of power swirling up from the ground.

Gaze snapping to the spider thing galloping toward them and then back to the shimmering portal forming in the north corner of the glade, she did some quick calculations and knew there was a chance the Avatars would not make it in time.

She glanced over her shoulder and briefly met Gryton's eyes. "You can curse me out in the afterlife if this doesn't work."

Erika lunged forward and broke into a sprint, running like all hell was breaking loose. Because that's what would happen if the atomic spider reached Gryton. She and the spider closed the distance swiftly.

It wasn't until the spider's giant legs took up her field of vision that it occurred to her the assassin spell couldn't see her. Or, perhaps, it didn't care, it was so focused on its primary target.

Putting on a burst of speed, she leaped at it. And then gasped out a surprised grunt a moment later when she fell through its leg. Having expected more substance to the appendage, she was shocked to find herself falling forward into the slightly denser core of its body.

All around her, the spell shrieked, deafening in its intensity. Gasping and choking, she gagged on the magic.

So much power. The normal tingling that accompanied her feeding was now a burning under her skin.

She screamed along with the assassin spell, but her gift continued to absorb more and more of the golden energy until the spell turned pallid. The spider's legs crumpled under it as it collapsed around her. She could see through it now, see the Avatars rushing toward her from one direction and the soldiers from another.

And farther back, Gryton stood with a surprised look on his face.

She'd never seen an expression quite like that on his face before. If she'd had the concentration, she would have peered into his head to see what he was thinking, but as it was, all she could do was slump forward onto the ground as her vision sparkled with snow and her body burned.

Blessedly, the sensation of feeding stopped.

And then so too did everything else.

Ah, shit. Did I just die? This life was just getting interesting.

CHAPTER THIRTY-EIGHT

Gryton

He had hated the feeling of uselessness he felt at being unable to fight the djinn's assassin spell, but he'd needed time to study it, to learn how to fight it. But before he could understand its composition and find a weakness to attack, the Null had tossed herself into the spell spider.

He...

He hadn't recognized the feeling in his core, an icy cold sensation no fire elemental should ever feel. It took the long moments while the Null absorbed the djinn's spell for Gryton to fully understand the cold feeling.

It was fear.

But not for himself. He feared for someone else.

Not concern. Not unease. Fear.

Forbidden rages of the Divine Ones! He'd been afraid the Null would be killed.

Gryton rocked back on his heels. While he wanted to stand frozen as he processed the new and very unwelcome feeling, he needed to study the remains of the spell before it dissipated completely. And he also needed to check on the Null to be certain she lived.

He...

He would need her later if he had any hope of killing the Lady of Battles and the Lord of the Underworld. It was that simple. His welfare was tied to hers. Of course he should feel some concern for what befell her until his mission was complete.

His sire and dam were already with the Null when he approached.

"How is she?" he found himself asking instead of studying the remains of the spell.

Lillian was leaning over Erika, her fingers at her throat. "If she wasn't a Null, I'd use magic to determine her condition, but she's already gorged herself on the djinn's power. The last thing she needs is more magic entering her overtaxed body."

He knelt next to them. "But she'll recover?"

"Of course I'll recover," the Null said, her voice not much more than a gravelly growl. "Balls! I hurt."

The tightly coiled ball of fear eased its icy grip on his heart, and he plastered a disdainful look on his face. "Ah. I see you're alive. I had hoped for a coma at least. So much for the few days of peace I'd been hoping for."

"Shit out of luck. I'll be back on my feet sooner than you can direct a glower at me."

She started to sit up but grabbed her head and groaned. Gryton slipped an arm under her shoulders so she wouldn't fall back and crack her thick skull.

"Easy," he muttered as he helped lower her back to the ground.

"Actually, a coma doesn't sound so bad. A nice nap. A few days' rest."

"You've done enough. Stay here, Erika. I'll go see what the lovely Vaspara has to tell us." Gryton turned and started over toward the fallen captain only to run up against twelve humans pointing their guns at him.

Sighing, he halted and glanced over his shoulder at his Avatar parents.

"They have orders to shoot you if you try to go anywhere without Private Emerson," Gregory added helpfully.

Pressing his lips into a narrow, humorless line, Gryton regarded his sire and then looked back at the Null.

"Nope." His mother stepped in front of him, blocking his view of the human. "You will not grab the poor woman and drag her caveman style over to the captain just so you can interrogate her."

The Sorceress started toward where Vaspara was still slumped and called back over her shoulder, "You will stay with Erika while your father and I investigate the Battle Goddess's assassin to see what other trick or traps she might be harboring."

"I saw one of the blood witch's twisted spells controlling Vaspara when she first attacked me," Gryton said to his mother's retreating back.

"I would expect as much, given what you, Anna, and

Obsidian have already shared with us about that place." His mother paused and glanced over her shoulder. "We'll update you as soon as we know more."

"Thank you." The words felt strange on his tongue but not as odd as the earlier feeling of fear. It was unsettling. He didn't even glower as the guards herded him back to Private Emerson and then encircled them.

Shortly after his parents went to check on Vaspara, Anna and Obsidian arrived with another company of human soldiers. Their arrival offered him a distraction from his unsettling thoughts. But the newly-made Rasoren and Kyrsu soon approached the Avatars.

Gryton knelt next to Erika while he watched the others. He wanted to know if Vaspara would survive, but he also found he didn't want to leave his Null keeper when she was so weak. He raised his helmet's visor and looked down at Erika.

She blinked up at him as if trying to bring him into focus.

"Howdy."

"Hello," he offered. "Erika, are you—"

"I will be fine, Hot Stuff." Her laughter turned into a moan.

If he could heal her, he would have. But healing was never one of his powers, and the last thing she needed was more magic.

She cleared her throat. "There is one silver lining in all this."

"Hmmm?"

"I finally got you to call me by my name. We can work on rank and surname later."

He rolled his eyes and then forced his attention to the others before he revealed something even more damning to the human. "Rest now, Null. I'm sure you'll be back to feeding on me in no time."

"You got that right." She closed her eyes after that, and while he sensed she wasn't asleep, she wasn't aware of her surroundings either.

Convinced that she would not die, he turned his attention to his other concerns.

While he'd never lowered his guard enough to form friendships, Vaspara was one of the captains he'd trusted the most. He somehow doubted it was random chance that Taryin had used Vaspara to deliver the assassin spell. And if Vaspara had been successful, she would have died moments after him, along with everyone else on this planet.

He forced his fists to relax. That Vaspara was here must mean she'd still been loyal to him even after he'd defected. Otherwise, the Battle Goddess wouldn't have sent one of her most skilled captains on this suicide mission.

But where was Sorac?

The firedrake was never far from the succubus if there was a dangerous mission. Gryton remembered the coiling, red-brown ropes of blood magic that had covered Vaspara when he'd first seen her.

Sorac must be dead. Otherwise, there was no way he'd allow the blood witch to have Vaspara. While the firedrake and the succubus always hid it well, he'd been certain they were in love with each other. It was their one significant weakness. And had likely been exploited in some fashion to defeat the two.

He only hoped Sorac's death had been swift.

Soft conversation drifted on the breeze and Gryton listened without difficulty.

Anna was leaning over Vaspara. "She didn't have this blood magic taint last time we faced her and Sorac in battle during the raid on Lord Draydrak's island."

"No," Obsidian agreed. "This is new and terribly powerful. The witch is learning new skills." With that ominous statement, the big gargoyle stepped back to allow Lillian and Gregory to better examine the unconscious succubus.

"Help me up," Erika hissed, drawing his gaze back to her upraised hand.

"Wait until one of your human medical teams get here."

"Help me up, or I swear to God—"

"Fine, but if you faint, I will toss you over my shoulder and lug you back to my cage and lock you in until you recover." Gryton reached down and hoisted her up.

"I don't faint."

"Good." He paused and then lowered his voice so the other guards standing around wouldn't hear. "But you should know the amount of energy one of your kind can absorb varies from Null to Null. So does recovery time. I also remember reading a Null's abilities grow stronger with use and age. The older, or the more battles they've seen, the more magic they can absorb. You're still very young in this lifetime. Have a care you don't overindulge and get yourself killed."

"Ah. Knew you cared."

He glowered at her. "Do I need to remind you it has nothing to do with your welfare and everything to do with mine?"

"Liar. Been in your head. I know it's more than that." She grinned suddenly. "Come on. Let's go see this Vaspara."

With a disgruntled huff, Gryton took more of her weight and helped her walk, the rest of the guard unit flanking them. They reached the outskirts of the other group in time to hear Anna speaking.

"She was strict," Anna agreed, "but never unfair. There are other captains I'd wish dead first."

"Vaspara was a loyal and respected woman. I vouch for her as well," Gryton offered. "Not that my word means anything to any of you."

He felt when the Null touched his thoughts for a few moments before she spoke.

"From what I can see in Gryton's memories, she isn't loathsome like many of the Battle Goddess's army. And, hell. No one deserves that repulsive blood magic crawling around underneath their skin. Let me absorb the energy and free her from that at least."

"As unpleasant as that spell likely is for Vaspara, you've already overtaxed yourself," Anna said, saving Gryton from having to mention his own worry again. "You need to rest and recover, and then after Command has talked this over, you can see about destroying the blood magic spell if that's how they want to handle this."

"No." Lillian's single word rang with challenge, her firm tone reminding them all she was the Sorceress and there was no room for argument. "Erika will deal with the tainted magic now."

Gryton spun to face his mother, his one brow raised in silent demand.

"I'm uncertain that what remains of the spell can't spy

upon us. We kill it now. If Erika accidentally kills the succubus, so be it. We already have enough knowledge of the djinn and the Battle Goddess's plans to know what they plan next."

Keeping his face neutral took some work, but he did, knowing they were all suddenly putting on an act for the benefit of anyone watching through the blood magic spell controlling Vaspara.

Erika glanced down at Vaspara again. "Magical malware. On it."

She slowly lowered herself to kneel next to the succubus, pausing once to look up at the Sorceress. "You sure that coiling magic shit can't infect me?"

"Very certain. All magic is just energy at its most basic level. Energy is neither good nor evil. And while it can take on the attributes of those who use it, as a Null, you simply draw out the energy and the rest of the magic's nature just fades to nothing."

"Hmmm." Erika hesitated and then with a muttered 'oh, hell' she swiftly snatched up Vaspara's nearest hand.

A jolt ran through the succubus's body. In the next moment, she was jerking and thrashing as if in the grip of an invisible predator. Gryton knew this was no external predator.

Anna and Obsidian both moved forward to hold her down, only to be knocked back by a wave of Lillian's power. "No one else approaches. The blood magic senses the Null. It's trying to move to a new host to escape being destroyed."

As if to reinforce his mother's words, a twisting tendril of reddish-brown magic rose above Vaspara's skin and thrashed in the air, seeking the nearest warm body. When one reached for him, he burned it to ash.

"I have this," Erika said. "Step back, Hot Stuff."

"Its existence insults my delicate sensibilities," he said dryly.

"Well, we can't have that, now can we?" She reached out with her other hand and locked her fingers around the thickest tendril and began squeezing. "Die you little bastards."

CHAPTER THIRTY-NINE

Vaspara

She blinked. Then blinked again. She was staring up at a soft blue sky with puffy white clouds. Not the teal tone of home. Then Vaspara remembered. She'd been enslaved and sent to a planet in the Mortal Realm to assassinate Gryton and kill as many of the Avatars' allies as possible.

It was doubtful Gryton's death throes would have been enough to kill the Avatars, but they would have spent vast amounts of power to save themselves, thus weakening them and making them easier prey for the Lady of Battles.

But nothing had gone as planned.

And Vaspara wasn't upset by that in the least.

The djinn's assassin spell was gone, as was Taryin's

tainted magic. Vaspara breathed deeply. She felt so free. So clean.

Was she dead? She looked around and found herself surrounded by strangers. Humans mostly. A dryad and a gargoyle. Ah… they were the Avatars; she could feel their power.

While she was alive, she probably wouldn't be for long.

Sighing, she closed her eyes and waited to be struck dead.

"My sire and dam will not kill you, Vaspara. They have something else planned."

The voice was one she knew well: Gryton.

She opened her eyes again. "I can't believe I never knew you were the Avatars' son until the djinn told me."

"It's a complicated story. It might take a while to tell." Gryton squatted next to her, a slanted smile on his lips.

Some instinct dragged her gaze away from Gryton to a female next to him. A slight shimmering surrounded her, rising off her body like heat, but it wasn't heat. It was magic. The purest, most untainted magic she'd ever encountered. She couldn't even determine what element the female was channeling.

"She's a Null." Gryton offered. "She drank the djinn's assassin spell meant for me and devoured Blood Witch Taryin's spell like a sweet treat after dinner. I imagine my sire and dam will want to explain the rest to you. They have plans you might be interested in hearing."

"Plans?" Vaspara glanced back at the Avatars, noting the Sorceress's surprisingly friendly expression. The Gargoyle Protector's wasn't as friendly, but he wasn't trying to kill her either, so she slowly sat up.

That was when she spotted Anna and Obsidian.

"Hello Vaspara," Anna said with a grin. "I have to say, I'm surprised you and Sorac didn't just pretend to be dead along with the rest of the unit the Battle Goddess sent after us."

Vaspara felt her throat tightening even as words poured out of her. "We did try. Sorac and I even escaped with his clutch and the djinn, but we were hunted down and captured."

Words just kept pouring out of her. She wasn't sure who was more surprised, her enemies or herself.

By the time she'd divulged everything she knew, Vaspara even admitted that she would have joined the Avatars if she had a choice. But she didn't. If she didn't die Sorac and his little ones would be punished for her betrayal.

"Please kill me. Show me that much mercy. If you kill me now, Captain Bervicta will sense my death and carry the news back to the Battle Goddess. Sorac will live to raise our draklings."

"Well," the Sorceress said in a cheerful tone. "Isn't it lucky for you I'm planning to let you escape with news that we have a Null on our side? I imagine that bit of news will save your life and restore your worth in the eyes of the Battle Goddess."

"They'll know I lied as soon as the blood witch enslaves me again."

Smiling, the Sorceress tilted her head. "You can't lie about what you don't remember. I'll take all your memories of this meeting, add a little spell of my own, create some fake memories to aid the deception, and then turn you loose. As far as you'll know, you blacked out for a short time while the Null was destroying the blood witch's work. Then you came to just as the Null was finishing off the djinn's assassin spell."

"I still don't see how any of that will hold up to scrutiny. The Lady of Battles or Blood Witch Taryin will sense your tampering."

The Sorceress laughed. "I gave birth to both the Twins. Gregory and I know their limits well. As for the blood witch, I've destroyed thousands of her kind. She'll not sense my subtle spell. I can do this."

Vaspara nodded, knowing she had to trust them. "Very well. Do whatever you need to destroy them."

The Sorceress nodded benevolently. "In return for your help, I'll do everything in my power to free the draklings before the final battle."

"Thank you. They are innocent and don't deserve what the Battle Goddess and Blood Witch Taryin have planned."

"There is one other thing I need you to do for me."

Vaspara nodded.

"I will have you carry a spell to the djinn for me. Do you agree to this?"

Vaspara would do anything to save and free Sorac and

the little ones, and the Sorceress was offering her a chance. Her gaze returned to the Null.

A Null of all things! A being even blood witches feared. Beings designed to contain a raging djinn.

For the first time since her capture, Vaspara felt hope.

"I'll do anything you need."

"Good," the Sorceress said. "Let's get started."

Gryton cleared his throat. Drawing everyone's attention back to him. "There's just one flaw in my mother's plan."

The Sorceress nodded in understanding and Gryton continued.

"For Bervicta to believe any of this, we will have to make this look real. If you escape without a scratch, Bervicta will be suspicious. I'm afraid I will have to do some damage before you escape."

Vaspara nodded, her eyes calm and knowing. "I'm a captain. I didn't get that title without experiencing a lot of pain along the way."

Gryton nodded. "And what's a little more pain for a better future?"

CHAPTER FORTY

Bervicta

It was taking too long. Vaspara should have completed the mission by now. Or failed. And by the earlier sounds of battle and no raging inferno rising into the sky afterward, Bervicta knew her friend had failed in her mission.

There was only one problem. Bervicta hadn't sensed Vaspara's death. She would have. They'd trained together, combining their personal magic many times. There would have been a resonance at the succubus's death. But there had been none.

Had Vaspara been captured? The blood magic and the djinn's spell should have forced Vaspara to complete her mission or die trying. A succubus, no matter how well trained, couldn't withstand a djinn's power.

Either way, something had gone drastically wrong.

But what?

Birds to the east of Bervicta's position took to the air, crying a warning. Sharp eyes scanning the forest, she moved closer to where the birds had taken flight. Even expecting something to emerge from the forest, she didn't recognize the figure staggering toward her until it came closer.

It was Vaspara, but her normally blonde hair had been burned away and two-thirds of her armor had been blackened, the exposed bits of skin red and oozing.

"By the Goddess!" The harpy wasn't sure if she was beseeching the Lady of Battles or the mother goddess at that moment. She rushed forward and steadied the succubus. "What happened?"

"Gryton..." Vaspara's voice broke, even it sounded damaged. "Gryton has a Null. She serves him, protects him."

Vaspara doubled over and coughed up blood. When she straightened, she continued in a broken whisper. "We need to keep moving. The Null destroyed Captain Taryin's magic and inadvertently freed me to act of my own free will. I escaped, barely, while the Null and the Avatars dealt with the djinn's spell. But they won't be far behind. We need to run."

"No. We need to fly." Bervicta stretched her still healing wing and eyed the succubus.

"You'll never be able to get us both off the ground, not with that wing. Go. Save yourself." Vaspara grimaced as she braced an arm against a tree. "I won't prove much of an opponent, but maybe I can slow them down long enough for you to escape."

"Fine." Bervicta unbuckled her harness and discarded it and her sword.

"What are you doing?"

She began unbuckling her armor next. "Getting rid of extra weight. The less weight, the better with this wing."

When Bervicta had shed all extra weight, she leaped into the air and flapped her wings.

"Good luck, my friend," Vaspara said as she pushed away from the tree and drew her own sword. "I'll try to slow them as much as I'm able."

"About that..." Bervicta seized Vaspara with her long talon-tipped toes, digging deep for a secure grip.

Vaspara screamed but bit the sound off in the next moment. Not that it mattered. Vaspara would have left a blood scent a gargoyle still in his mother's hamadryad could have followed.

Beating her wings harder, Bervicta gained speed and dragged herself and her burden through the forest. She could hear men not far behind. Her injured wing grew tired, but she pushed past the exhaustion, then the pain, and after that, she gritted her teeth and ignored the agony burning down her back.

But harpies were known to be strong-willed and stubborn.

Ahead she glimpsed the still active portal. The humans were just behind her now, their machines roaring above the trees. She put on a last desperate burst of speed.

Ten wingbeats later, Bervicta came in for a crash land-ing. She and Vaspara rolled across the ground, finally stopping just a few body lengths from the portal. With a snarl of pain and will, she waved her hand, calling on her magic to awaken the dormant portal.

As the magic sparked to life, Bervicta climbed to her feet and grabbed Vaspara's arm and then hauled her up over her shoulder. Grunting at the new pain shooting down her spine, the harpy cursed and ran through the portal's horizon as the soldiers came rushing up behind her.

Turning, she grinned at them as she willed the portal to close.

"We'll have to play some other time, lovely, lovely men." She cupped one of her breasts as she grinned back at them through the rapidly closing portal.

"They probably don't even understand your words," Vaspara mumbled.

"Likely not. But they're males. I imagine they understood my meaning."

Vaspara's snort turned into a moan. "Goddess! Just put me down. I feel like my head will explode."

Bervicta did as she was told and slowly lowered Vaspara to the ground. "You look terrible. But you'll be good as new as soon as I get you to Sorac or the djinn."

You just have to live long enough for that, Bervicta whispered in the privacy of her own mind. But going by how bad Vaspara looked, Bervicta wasn't at all certain the succubus would live long enough to reach help.

CHAPTER FORTY-ONE

Gryton

"They made it through the gate," Major Resnick informed the group after he'd gotten off the radio.

Gryton merely nodded at the news. He hadn't been surprised that Vaspara had made it once she met up with the winged female. Bervicta always completed a mission. He felt a touch of pride that the two had kept ahead of Major Resnick's men without the humans having to stall and pretend difficulty in the hunt.

A disturbance in the shadows along the maze's north wall warned Gryton they were about to get another visitor.

Thayn appeared in the glade a moment later. "The plan is in motion."

As a group, everyone else in the glade turned to gaze questioningly at the gargoyle.

"We must return to the Magic Realm tonight," he explained. "Now that the Lady of Battles knows we have a Null, she will be swift to mobilize her army. She can't risk allowing the Null to fully mature."

Thayn looked pleased by the turn of events, Gryton noticed. And not for the first time, he suspected the elder had something else planned. Come to think of it, where had he been during the attack?

"Pretty sure my superiors aren't just going to allow me to go at your command. They must discuss this newest development since it changes a few things."

Thayn grinned. "I think they will see reason. The longer we wait to go, the greater the likelihood the war will spill across the Veil and impact your Earth."

"Well, since you put it that way..."

CHAPTER FORTY-TWO

Gryton

Thayn wasn't wrong. The humans had seen the reason they needed to move up their plans, and once the orders had been given, their soldiers interacted much like any unit Gryton himself had trained.

As soon as the humans were ready, the Avatars created one of the great portal spells to carry the expedition—aptly named Lethal Crossing by the humans—into the Magic Realm. At first, he'd been concerned Private Erika Emerson's gift would activate and destabilize the spell when it was time for her to cross the threshold.

But they'd discovered a benefit in the djinn's assassin spell. Erika had gorged herself on that power, and her body had been too busy radiating all that purified energy back into the surrounding environment to be interested in the magic that powered the portal spell.

Now he dug the toe of his boot into the soft loam of the forest and breathed deeply of the fresh air. He'd missed the clean scent of green growing things, loam, and dampness. The atmosphere of the Magic Realm was just so much sweeter on his tongue.

"You missed this place, didn't you?" Erika stated, drawing his attention back to where she was helping to set up tents that would be the first structures in the humans' so-called forward operating base, or FOB. The humans did so love shortening names and titles. He was half surprised they hadn't shortened his name to Gry or Ton.

"Can I get some help over here, Hot Stuff?"

Ah, yes. How could he forget? His keeper already had several silly nonsense names for him.

He glowered at her more out of routine than annoyance.

"The base will not build itself," she added.

"You're assuming Lord Death will even allow humans this close to his territory."

Erika stopped what she was doing and joined him at the edge of the forest. A few body lengths from the last tree, a cliff wall dropped away to the ocean below. Far out across an expanse of blue-green water sat a vast island. Even over the distance, its size was impressive.

"The Avatars and Thayn seemed to think everything will go according to plan." Erika cocked a hip and leaned against a tree. "And if you're worried about this so-called Lord Death coming to kill you, I'm told Nulls are also known as god-killers. I'll eat him if he tries to do something unwarranted to you."

Snorting, he just shook his head at her ignorance. "You are a child and nowhere near ready to take on a demigod."

"Not yet. But I will be." She paused and looked thoughtful. "Hmmm. And as for old enough, if what the Avatars and Thayn say is true, I'm plenty old enough."

"That doesn't count."

She winked at him. "Still older than you."

"Oh, shut up." But a foolish grin ruined his attempt to scold her. To hide it, he looked back out over the water.

The human didn't leave to return to her work, though. "Penny for your thoughts."

"I don't even know what a penny is. As for my thoughts, you regularly read them anyway."

"The novelty is wearing off. Figured I'd just ask this time."

He sighed and turned to her. "They are somewhere between disbelief and denial. I've avoided Lord Death for over six thousand years. Yet here I am, willingly entering his domain, not to fight, but to surrender."

"Well, at least you shouldn't have to wait long to learn your fate." She glanced at her watch. "Thayn said the gargoyle scouts would make the flight to the island and back in less than an hour. It's been close to an hour now. The only thing we don't know is how long it will take Lord Draydrak to plan a response."

"It's the response that concerns me. Not the gargoyle scouts."

"Maybe this Lord Draydrak will surprise you? Thayn is fun. And Anna and Obsidian say the demigod is nothing like his sister. I think I even heard Anna describe him as kind and soft-spoken of all things. Who knows, maybe you and your older brother will be friends."

"He's not my brother in the sense you speak. The Divine Ones created him using their Avatars as hosts."

"Yeah, well, it's complicated—so I'm just going to go with brother."

Gryton snorted. And as for being friends with Death? He held back another snort of disbelief. No. They were the opposite of friends.

Besides, Gryton didn't have friends.

His thoughts spun off in another direction and he frowned. Well, perhaps that statement wasn't as true as it once had been.

He turned to gaze upon the Null—Erika, he acknowledged. He'd begun to call her by her name in his own thoughts.

While he hadn't set out to become friends, something like friendship was growing up between them, and no matter how hard he tried, he didn't seem able to weed it out.

Perhaps it was only natural and not a sign of some internal flaw in his composition. She was the first person besides his mother to risk her life to save his.

Only recently had his mother's hamadryad saved him. Then his mother had begun to train him to better control his feral magic. And now the Null had acted to save him as well. Never in his long life had anyone cared to protect him.

It was... nice.

It was also a weakness that he didn't like.

He huffed. Being around soft-hearted beings was making him equally soft. The fastest way to get killed was to lose his edge. He couldn't allow that to happen. He couldn't let friendship grow up even more between them.

Erika started to laugh as she pushed away from the tree. "If it puts your mind at ease, think of it as me risking my ass to save all the rest of the Earth instead of just you. By the way, I'd do it again. Save the Earth, I mean."

He arched a brow. He knew there was more to it than that. Their soul-binding had grown strong enough that he could look into her mind and feel some of what she felt. And right this moment it allowed him to sense she was becoming attached to him.

He'd find a way to use that.

Erika just snorted and slapped the back of his head. "I can still hear your thoughts, Hot Stuff."

"I know. I just like to see if I can get a rise out of you."

"Hmmm. Think I'm rubbing off on you, Hot Stuff."

"No doubt," he said, about to say more when the wings of a hundred Legion gargoyles appeared to blacken the sky as they dropped their shadow magic. A moment later, the first of them landed on the cliff.

Gryton's grin vanished.

Fate had just turned her full attention back to him. And that had never been a good thing in his experience.

CHAPTER FORTY-THREE

Lillian

At last, the summons came. Lillian wasn't sure who was more uneasy, her mate or her son. But the time to face Lord Death had come. A hundred gargoyles—an honor guard—escorted them. Thayn led the flight. Anna and Obsidian flew to either side of him. Next came Gryton and Private Erika Emerson on their gargoyle mounts.

Gryton's mount for the flight was Truth in Shadows, the gargoyle who had played herald and announced the return of Anna and Obsidian.

The other gargoyle was the youngster called Oath. Lillian was rather sure Obsidian had called in favors among his personal friends to find mounts for the Null and the fire elemental.

Oath was the more boisterous of the two, asking Private Emerson about her family and life on Earth. Erika graciously answered all the youth's questions. They'd both been awkward in the flight's beginning, Erika having never ridden gargoyle-back before and Oath being young and still inexperienced with a rider.

Gregory followed close on Oath's tail, and Lillian positioned herself near Truth and Gryton. Behind Lillian, Major Resnick and his team had been strapped into saddles for the flight to the island. There had been much cursing and grumbling when they'd learned they would be flying gargoyle-back, but they'd been good sports about it once they realized there were no boats.

For their part, the Legion gargoyles were good-natured about carrying the humans.

Even burdened with riders, the flight was short, and soon the group was dropping out of the sky to sweep over beautiful white sand beaches. As the gargoyles winged their way higher up into the island's interior, Lillian gazed upon the gardens and streams and pools spreading out in all directions, as far as the eye could see. It was just like she remembered.

She'd missed this place and its guardian. So had Gregory. His joy at returning to what he considered a second home outside of the Spirit Realm was flowing along their mental link. While they'd helped the Divine Ones birth Lord Death, Lillian and her other half had come to see Lord Draydrak as a brother. After all, they were all created by the Divine Ones.

It was nice to be home.

Thayn winged his way higher into the island until the central temple grew large. Circling, the group came in for a landing one by one. She and Gregory came in right behind Gryton and Erika, but their son was already off Truth's back and several feet away before Lillian had even folded her wings.

Erika and Oath had landed without incident.

Before she could check over the rest of the group, the sound of massive hooves on stone reached her. She looked to the south to see Draydrak galloping toward them.

"Fuck me! I know I was told that he was centaur-like, but no one said he was half the size of a mountain," Erika muttered to Gryton loud enough for all to hear.

"Shh," Lillian soothed, hoping to calm the other woman. "He's a friend and won't hurt you."

"What about Gryton?"

"Gregory and I will talk to him and smooth things over."

Lord Draydrak skidded to a halt in a spray of sand and grit. Bending his head, he pointed his muzzle toward them as he studied the group, his eyes searching.

"Ah, the Avatars have returned. Both the new and the old. And they've come with an unexpected player. The Divine Ones have been busy." Lord Draydrak flashed them all an evil-looking grin.

"Gryton, it was never your death I sought."

Faster than Lillian could weave a spell or even cry out a warning, Lord Draydrak reached down and scooped up Erika in one of his giant hands.

"It was hers," Draydrak bellowed, "And you did so

conveniently bring me the one thing that can kill Death. I can't allow that to happen." Then he spun on his hindquarters and galloped in the opposite direction. Spreading his wings wide, he caught a current and soared into the air, heading toward the island's east shore and the ocean.

Erika screamed in pain and fear.

"He will drown the Null!" Gregory shouted and then bolted into motion, spreading his wings to give chase.

The other legion gargoyles scattered as Major Resnick and his men shouted out warnings and curses, their weapons trained on the retreating forms of Lord Death and Gregory. But there was nothing they could do to save the Null.

Instinctively, Lillian began summoning magic, weaving battle spells even as she wondered how she had miscalculated so badly. Her eyes tracked toward Thayn, where he stood off to one side.

Lord Draydrak did nothing the eldest of the gargoyles did not know about.

He had to have known what Lord Death had planned. She'd never thought their oldest friend would deceive them in such a way. Betrayal was bitter in her mouth.

Beside her, Anna and Obsidian shook off their surprise and began summoning power as they took to the air. Moments later they were racing in pursuit of Draydrak. They, at least, were still true allies.

But Lillian was the Sorceress. She did not need to physically chase after the enemy to hunt him.

She wasn't the only one not giving chase. Beside her, Gryton was calling on power, waves of molten fire licking between the scales of his armor. That had surprised her for a moment. She'd thought he'd have given chase. Then she realized he lacked wings, and no one would win a foot race against Lord Draydrak.

But there were other ways to win.

She called on a greater flow of magic from the Spirit Realm, then spread her wings, allowing the opposing magics to create currents in the air and lift her up. Draydrak's betrayal would cost him greatly.

Even as the need for revenge burned in her soul, her heart was heavy with the knowledge she'd failed the human woman. Lillian's attack would be too late to save Erika if the Lord of the Underworld wanted the Null dead.

If he wanted her dead...

If...

Oh!

She reached for Lord Death. His mental shields admitted her, and then she was within his mind, that calm, soothing place where rational thought ruled. There was no hatred or animosity flowing from Draydrak despite his earlier outward aggression and harsh words.

Lillian's eyes widened in understanding at what she found in his mind. Draydrak wasn't harming Erika, not yet. This was all an elaborate trick. Or a trap. He wanted them to chase him.

No. He wanted Gryton to chase him.

Then it all clicked, coming together. The real reason Lord Draydrak had been hunting Gryton all these years.

It wasn't to kill him; it was to—

"Gryton wait! It's a trick!"

A wave of heat hit her, blowing her backward and sending her crashing to the ground. All around, legion gargoyles and Resnick and his men were knocked to the ground by hurricane-force winds that had suddenly materialized out of nowhere. Spitting sand from her mouth, she scrambled to her feet.

She squinted between her lashes, seeking her son even as her magic snapped a protective shield around her. Within moments, she found Gryton.

He was still where he'd been. But now fire rolled off him. The scales of his body armor cracked open along his back, his elemental magic expanding out around him in an ever-enlarging circle. Within heartbeats, the tall wall of fire split in two, taking the form of a pair of vast wings.

"Gryton, wait! He wants you to attack him! Stay! Let us rescue Erika! Calm yourself!"

"No!" His denial came out more roar than word.

"This is what Lord Draydrak wants!"

But it was too late. Gryton was beyond hearing her or anyone else.

The dragon was only interested in one thing: rescuing his maiden.

Roaring his fury, the elemental dragon ripped its way free of Gryton's body. A narrow, angular head on a long sinuous neck towered over Lillian. His form continued to solidify. Broad shoulders merged into a powerful chest wrapped with muscle. The vast wings cast a growing shadow as the dragon grew in size.

"Our son is breathtaking," Lillian whispered to Gregory along their mental link a moment before the massive dragon covered with fire-gilded burgundy and gold scales

gathered his powerful hindquarters and launched himself after Lord Draydrak with an earth-shaking roar.

"Breathtakingly pissed off by the sound," Gregory corrected.

"Indeed," Lillian agreed as she raced after her elemental dragon son. It was clear he was hellbent on turning this world to ash in his quest to save the life of his Null.

THE END

The story continues in Sorceress Eternal, the final book in the Gargoyle & Sorceress Tales.

Hey before you go, can I interest you in signing up for my author newsletter? You get my free starter library as a gift for joining.

http://lisablackwood.com/join-the-newsletter-here/

Did you enjoy Scion of the Sorceress? If you have a moment and wouldn't mind leaving a review, that would be greatly appreciated. Reviews help other readers to decide if a book is something they would like. It doesn't

need to be long. Even a few words is tremendously
helpful.

None of this would have been possible without, you, my
readers. You're awesome! Thank You!

Bye for now,
Lisa Blackwood

ABOUT THE AUTHOR

Lisa Blackwood is the author of the bestselling Gargoyle and Sorceress urban fantasy series. Her work has also landed on the Wall Street Journal and the USA Today Bestseller lists as part of the Dominion Rising Anthology. When she's not reading and writing, she also enjoys gardening and spending time with her horse and her dogs.

At present, she grudgingly lives in a small town in Southern Ontario, though she would much rather live deep in a dark forest, surrounded by majestic old-growth trees. Since she cannot live her fantasy, she decided to write fantasy instead.

BOOKS BY LISA BLACKWOOD

Gargoyle & Sorceress

Dawn of the Sorceress

Sorceress Awakening

Sorceress Rising

Sorceress Hunting

Sorceress at War

Sorceress Enraged

Legacy of the Sorceress

Sorcery & Firedrakes

Scion of the Sorceress

Sorceress Eternal

In Deception's Shadow Series (Epic Fantasy Romance)

Betrayal's Price

Herd Mistress

Maiden's Wolf

Death's Queen

The Prince's Gryphon (forthcoming)

Ishtar's Legacy Series (Epic Fantasy Romance)

Ishtar's Blade

The Blade's Beginning (short story)

Blade's Honor

Blade's Destiny

The Blade's Shadow

First Queen of the Gryphons

The King of the Anunnaki (forthcoming)

The Anunnaki's Blade (forthcoming)

Huntress vs Huntsman (Epic Fantasy Romance)

Master of the Hunt

Night Huntress

Dragon Archer

Soul Mage (forthcoming)

www.ingramcontent.com/pod-product-compliance
Lightning Source LLC
Chambersburg PA
CBHW030800210726
48290CB00002B/361